"Who the devil are you?"

Elisabeth whirled around and stared into furious gray eyes. The man was remarkable—rugged yet polished in his Victorian way. His vest bore a watch chain, and his odd, stiff collar was open. For some confounding reason, Elisabeth found herself wanting to touch him.

The stranger's eyes raked her figure, leaving fire in their wake. "I asked you a question," he snapped.

Elisabeth gave herself an inward shake. This guy was a dream—or a delusion—and yet she felt a staggering attraction to him. She tried to keep her voice calm as she gazed into his hard, autocratic face. "I'm Elisabeth McCartney. And either I'm dreaming, or you are. In any case, I need to get back to where I belong."

His dark eyebrows drew together. "I, for one, am not dreaming," he pronounced. "And *you* won't be going anywhere...."

Also available from MIRA Books and
LINDA LAEL MILLER

STATE SECRETS
USED-TO-BE LOVERS
JUST KATE
ONLY FOREVER
DARING MOVES
MIXED MESSAGES
GLORY, GLORY

Coming soon

HERE AND THEN

LINDA LAEL MILLER

THERE AND NOW

MIRA BOOKS

ISBN 1-55166-283-3

THERE AND NOW

Copyright © 1992 by Linda Lael Miller.

Printed in U.S.A.

For Darlene Layman,
the best darn secretary ever,
and her very nice husband, Lloyd

PINE RIVER, WASHINGTON 1892	PINE RIVER, WASHINGTON 1992
Population: 300	Population: 5,500
4 saloons	1 tavern/pool hall
1 U.S. Marshal	5 full-time police officers
One-room schoolhouse	1 elementary school, 1 high school and 1 junior college
1 doctor— Jonathan Fortner, M.D.	15 physicians and 1 hospital
2 churches	6 churches
3 livery stables	4 full-service filling stations
172 horses (within the city limits)	53 horses (outside the city limits)

1

Elisabeth McCartney's flagging spirits lifted a little as she turned past the battered rural mailbox and saw the house again.

The white Victorian structure stood at the end of a long gravel driveway, flanked by apple trees in riotous pink-white blossom. A veranda stretched around the front and along one side, and wild rose bushes, budding scarlet and yellow, clambered up a trellis on the western wall.

Stopping her small station wagon in front of the garage, Elisabeth sighed and let her tired aquamarine eyes wander over the porch, with its sagging floor and peeling paint. Less than two years before, Aunt Verity would have been standing on the step, waiting with smiles and hugs. And Elisabeth's favorite cousin, Rue, would have vaulted over the porch railing to greet her.

Elisabeth's eyes brimmed with involuntary tears. Aunt Verity was dead now, and Rue was God only knew where, probably risking life and limb for some red-hot news story. The divorce from Ian, final for just a month, was a trauma Elisabeth was going to have to get through on her own.

With a sniffle, she squared her shoulders and drew a deep breath to bolster her courage. She reached for her purse and got out of the car, pulling her suitcase after her. Elisabeth had gladly let Ian keep their ultramodern plastic-

and-smoked-glass furniture. Her books, tapes and other personal belongings would be delivered later by a moving company.

She slung her purse strap over her shoulder and proceeded toward the porch, the high grass brushing against the knees of her white jeans as she passed. At the door, with its inset of colorful stained glass, Elisabeth put down the suitcase and fumbled through her purse for the set of keys the real-estate agent had given her when she stopped in Pine River.

The lock was old and recalcitrant, but it turned, and Elisabeth opened the door and walked into the familiar entryway, lugging her suitcase with her.

There were those who believed this house was haunted—it had been the stuff of legend in and around Pine River for a hundred years—but for Elisabeth, it was a friendly place. It had been her haven since the summer she was fifteen, when her mother had died suddenly and her grieving, overwhelmed father had sent her here to stay with his somewhat eccentric widowed sister-in-law, Verity.

Inside, she leaned back against the sturdy door, remembering. Rue's wealthy parents had been divorced that same year, and Elisabeth's cousin had joined the fold. Verity Claridge, who told fabulous stories of ghosts and magic and people traveling back and forth between one century and another, had taken both girls in and simply loved them.

Elisabeth bit her lower lip and hoisted her slender frame away from the door. It was too much to hope, she thought with a beleaguered smile, that Aunt Verity might still be wandering these spacious rooms.

With a sigh, she hung her shoulder bag over the newel post at the base of the stairway and hoisted the suitcase.

At the top of the stairs were three bedrooms, all on the right-hand side of the hallway. Elisabeth paused, looking curiously at the single door on the left-hand side and touched the doorknob.

Beyond that panel of wood was a ten-foot drop to the sun-porch roof. The sealed door had always fascinated both her and Rue, perhaps because Verity had told them such convincing stories about the world that lay on the other side of it.

Elisabeth smiled and shook her head, making her chin-length blond curls bounce around her face. "You may be gone, Auntie," she said softly, "but your fanciful influence lives on."

With that, Elisabeth opened the door on the opposite side of the hallway and stepped into the master suite that had always been Verity's. Although the rest of the house was badly in need of cleaning, the real-estate agent had sent a cleaning crew over in anticipation of Elisabeth's arrival to prepare the kitchen and one bedroom.

The big four-poster had been uncovered and polished, made up with the familiar crocheted ecru spread and pillow shams, and the scent of lemon furniture polish filled the air. Elisabeth laid the suitcase on the blue-velvet upholstered bench at the foot of the bed and tucked her hands into the back pockets of her jeans as she looked around the room.

The giant mahogany armoire stood between two floor-to-ceiling windows covered by billowing curtains of Nottingham lace, waiting to receive the few clothes Elisabeth had brought with her. A pair of Queen Anne chairs, upholstered in rich blue velvet, sat facing the little brick fireplace, and a chaise longue covered in cream-colored brocade graced the opposite wall. There was also a desk—

Verity had called it a secretary—and a vanity table with a seat needle-pointed with pale roses.

Pushing her tousled tresses back from her face with both hands, Elisabeth went to the vanity and perched on the bench. A lump filled her throat as she recalled sitting here while Verity styled her hair for a summer dance.

With a hand that trembled slightly, Elisabeth opened the ivory-inlaid jewel box. Verity's favorite antique necklace, given to her by a friend, lay within.

Elisabeth frowned. *Odd,* she reflected. She'd thought Rue had taken the delicate filigree necklace, since she was the one who loved jewelry. Verity's modest estate—the house, furnishings, a few bangles and a small trust fund—had been left to Elisabeth and Rue in equal shares, and then the cousins had made divisions of their own.

Carefully, Elisabeth opened the catch and draped the necklace around her neck. She smiled sadly, recalling Verity's assertions that the pendant possessed some magical power.

Just then, the telephone rang, startling her even though the agent at the real-estate office had told her service had been connected and had given her the new number.

"Hello?" she said into the receiver of the French phone sitting on the vanity table.

"So you made it in one piece." The voice belonged to Janet Finch, one of Elisabeth's closest friends. She and Janet had taught together at Hillsdale Elementary School in nearby Seattle.

Elisabeth sagged a little as she gazed into the mirror. The necklace looked incongruous with her Seahawks sweatshirt. "You make it sound like I crawled here through a barrage of bullets," she replied. "I'm all right, Janet. Really."

Janet sighed. "Divorce is painful, even if it was your

own idea," she insisted quietly. "I just think it would have been better if you'd stayed in Seattle, where your friends are. I mean, who do you know in that town now that your aunt is gone and Rue is off in South Africa or Eastern Europe or wherever she is?"

Through the windows, Elisabeth could see the neighbor's orchard. It was only too true that most of her friends had long since moved away from Pine River and her life had been in Seattle from the moment she'd married Ian. "I know myself," she answered. "And the Buzbee sisters."

Despite her obvious concerns, Janet laughed. Like Elisabeth, she was barely thirty, but she could be a real curmudgeon at times. "The Buzbee sisters? I don't think you've told me about them."

Elisabeth smiled. "Of course, I have. They live across the road. They're spinsters, but they're also card-carrying adventurers. According to Aunt Verity, they've been all over the world—they even did a joint hitch in the Peace Corps."

"Fascinating," Janet said, but Elisabeth couldn't tell whether she meant it or not.

"When you come down to visit, I'll introduce you," Elisabeth promised, barely stifling a yawn. Lately, she'd tired easily; the emotional stresses and strains of the past year were catching up with her.

"If that's an invitation, I'm grabbing it," Janet said quickly. "I'll be down on Friday night to spend the weekend helping you settle in."

Elisabeth smiled, looking around the perfectly furnished room. There wasn't going to be a tremendous amount of "settling in" to do. And although she wanted to see Janet, she would have preferred to spend that first weekend alone, sorting through her thoughts and absorbing the special ambiance of Aunt Verity's house. "I'll make spaghetti and meatballs," she said, resigned. "Call me when you get to Pine River and I'll give you directions."

"I don't need directions," Janet pointed out reasonably. "You were married in that house, in case you've forgotten, and I was there." Her voice took on a teasing note. "You remember. Rue and I and two of your friends from college were all dressed alike, in floaty pink dresses and picture hats, and your cousin said it was a shame we couldn't sing harmony."

Elisabeth chuckled and closed her eyes. How she missed Rue, with her quick, lethal wit. She drew a deep breath, let it out, and made an effort to sound cheerful so Janet wouldn't worry about her any more than she already did. "I'll be looking for you on Friday, in time for dinner," Elisabeth said. And then, after quick good-byes, she hung up.

With a sigh of relief, Elisabeth crossed the room to the enormous bed, kicked off her sneakers and stretched out, her hands cupped behind her head. Looking up at the intricately crocheted canopy, she felt a sense of warm well-being wash over her.

She would make a list and shop for groceries later, she promised herself. Right now she needed to rest her eyes for a few moments.

She must have drifted off, because when the music awakened her, the spill of sunlight across the hooked rug beside the bed had receded and there was a slight chill in the air.

Music.

Elisabeth's heart surged into her throat as she sat up and looked around. There was no radio or TV in the room, and yet the distant, fairylike notes of a piano still teased her ears, accompanied by a child's voice.

"Twinkle, twinkle, little star
how I wonder what you are...."

Awkwardly, Elisabeth scrambled off the bed to pursue the sound, but it ceased when she reached the hallway.

All the same, she hurried downstairs.

The small parlor, where Aunt Verity's spinet was kept, was empty, and the piano itself was hidden beneath a large canvas dust cover. Feeling a headache begin to pulse beneath her right temple, Elisabeth checked the big, old-fashioned radio in the large parlor and the portable TV set on the kitchen counter.

Neither was on.

She shoved her hands through her already-mussed hair. Maybe her friends were right to be concerned. Maybe the divorce was affecting her more deeply than she'd ever guessed.

The thing to do, she decided after a five-minute struggle to regain her composure, was to get her purse and drive into Pine River for groceries. Since she'd left her shoes behind, she started up the rear stairway.

An instant after Elisabeth reached the second floor, the piano music sounded clearly again, thunderous and discordant. She froze, her fingers closed around Aunt Verity's pendant.

"I don't want to practice anymore," a child's voice said petulantly. "It's sunny out, and Vera and I are having a picnic by the creek."

Elisabeth closed her eyes, battling to retain her equilibrium. The voice, like the music, was coming from the other side of the door Aunt Verity had told so many stories about.

As jarring as the experience was, Elisabeth had no sense of evil. It was her own mental state she feared, not the ghosts that supposedly populated this old house. Perhaps in her case, the result of a broken dream had been a broken mind.

She walked slowly along the highway, gripped the doorknob and rattled it fiercely. The effort to open the door was hopeless, since the passage had been sealed long ago, but Elisabeth didn't let up. "Who's there?" she cried.

She wasn't crazy. Someone, somewhere, was playing a cruel joke on her.

Finally exhausted, she released her desperate hold on the knob, and asked again plaintively, "Please. Who's there?"

"Just us, dear," said a sweet feminine voice from the top of the main stairway. The music had died away to an echo that Elisabeth thought probably existed only in her mind.

She turned, a wan smile on her face, to see the Buzbee sisters, Cecily and Roberta, standing nearby.

Roberta, the taller and more outgoing of the two, was holding a covered baking dish and frowning. "Are you quite all right, Elisabeth?" she asked.

Cecily was watching Elisabeth with enormous blue eyes. "That door led to the old part of the house," she said. "The section that was burned away in 1892."

Elisabeth felt foolish, having been caught trying to open a door to nowhere. She managed another smile and said, "Miss Cecily, Miss Roberta—it's so good to see you."

"We've brought Cecily's beef casserole," Roberta

said, practical as ever. "Sister and I thought you wouldn't want to cook, this being your first night in the house."

"Thank you," Elisabeth said shakily. "Would you like some coffee? I think there might be a jar of instant in one of the cupboards...."

"We wouldn't *think* of intruding," said Miss Cecily.

Elisabeth led the way toward the rear stairway, hoping her gait seemed steady to the elderly women behind her. "You wouldn't be intruding," she insisted. "It's a delight to see you, and it was so thoughtful of you to bring the casserole."

From the size of the dish, Elisabeth figured she'd be able to live on the offering for a week. The prospective monotony of eating the same thing over and over didn't trouble her; her appetite was small these days, and what she ate didn't matter.

In the kitchen, Elisabeth found a jar of coffee, probably left behind by Rue, who liked to hole up in the house every once in a while when she was working on a big story. While water was heating in a copper kettle on the stove, Elisabeth sat at the old oak table in the breakfast nook, talking with the Buzbee sisters.

She neatly skirted the subject of her divorce, and the sisters were too well-mannered to pursue it. The conversation centered on the sisters' delight at seeing the old house occupied again. Through all of it, the child's voice and the music drifted in Elisabeth's mind, like wisps of a half-forgotten dream. *Twinkle, twinkle...*

Trista Fortner's small, slender fingers paused on the piano keys. Somewhere upstairs, a door rattled hard on its hinges. "Who's there?" a feminine voice called over the tremendous racket.

Trista got up from the piano bench, smoothed her

freshly ironed poplin pinafore and scrambled up the front stairs and along the hallway.

The door of her bedroom was literally clattering in its frame, the knob twisting wildly, and Trista's brown eyes went wide. She was too scared to scream and too curious to run away, so she just stood there, staring.

The doorknob ceased its frantic gyrations, and the woman spoke again, "Please. Who's there?"

"Trista," the child said softly. She found the courage to touch the knob, to twist her wrist. Soon, she was peering around the edge.

There was nothing at all to see, except for her bed, her dollhouse, the doorway that led to her own private staircase leading into the kitchen and the big, wooden wardrobe that held her clothes.

At once disappointed and relieved, the eight-year-old closed the door again and trooped staunchly back downstairs to the piano.

She sighed as she settled down at the keyboard again. If she mentioned what she'd heard and seen to Papa, would he believe her? The answer was definitely no, since he was a man of science. He would set her down in his study and say, "Now, Trista, we've discussed this before. I know you'd like to convince yourself that your mother could come back to us, but there are no such things as ghosts. I don't want to hear any more of this foolishness from you. Is that clear?"

She began to play again, dutifully. Forlornly.

A few minutes later, Trista glanced at the clock on the parlor mantel. Still half an hour left to practice, then she could go outside and play with Vera. She'd tell her best friend there was a ghost in her house, she supposed, but only after making her swear to keep quiet about it.

On the other hand, maybe it would be better if she

didn't say anything at all to anybody. Even Vera would think Trista was hearing things just because she wanted her mama to come back.

"Twinkle, twinkle," she muttered, as her fingers moved awkwardly over the keys.

"My, yes," Roberta Buzbee went on, dusting nonexistent crumbs from the bosom of her colorful jersey print dress. "Mama was just a little girl when this house burned."

"She was nine," Miss Cecily put in solemnly. She shuddered. "It was a dreadful blaze. The doctor and his poor daughter perished in it, you know. And, of course, that part of the house was never rebuilt."

Elisabeth swallowed painfully, thinking of the perfectly ordinary music she'd heard—and the voice. "So there was a child," she mused.

"Certainly," Roberta volunteered. "Her name was Trista Anne Fortner, and she was Mama's very best friend. They were close in age, you know, Mama being a few months older." She paused to make a tsk-tsk sound. "It was positively tragic—Dr. Fortner expired trying to save his little girl. It was said the companion set the fire— she was tried for murder and hanged, wasn't she, Sister?"

Cecily nodded solemnly.

A chill moved through Elisabeth, despite the sunny warmth of that April afternoon, and she took a steadying sip from her coffee cup. *Get a grip, Elisabeth,* she thought, giving herself an inward shake. *Whatever you heard, it wasn't a dead child singing and playing the piano. Aunt Verity's stories about this house were exactly that—stories.*

"You look pale, my dear," Cecily piped up.

The last thing Elisabeth needed was another person to

worry about her. Her friends in Seattle were doing enough of that. "I'll be teaching at the Pine River school this fall," she announced, mainly to change the subject.

"Roberta taught at the old Cold Creek schoolhouse," Cecily said proudly, pleased to find some common ground, "and I was the librarian in town. That was before we went traveling, of course."

Before Elisabeth could make a response, someone slammed a pair of fists down hard on the keys of a piano.

This time, there was no possibility that the sound was imaginary. It reverberated through the house, and both the Buzbee sisters flinched.

Very slowly, Elisabeth set her coffee cup on the counter. "Excuse me," she said when she was able to break the spell. The spinet in the parlor was still draped, and there was no sign of anyone.

"It's the ghost," said Cecily, who had followed Elisabeth from the kitchen, along with her sister. "After all this time, she's still here. Well, I shouldn't wonder."

Elisabeth thought again of the stories Aunt Verity had told her and Rue, beside the fire on rainy nights. They'd been strange tales of appearances and disappearances and odd sounds, and Rue and Elisabeth had never passed them on because they were afraid their various parents would refuse to let them go on spending their summers with Verity. The thought of staying in their boarding schools year round had been unbearable.

"Ghost?" Elisabeth croaked.

Cecily was nodding. "Trista has never rested properly, poor child. And they say the doctor looks for her still. Folks have seen his buggy along the road, too."

Elisabeth suppressed a shudder.

"Sister," Roberta interceded somewhat sharply. "You're upsetting Elisabeth."

"I'm fine," Elisabeth lied. "Just fine."

"Maybe we'd better be going," said Cecily, patting Elisabeth's arm. "And don't worry about poor little Trista. She's quite harmless, you know."

The moment the two women were gone, Elisabeth hurried to the old-fashioned black telephone on the entryway table and dialed Rue's number in Chicago.

An answering machine picked up on the third ring. "Hi, there, whoever you are," Rue's voice said energetically. "I'm away on a special project, and I'm not sure how long I'll be gone this time. If you're planning to rob my condo, please be sure to take the couch. If not, leave your name and number and I'll get in touch with you as soon as I can. Ciao, and don't forget to wait for the beep."

Elisabeth's throat was tight; even though she'd known Rue was probably away, she'd hoped, by some miraculous accident, to catch her cousin between assignments. "Hi, Rue," she said. "It's Beth. I've moved into the house and—well—I'd just like to talk, that's all. Could you call as soon as you get in?" Elisabeth recited the number and hung up.

She pushed up the sleeves of her shirt and started for the kitchen. Earlier, she'd seen cleaning supplies in the broom closet, and heaven knew, the place needed some attention.

Jonathan Fortner rubbed the aching muscles at his nape with one hand as he walked wearily through the darkness toward the lighted house. His medical bag seemed heavier than usual as he mounted the back steps and opened the door.

The spacious kitchen was empty, though a lantern glowed in the center of the red-and-white-checked tablecloth.

Jonathan set his bag on a shelf beside the door, hung up his hat, shrugged out of his suitcoat and loosened his string tie. Sheer loneliness ached in his middle as he crossed the room to the stove with its highly polished chrome.

His dinner was congealing in the warming oven, as usual. Jonathan unfastened his cuff links, dropped them into the pocket of his trousers and rolled up his sleeves. Then, taking a kettle from the stove, he poured hot water into a basin, added two dippers of cold from the bucket beside the sink and began scrubbing his hands with strong yellow soap.

"Papa?"

He turned with a weary smile to see Trista standing at the bottom of the rear stairway, wearing her nightgown. "Hello, Punkin," he said. A frown furrowed his brow. "Ellen's here, isn't she? You haven't been home alone all this time?"

Trista resembled him instead of Barbara, with her dark hair and gray eyes, and it was a mercy not to be reminded of his wife every time he looked at his daughter.

"Ellen had to go home after supper," Trista said, drawing back a chair and joining Jonathan at the table as he sat down to eat. "Her brother Billy came to get her. Said the cows got out."

Jonathan's jawline tightened momentarily. "I don't know how many times I've told that girl..."

Trista laughed and reached out to cover his hand with her own. "I'm big enough to be alone for a few hours, Papa," she said.

Jonathan dragged his fork through the lumpy mashed potatoes on his plate and sighed. "You're eight years old," he reminded her.

"Maggie Simpkins is eight, too, and she cooks for her father and all her brothers."

"And she's more like an old woman than a child," Jonathan said quietly. It seemed he saw elderly children every day, though God knew things were better here in Pine River than in the cities. "You just leave the housekeeping to Ellen and concentrate on being a little girl. You'll be a woman soon enough."

Trista looked pointedly at the scorched, shriveled food on her father's plate. "If you want to go on eating that awful stuff, it's your choice." She sighed, set her elbows on the table's edge and cupped her chin in her palms. "Maybe you should get married again, Papa."

Jonathan gave up on his dinner and pushed the plate away. Just the suggestion filled him with loneliness—and fear. "And maybe you should get back to bed," he said brusquely, avoiding Trista's eyes while he took his watch from his vest pocket and frowned at the time. "It's late."

His daughter sighed again, collected his plate and scraped the contents into the scrap pan for the neighbor's pigs. "Is it because you still love Mama that you don't want to get another wife?" Trista inquired.

Jonathan went to the stove for a mug of Ellen's coffee, which had all the pungency of paint solvent. There were a lot of things he hadn't told Trista about her mother, and one of them was that there had never really been any love between the two of them. Another was that Barbara hadn't died in a distant accident, she'd deliberately abandoned her husband and child. Jonathan had gone quietly to Olympia and petitioned the state legislature for a divorce. "Wives aren't like wheelbarrows and soap flakes, Trista," he said hoarsely. "You can't just go to the mercantile and buy one."

"There are plenty of ladies in Pine River who are sweet

on you," Trista insisted. Maybe she was only eight, but at times she had the forceful nature of a dowager duchess. "Miss Jinnie Potts, for one."

Jonathan turned to face his daughter, his cup halfway to his lips, his gaze stern. "To bed, Trista," he said firmly.

She scampered across the kitchen in a flurry of dark hair and flannel and threw her arms around his middle. "Good night, Papa," she said, squeezing him, totally disarming him in that way that no other female could. "I love you."

He bent to kiss the top of her head. "I love you, too," he said, his voice gruff.

Trista gave him one last hug, then turned and hurried up the stairs. Without her, the kitchen was cold and empty again.

Jonathan poured his coffee into the iron sink and reached out to turn down the wick on the kerosene lantern standing in the center of the table. Instantly, the kitchen was black with gloom, but Jonathan's steps didn't falter as he crossed the room and started up the stairs.

He'd been finding his way in the dark for a long time.

2

Apple-blossom petals blew against the dark sky like snow as Elisabeth pulled into her driveway early that evening, after making a brief trip to Pine River. Her khaki skirt clung to her legs as she hurried to carry in four paper bags full of groceries.

She had just completed the second trip when a crash of thunder shook the windows in their sturdy sills and lightning lit the kitchen.

Methodically, Elisabeth put her food away in the cupboards and the refrigerator, trying to ignore the sounds of the storm. Although she wasn't exactly afraid of noisy weather, it always left her feeling unnerved.

She had just put a portion of the Buzbee sisters' casserole in the oven and was preparing to make a green salad when the telephone rang. "Hello," she said, balancing the receiver between her ear and shoulder so that she could go on with her work.

"Hello, darling," her father said in his deep and always slightly distracted voice. "How's my baby?"

Elisabeth smiled and scooped chopped tomatoes into the salad bowl. "I'm fine, Daddy. Where are you?"

He chuckled ruefully. "You know what they say—if it's Wednesday, this must be Cleveland. I'm on another business trip."

That was certainly nothing new. Marcus Claridge had

been on the road ever since he had started his consulting business when Elisabeth was little. "How are Traci and the baby?" she asked. Just eighteen months before Marcus had married a woman three years younger than Elisabeth, and the couple had an infant son.

"They're terrific," Marcus answered awkwardly, then cleared his throat. "Listen, I know you're having a rough time right now, sweetheart, and Traci and I were thinking that...well...maybe you'd like to come to Lake Tahoe and spend the summer with us. I don't like to think of you burrowed down in that spooky old house...."

Elisabeth laughed, and the sound was tinged with hysteria. She didn't dislike Traci, who invariably dotted the *i* at the end of her name with a little heart, but she didn't want to spend so much as an hour trying to make small talk with the woman, either. "Daddy, this house isn't spooky. I love the place, you know that. Who told you I was here, anyway?"

Her father sighed. "Ian. He's very worried about you, darling. We all are. You don't have a job. You don't know a soul in that backwoods town. What do you intend to do with yourself?"

She smiled. Trust Ian to make it sound as if she were hiding out in a cave and licking her wounds. "I've been substitute teaching for the past year, Daddy, and I *do* have a job. I'll be in charge of the third grade at Pine River Elementary starting in early September. In the meantime, I plan to put in a garden, do some reading and sewing—"

"What you need is another man."

Elisabeth rolled her eyes. "Even better, I could just step in front of a speeding truck and break every bone in my body," she replied. "That would be quicker and not as messy."

"Very funny," Marcus said, but there was a grudging

note of amused respect in his tone. "All right, baby, I'll leave you alone. Just promise me that you'll take care of yourself and that you'll call and leave word with Traci if you need anything."

"I promise," Elisabeth said.

"Good."

"I love you, Daddy—"

The line went dead before Elisabeth had completed the sentence. "Say hello to Traci and the baby for me," she finished aloud as she replaced the receiver.

After supper, Elisabeth washed her dishes. By then, the power was flickering on and off, and the wind was howling around the corners of the house. She decided to go to bed early so she could get a good start on the cleaning come morning.

Since she'd showered before going to town, Elisabeth simply exchanged her skirt and blouse for an oversize red football jersey, washed her face, scrubbed her teeth and went to bed. Her hand curved around the delicate pendant on Aunt Verity's necklace as she settled back against her pillows.

Lightning filled the room with an eerie light, but Elisabeth felt safe in the big four-poster. How many nights had she and Rue come squealing and giggling to this bed, squeezing in on either side of Aunt Verity to beg her for a story that would distract them from the thunder?

She snuggled down between crisp, clean sheets, closed her eyes and sighed. She'd been right to come back here; this was home, the place where she belonged.

The scream brought her eyes flying open again.

"Papa!"

Elisabeth bolted out of bed and ran into the hallway. Another shriek sounded, followed by choked sobs.

It wasn't the noise that paralyzed Elisabeth, however;

it was the thin line of golden light glowing underneath the door across the hall. That door that opened onto empty space.

She leaned against the jamb, one trembling hand resting on the necklace, as though to conjure Aunt Verity for a rescuer. "Papa, Papa, where are you?" the child cried desperately from the other side.

Elisabeth pried herself away from the woodwork and took one step across the hallway, then another. She found the knob, and the sound of her own heartbeat thrumming in her ears all but drowned out the screams of the little girl as she turned it.

Even when the door actually opened, Elisabeth expected to be hit with a rush of rainy April wind. The soft warmth that greeted her instead came as a much keener shock.

"My God," she whispered as her eyes adjusted to a candle-lit room where there should have been nothing but open air.

She saw the child, curled up at the very top of a narrow bed. Then she saw what must be a dollhouse, another door and a big, old-fashioned wardrobe. As she stood there on the threshold of a world that couldn't possibly exist, the little girl moved, her form illuminated by the light that glowed from an elaborate china lamp on the bedside table.

"You're not Papa," the child said with a cautious sniffle, edging farther back against the intricately carved headboard.

Elisabeth swallowed. "N-no," she allowed, extending one toe to test the floor. Even now, with this image in front of her, complete in every detail, her five senses were telling her that if she stepped into the room, she would plummet onto the sun-porch roof and break numerous bones.

The little girl dragged the flannel sleeve of her night-gown across her face and sniffled again. "Papa's probably in the barn. The animals get scared when there's a storm."

Elisabeth hugged herself, squeezed her eyes tightly shut and stepped over the threshold, fully prepared for a plunge. Instead, she felt a smooth wooden floor beneath her feet. It seemed to her that "Papa" might have been more concerned about a frightened daughter than frightened animals, but then, since she had to be dreaming the entire episode, that point was purely academic.

"You're the lady, aren't you?" the child asked, drawing her knees up under the covers and wrapping small arms around them. "The one who rattled the doorknob and called out."

This isn't happening, Elisabeth thought, running damp palms down her thighs. *I'm having an out-of-body experience or something.* "Y-yes," she stammered after a long pause. "I guess that was me."

"I'm Trista," the girl announced. Her hair was a dark, rich color, her eyes a stormy gray. She settled comfortably against her pillows, folding her arms.

Trista. The doctor's daughter, the child who died horribly in a raging house fire some seventy years before Elisabeth was even born. "Oh, my God," she whispered again.

"You keep saying that," Trista remarked, sounding a little critical. "It's not truly proper to take the Lord's name in vain, you know."

Elisabeth swallowed hard. "I k-know. I'm sorry."

"It would be perfectly all right to give me yours, however."

"What?"

"Your name, goose," Trista said good-naturedly.

"Elisabeth. Elisabeth McCartney—no relation to the

Beatle.'' As she spoke, Elisabeth was taking in the frilly chintz curtains at the window, the tiny shingles on the roof of the dollhouse.

Trista wrinkled her nose. ''Why would you be related to a bug?''

Elisabeth would have laughed if she hadn't been so busy questioning her sanity. *I refuse to have a breakdown over you, Ian McCartney,* she vowed silently. *I didn't love you that much.* ''Never mind. It's just that there's somebody famous who has the same last name as I do.''

Trista smoothed the colorful patchwork quilt that covered her. ''Which are you?'' she demanded bluntly. ''My guardian angel, or just a regular ghost?''

Now Elisabeth did laugh. ''Is there such a thing as a 'regular ghost'?'' she asked, venturing farther into the room and sitting down on the end of Trista's bed. At the moment, she didn't trust her knees to hold her up. ''I'm neither one of those things, Trista. You're looking at an ordinary, flesh-and-blood woman.''

Trista assessed Elisabeth's football jersey with a puzzled expression. ''Is that your nightdress? I've never seen one quite like it.''

''Yes, this is my—nightdress.'' Elisabeth felt lightheaded and wondered if she would wake up with her face in the rain gutter that lined the sun-porch roof. She ran one hand over the high-quality workmanship of the quilt. If this was an hallucination, she reflected, it was a remarkably vivid one. ''Go to sleep now, Trista. I'm sure it's very late.''

Thunder shook the room and Trista shivered visibly. ''I won't be able to sleep unless I get some hot milk,'' she said, watching Elisabeth with wide, hopeful eyes.

Elisabeth fought an urge to enfold the child in her arms, to beg her to run away from this strange house and never,

ever return. She stood, the fingers of her right hand fidgeting with the necklace. "I'll go and make some for you." She started back toward the door, but Trista stopped her.

"It's that way, Elisabeth," she said, pointing toward the inner door. "I have my own special stairway."

"This is getting weirder and weirder," Elisabeth muttered, careful not to stub her toe on the massive dollhouse as she crossed to the other door and opened it. "Let's see just how far this delusion goes," she added, finding herself at the top of a rear stairway. Her heart pounded so hard, she thought she'd faint as she made her way carefully down to the lower floor.

She wouldn't have recognized the kitchen, it was so much bigger than the one she knew. A single kerosene lantern burned in the center of the oak table, sending up a quivering trail of sooty smoke. There were built-in cabinets and bins along one wall, and the refrigerator and the stove were gone. In their places were an old-fashioned wooden icebox and an enormous iron-and-chrome monster designed to burn wood. The only thing that looked familiar was the back stairway leading into the main hallway upstairs.

Elisabeth stood in the middle of the floor, holding herself together by sheer force of will. "This is a dream, Beth," she told herself aloud, grasping the brass latch on the door of the icebox and giving it a cautious wrench. "Relax. This is *only a dream.*"

The door opened and she bent, squinting, to peer inside. Fortunately, the milk was at the front, in a heavy crockery pitcher.

Elisabeth took the pitcher out of the icebox, closed the door with a distracted motion of one heel and scanned the dimly lit room again. "Wait till you tell Rue about this," she chattered on, mostly in an effort to comfort herself.

"She'll want to do a documentary about you. You'll make the cover of the *Enquirer,* and tabloid TV will have a heyday—"

"Who the hell are you?"

The question came from behind her, blown in on a wet-and-frigid wind. Elisabeth whirled, still clutching the pitcher of cream-streaked milk to her bosom, and stared into the furious gray eyes of a man she had never seen before.

A strange sensation of being wrenched toward him spiritually compounded Elisabeth's shock.

He was tall, close to six feet, with rain-dampened dark hair and shoulders that strained the fabric of his suitcoat. He wore a vest with a gold watch chain dangling from one pocket, and his odd, stiff collar was open.

For some confounding reason, Elisabeth found herself wanting to touch him—tenderly at first, and then with the sweet, dizzying fury of passion.

She gave herself an inward shake. "This is really authentic," Elisabeth said. "I hope I'll be able to remember it all."

The stranger approached and took the endangered pitcher from Elisabeth's hands, setting it aside on the table. His eyes raked her figure, taking in every fiber of the long football jersey that served as her favorite nightgown, leaving gentle fire in their wake.

"I asked you a question," he snapped. "Who the devil are you?"

Elisabeth gave an hysterical little burst of laughter. The guy was a spirit—or more likely a delusion—and she felt a staggering attraction to him. She *must* be 'round the bend. "Who I am isn't the question at all," she answered intractably. "The question is, are you a ghost or am *I* a ghost?" She paused and spread her hands, reasoning that there was no sense in fighting the dream. "I mean, who ya gonna call?"

The man standing before her—Elisabeth could only assume he was the "Papa" Trista had been screaming for—puckered his brow in consternation. Then he felt her forehead with the backs of four cool fingers.

His touch heated Elisabeth's skin and sent a new shock splintering through her, and Elisabeth fairly leapt backward. Hoping it would carry her home to the waking world, like some talisman, she brought the pendant from beneath her shirt and traced its outline with her fingers.

"What is your name?" the man repeated patiently, as though speaking to an imbecile.

Elisabeth resisted an impulse to make a suitable noise with a finger and her lower lip and smiled instead. She had a drunken feeling, but she assured herself that she was bound to wake up any minute now. "Elisabeth McCartney. What's yours?"

"Dr. Jonathan Fortner," was the pensive answer. His steely eyes dropped to the pendant she was fiddling with and went wide. In the next instant, before Elisabeth had had a chance even to brace herself, he'd gripped the necklace and ripped it from her throat. "Where did you get this?" he demanded, his voice a terrifying rasp.

Elisabeth stepped back again. Dream or no dream, she'd felt the pull of the chain against her nape, and she was afraid of the suppressed violence she sensed in this man. "It—it belonged to my aunt—and now it belongs to my cousin and me." She gathered every shred of courage she possessed just to keep from cowering before this man. "If you'll just give it back, please...."

"You're a liar," Dr. Fortner spat out, dropping the necklace into the pocket of his coat. "This pendant was my wife's—it's been in her family for generations."

Elisabeth wet her lips with the tip of her tongue. This whole experience, whatever it was, was getting totally out of hand. "Perhaps it belonged to your—your wife at one time," she managed nervously, "but it's mine now. Mine and my cousin's." She held out one palm. "I want it back."

He looked at her hand as though he might spit in it, then pressed her into a chair. Her knees were like jelly, and she couldn't be sure whether this was caused by her situation or the primitive, elemental tug she felt toward this man.

"Papa?" Trista called from upstairs.

Dr. Fortner's lethal glance followed the sound. He stood stock still for a long moment, then shrugged out of his coat and hung it from a peg beside the door. "Everything is all right," he called back. "Go to sleep."

Elisabeth swallowed the growing lump in her throat and started to rise from the chair. At one quelling glance from Dr. Fortner, however, she thought better of it and sank back to her seat. She watched with rounded eyes as her reluctant host sat down across from her.

"Who are you?" he asked sternly.

He was a remarkable man, ruggedly handsome and yet polished, in a Victorian sort of way. The sort Elisabeth had fantasized about since puberty.

She tried to keep her voice even and her manner calm. "I told you. I'm Elisabeth McCartney."

"All right, Elisabeth McCartney—what are you doing here, dressed in that crazy getup, and why were you wearing my wife's necklace?"

"I was—well, I don't know what I'm doing here, actually. Maybe I'm dreaming, maybe I'm a hologram or an astral projection...."

His dark eyebrows drew together for a moment. "A what?"

She sighed. "Either I'm dreaming or you are. Or maybe both of us. In any case, I think I need Aunt Verity's necklace to get back where I belong."

"Then it looks like you won't be going anywhere for a while. And I, for one, am not dreaming."

Elisabeth gazed into his hard, autocratic face. Doubtless, the pop-psychology gurus would have something disturbing to say about the irrefutable appeal this man held for her. "You're probably right. I don't see how you could possibly have the sensitivity to dream. Alan Alda, you definitely aren't. It must be me."

"Papa, is Elisabeth still here?"

The doctor's eyes scoured Elisabeth, then softened slightly. "Yes, Punkin, she's still here."

"She was going to bring me some warm milk," Trista persisted.

Jonathan glowered at Elisabeth for a moment, then gestured toward the pitcher. She stumbled out of her chair and proceeded to the wall of cupboards where, with some effort, she located a store of mugs and a small pan.

She poured milk into the kettle, shaking so hard, it was a wonder she didn't spill the stuff all over the floor, and set it on the stove to heat. She glanced toward the doctor's coat, hanging nearby on a peg, and gauged her chances of getting the necklace without his noticing.

They didn't seem good.

"If you want that milk to heat, you'll have to stoke up the fire," he said.

Elisabeth stiffened. The stove had all kinds of lids and doors, but she had no idea how to reach in and "stoke" the flames to life. And she really didn't want to bend over in her nightshirt. "Maybe you could do that," she said.

He took a chunk of wood from a crude box beside the stove, opened a little door in the front and shoved it inside. Then he reached for a poker that rested against the wall and jabbed at the embers and the wood until a snapping blaze flared up.

Elisabeth, feeling as stirred and warm as the coals at the base of the rejuvenated fire, lifted her chin to let him know she wasn't impressed and waited for the milk to heat.

Dr. Fortner regarded Elisabeth steadily. "I'm sure you're some kind of lunatic," he said reasonably, "though I'll be damned if I can figure out how you ended up in Pine River. In any case, you'll have to spend the night. I'll turn you over to the marshal in the morning."

Elisabeth was past wondering when this nightmare was going to end. "You'd actually keep me here all night? I'm a lunatic, remember? I could take an ax and chop you to bits while you sleep. Or put lye down your well."

By way of an answer, he strode across the room, snatched the pan from the stove and poured the milk into a mug. Then, after setting the kettle in the sink, he grasped Elisabeth's elbow in one hand and the cup in the other and started toward the stairs, stopping only to blow out the lamp.

The suitcoat, Elisabeth noticed, was left behind, on its peg next to the door.

He hustled Elisabeth through the darkness and up the steep, narrow, enclosed staircase ahead of him. Her knees trembled with a weird sort of excitement as she hustled along. "I'm not crazy, you know," she insisted, sounding a little breathless.

He opened the door to Trista's room and carried the milk inside, only to find his daughter sleeping soundly, a big, yellow-haired rag doll clutched in her arms.

A fond smile touched Jonathan Fortner's sensual mouth, and he bent to kiss the child lightly on the forehead. Then, after setting the unneeded milk on the bedstand, he motioned for Elisabeth to precede him into the hallway.

The fact that she'd originally entered the Twilight Zone from that door was not lost on Elisabeth. She rushed eagerly through it, certain she'd awaken on the other side in her own bed.

Instead, she found herself in a hallway that was familiar and yet startlingly different from the one she knew. There was a painted china lamp burning on a table, and grim photographs stuck out from the walls, their wire hangers visible. The patterned runner on the floor was one Elisabeth had never seen before.

"It must have been the beef casserole," she said.

Dr. Fortner gave her a look and propelled her down the hall to the room next to the one she was supposed to be sleeping in. "Get some rest, Miss McCartney. And remember—if you get up and start wandering around, I'll hear you."

"And do what?" Elisabeth said as she pushed open the door and stepped into a shadowy room. In the real world, it would be the one she and Rue had always shared during their visits.

"And lock you in the pantry for the rest of the night," he replied flatly.

Even though the room was almost totally dark, Elisabeth knew the doctor wasn't kidding. He *would* lock her in the pantry, like a prisoner. But then, all of this was only happening in her imagination anyway.

He pulled back some covers on a bed and guided her into it, and Elisabeth went without a struggle, pursued by odd and erotic thoughts of him joining her. None of this was like her at all; Ian had always complained that she wasn't passionate enough. She decided to simply close her eyes and put the whole crazy episode out of her mind. In the morning, she would wake up in her own bed.

"Good night," Dr. Fortner said. The timbre of his voice was rich and deep, and he smelled of rain and horses and pipe tobacco.

Elisabeth felt a deep physical stirring, but she knew nothing was going to come of it because, unfortunately, this wasn't that kind of dream. "Good night," she responded in a dutiful tone.

She lay wide awake for a long time, listening. Somewhere in the room, a clock was ticking, and rain pattered against the window. She heard a door open and close, and she imagined Dr. Fortner taking off his clothes. He'd do it methodically, with a certain rough, masculine grace.

Elisabeth closed her eyes firmly, but the intriguing images remained and her body began to throb. "Good grief, woman," she muttered, "this is a *dream*. Do you realize what Rue will say when she hears about this—and I know you'll be fool enough to tell her, too—she'll say, 'Get a life Bethie. Better yet, get a shrink.'"

She waited for a long time, then crept out of bed, grimacing as she opened the door. Fortunately, it didn't squeak on its hinges nor did the floorboards creak. Holding her breath, Elisabeth groped her way down the hall in the direction of the main staircase.

So much for your threats, Dr. Fortner, she thought smugly as she hurried through the large parlor and the dining room.

In the kitchen, she stubbed her toe trying to find the matches on the table and cried out in pain before she could stop herself. The fire was out in the stove and the room was cold.

Elisabeth snatched the coat from the peg and pulled it on, cowering in the shadows by the cabinets as she waited for Jonathan Fortner to storm in and follow up on his threat to lock her in the pantry.

When an estimated ten minutes had ticked past and he still hadn't shown up, Elisabeth came out of hiding, her fingers curved around the broken necklace in the coat's pocket. Slowly, carefully, she crept up the smaller of the two stairways and into Trista's room.

There she stood beside the bed for a moment, seeing quite clearly now that her eyes had adjusted again, looking down at the sleeping child. Trista was beautiful and so very much alive. Tears lined Elisabeth's lashes as she thought of all this little girl would miss by dying young.

She bent and kissed Trista's pale forehead, then crossed the room to the other door, the one she'd unwittingly stumbled through hours before. Eyes closed tightly, fingers clutching the necklace, she turned the knob and stepped over the threshold.

For almost a full minute she just stood there in the hallway, trembling, afraid to open her eyes. It was the feel of plush carpeting under her bare feet that finally alerted her to the fact that the dream was over and she was back in the real world.

Elisabeth began to sob softly for joy and relief. And maybe because she missed a man who didn't exist. When she'd regained some of her composure, she opened the door of her own room, stepped inside and flipped the switch. Light flooded the chamber, revealing the four-poster, the fireplace, the vanity, the Queen Anne chairs.

Suddenly, Elisabeth was desperately tired. She switched off the lights, stumbled to the bed and fell onto it face first.

When she awakened, the room was flooded with sunlight and her nose itched. Elisabeth sat up, pushing back her hair with one hand and trying to focus her eyes.

The storm was over, and she smiled. Maybe she'd take a long walk after breakfast and clear her head. That crazy dream she'd had the night before had left her with a sort of emotional hangover, and she needed fresh air.

She was passing the vanity table on her way to the bathroom when her image in the mirror stopped her where she stood. Shock washed over her as she stared, her eyes enormous, her mouth wide open.

She was wearing a man's suitcoat.

Her knees began to quiver and for a moment, she thought she'd be sick right where she stood. She collapsed onto the vanity bench and covered her face with both hands, peeking through her fingers at her reflection.

"It wasn't a dream," she whispered, hardly able to believe the words. She ran one hand down the rough woolen sleeve of the old-fashioned coat. "I was really there."

For a moment, the room dipped and swayed, and Elisabeth was sure she was going to faint. She pushed the bench back from the table and bent to put her head between her knees. "Don't swoon, Beth," she lectured herself. "There's a perfectly logical explanation for this. Okay, it beats the hell out of me what it could be, but there *is* an answer!"

Once she was sure she wasn't going to pass out, Elisabeth sat up again and drew measured breaths until she had achieved a reasonable sense of calm. She stared at her pale face in the mirror and at her startled blue eyes. But mostly she stared at Dr. Jonathan Fortner's coat.

She put her hand into the right pocket and found the necklace. Slowly lifting it out, she spread it gently on the vanity table. The necklace was broken near the catch, but the pendant was unharmed.

Elisabeth pulled in a deep breath, let it out slowly. Then, calmly, she stood up, removed Dr. Fortner's coat and proceeded into the bathroom.

During her shower and shampoo, she almost succeeded in convincing herself that she'd imagined the suitcoat as well as the broken necklace. But when she came out, wrapped in a towel, they were where she'd left them, silent proof that something very strange had happened to her.

With a lift of her chin, Elisabeth dressed in gray corduroy slacks and a raspberry sweater, then carefully blew her hair dry and styled it. She took the necklace with her when she went out of the room, but left the suitcoat behind.

In the hallway, her eyes locked on the door across the hall. She tried the knob, but it was rusted in place, and the plastic seal that surrounded the passage was unbroken.

"Trista?" she whispered.

There was no answer.

Elisabeth went slowly down the back staircase, recalling that there had been two of them in her "dream." She ate cereal, coffee and fruit while staring at the kitchen table, fetched her purse, got into her car and drove slowly along the puddled driveway toward the main road.

The house still needed cleaning, but Elisabeth's priorities had been altered slightly. Before she did anything else, she meant to have the necklace repaired.

3

"It should be ready by Friday morning," said the clerk in Pine River's one and only jewelry store, dropping Aunt Verity's necklace into a small brown envelope.

Elisabeth felt oddly deflated. She didn't know what was happening to her, but she suspected that the antique pendant was at the core of things, given Aunt Verity's stories, and she didn't want to let it out of her sight. "Thank you," she said with a sigh, and left the shop.

After doing a little more shopping at the supermarket, she drove staunchly back to the house, changed into old clothes, covered her hair with a bandanna and set to work dusting and sweeping and scrubbing.

She'd finished the large parlor and was starting on the dining room when the doorbell sounded. Elisabeth straightened her bandanna and smoothed her palms down the front of her frayed flannel shirt, then answered the rather peremptory summons.

Ian was standing on the porch, looking dapper in his three-piece business suit. His eyes assessed Elisabeth's work clothes with a patronizing expression that made her want to slap him.

Ironic as it was, he seemed to have no texture, no reality. It was as though *he* were the other-worldly being, not Jonathan.

"Hello, Bethie," he said.

She made no move to invite him in. "What do you want?" she asked bluntly. Her ex-husband was handsome, with his glossy chestnut hair and dark blue eyes, but Elisabeth had no illusions where he was concerned. To think she'd once believed he was an idealist!

He patted the expensive briefcase he carried under one arm. "Papers to sign," he said with a guileless lift of his eyebrows. "No big deal."

Reluctantly, Elisabeth stepped back out of the doorway. Since she didn't feel up to a sparring match with Ian, she didn't state the obvious: if Ian had left his very profitable seminars and taping sessions to deliver these papers personally, they were, indeed, a "big deal."

She saw his gaze sweep over the valuable antique furnishings as he stepped into the main parlor. Had his brain been an adding machine, it would have been spitting out paper tape.

"Your father called," he said, perching in a leather wing chair near the fireplace. "He's been worried about you."

Elisabeth kept her distance, standing with her arms folded. "I know. I talked to him."

Ian sighed and opened the briefcase on his lap, taking out a sheaf of papers. "I'm concerned about your inheritance, Bethie,—"

"I'll just bet you are," she interjected, holding her shoulders a little straighter.

He gave her a look of indulgent reprimand. "I have no intention of trying to take anything from you," he told her, shaking a verbal finger in her face. "It's just that I have questions about your ability to manage your share of the estate." He looked around again at the paintings, the substantial furniture and the costly knickknacks. "I don't think you realize what a bonanza you have here. You could easily be taken in."

"And your suggestion is...?" Elisabeth prompted dryly.

"That you allow my accountant to run an audit and give you some advice on how to manage—"

"Put the papers back in your briefcase, Ian. Neither Rue nor I want to sell this place or anything that's in it. Besides that, Rue's father had everything appraised soon after the will was read."

Ian's chiseled face was flushed. Clearly he was annoyed that he'd taken time away from his motivational company to visit his hopelessly old-fashioned ex-wife. "Elisabeth, you can't be serious about keeping this cavernous, drafty old house. Why, you could live anywhere in the world on your share of the take...."

Elisabeth walked to the front door and opened it, and Ian followed, somewhat unwillingly. Not for one moment did she believe the man had ever had her best interests at heart—he'd been planning to file for changes in the divorce agreement and get a piece of what he called "the take."

"Goodbye," she said.

"I'm getting married next Saturday," he replied, almost smugly, as he swept through the doorway.

"Congratulations," Elisabeth answered. "You'll understand if I don't send a sterling-silver pickle dish?" With that, she shut the door firmly and leaned against it, her arms folded.

Her throat thickened as she remembered her own wedding, right here in this marvelous old house, nearly a decade before. There had been flowers, old-fashioned dresses and organ music. Somehow, she'd missed the glaring fact that Ian didn't fit into the picture, with his supersophistication and jet-set values.

In retrospect, she saw that Ian had always been emotionally unavailable, just like her father, and she'd seen his cool distance as a challenge, something to surmount with her love.

After a few years, she'd realized her mistake—Ian didn't want children or a real home the way she did, and he cared far more about money than the ideals he touted in his lectures and books. Furthermore, there would be no breaching the emotional wall he'd built around his soul.

Elisabeth had quietly returned to teaching school, biding her time and saving her money until she'd built up the courage to file for a divorce and move out of Ian's luxury condo in Seattle.

With a sigh, she thrust herself away from the door and went back to her cleaning. The road to emotional maturity had been a painful, rocky one for her, but she'd learned who she was and what she wanted. To her way of thinking, that put her way out in front of the crowd.

Carefully, she removed Dresden figurines and Haviland plates from the big china closet in the dining room. As she worked, Elisabeth cataloged the qualities she would look for in a second husband. She wanted a gentle man, but he had to be strong, too. Tall, maybe, with dark hair and broad shoulders—

Elisabeth realized she was describing Jonathan Fortner and put down the stack of dessert plates she'd been about to carry to the kitchen for washing. Her hands were trembling.

He's not real, she reminded herself firmly. But another part of her mind argued that he was. She had his suitcoat to prove it.

Didn't she?

What with all the things that had been happening to her since her return to Pine River, Elisabeth was beginning to wonder if she really knew what was real and what wasn't. She hurried up the back stairs and along the hallway to her bedroom, ignoring the sealed doorway in the outside wall, and marched straight to the armoire.

After opening one heavy door, she reached inside and pulled out the coat, pressing it to her face with both hands. It still smelled of Jonathan, and the mingled scents filled Elisabeth with a bittersweet yearning to be near him.

Which was downright silly, she decided, since the man obviously lived in some other time—or some other universe. She would probably never see him again.

Sadly, she put the jacket back on its hanger and returned it to the wardrobe.

By Friday morning, Elisabeth had almost convinced herself that she *had* dreamed up Dr. Fortner and his daughter. Probably, she reasoned, she'd felt some deep, subconscious sympathy for them, learning that they'd both died right there in Aunt Verity's house. Her ideal man had no doubt been woven from the dreams, hopes and desperate needs secreted deep inside her, where a man as shallow as Ian could never venture.

As for the suitcoat, well, that had probably belonged to Verity's long-dead husband. No doubt, she had walked in her sleep that night and found the jacket in one of the trunks in the attic. But if that was true, why was the garment clean and unfrayed? Why didn't it smell of mothballs or mildew?

Elisabeth shook off the disturbing questions as she parked her car in front of Carlton Jewelry, but another quandary immediately took its place. Why was she almost desperately anxious to have Aunt Verity's necklace back in her possession again? Granted, it was very old and probably valuable, but she had never been much for bangles and beads, and money hardly mattered to her at all.

She was inordinately relieved when the pendant was poured from its brown envelope into the palm of her hand, fully restored to its former glory. She closed her fingers around it and shut her eyes for a second, and immediately, Jonathan's face filled her mind.

"Ms. McCartney?" the clerk asked, sounding concerned.

Elisabeth remembered herself, opened her eyes and got out her wallet to pay the bill.

When she arrived home an hour later with the makings for spaghetti, garlic bread and green salad, the moving company was there with her belongings. The two men carried in her books, tape collection, stereo, microwave oven, TV sets and VCR and boxes of seasonal clothes and shoes.

Elisabeth paid the movers extra to connect her VCR and set up the stereo, and made them tuna sandwiches and vegetable soup for lunch. When they were gone, she put on a Mozart tape and let the music swirl around her while she did up the lunch dishes and put away some of her things.

Knowing it would probably take hours or even days to find places for everything, Elisabeth stored her seasonal clothes in the small parlor and set about making her special spaghetti sauce.

Seeing her practical friend Janet again would surely put to rest these crazy fancies she was having, once and for all.

As promised, Janet arrived just when the sauce was ready to be poured over the pasta and served. She had straight reddish-brown hair that just brushed her shoulders and large hazel eyes, and she was dressed in a fashionable gray-and-white, pin-striped suit.

Elisabeth met her friend on the porch with a hug. "It's so good to see you."

Janet's expression was troubled as she studied Elisabeth. "You're pale, and I swear you've lost weight," she fretted.

Elisabeth grinned. "I'm *fine*," she said pointedly, bending to grasp the handle of the small suitcase Janet had set down moments before. "I hope you're hungry, because the sauce is at its peak."

After putting Janet's things in an upstairs bedroom, the two women returned to the kitchen. There they consumed spaghetti and salad at the small table in the breakfast nook, while an April sunset settled over the landscape.

From the first, Elisabeth wanted to confide in her friend, to show her the suitcoat and tell her all about her strange experience a few nights before, but somehow, she couldn't find the courage. They talked about Janet's new boyfriend and Rue's possible whereabouts instead.

After the dishes were done, Janet brought a video tape from her room and popped it into the VCR, while Elisabeth built a fire on the parlor hearth, using seasoned apple wood she'd found in the shed out back. An avid collector of black-and-white classics, Janet didn't rent movies, she bought them.

"What's tonight's feature?" Elisabeth asked, curling up at one end of the settee, while Janet sat opposite her, a bowl of the salty chips they both loved between them.

Janet gave a little shudder and smiled. *"The Ghost and Mrs. Muir,"* she replied. "Fitting, huh? I mean, since this house is probably haunted."

Elisabeth practically choked on the chip she'd just swallowed. "Haunted? Janet, that is really silly." The FBI warning was flickering on the television screen, silently ominous.

Her friend shrugged. "Maybe so, but a funny feeling came over me when I walked in here. It happened before, too, when I came to your wedding."

"That was a sense of impending doom, not anything supernatural," Elisabeth said.

Janet laughed. "You're probably right."

As they watched the absorbing movie, Elisabeth fiddled with the necklace and wondered if she wouldn't just turn around one day, like Mrs. Muir with her ghostly captain, and see Jonathan Fortner standing behind her.

The idea gave her a delicious, shivery sensation, totally unrelated to fear.

After the show was over and the chips were gone, Elisabeth and Janet had herbal tea in the kitchen and gossiped. When Elisabeth mentioned Ian's visit and his plans to remarry, Janet's happy grin faded.

"The sleaseball. How do you feel about this, Beth? Are you sad?"

Elisabeth reached across the table to touch her friend's hand. "If I am, it's only because the marriage I thought I was going to have never materialized. Like so many women, I created a fantasy world out of my own needs and desires, and when it collapsed, I was hurt. But I'm okay now, Janet, and I want you to stop worrying about me."

Janet looked at Elisabeth for a long moment and then nodded. "All right, I'll try. But I'd feel better if you'd come back to Seattle."

Elisabeth pushed back her chair and carried her empty cup and Janet's to the sink. "I played a part for so many years," she said with a sigh. "Now I need solitude to sort things out." She turned to face her friend. "Do you understand?"

"Yes," Janet answered, albeit reluctantly, getting out of her chair.

Elisabeth turned off the downstairs lights and started up the rear stairway, which was illuminated by the glow of the moon flooding in from a fanlight on the second floor. The urge to tell Janet about Jonathan was nearly overwhelming, but she kept the story to herself. There was no way practical, ducks-in-a-row Janet was going to understand.

Reaching her room, Elisabeth called out a good-night to her friend and closed the door. Everything looked so normal and ordinary and *real*—the four-poster, the vanity, the Queen Anne chairs, the fireplace.

She went to the armoire, opened it and ferreted out the suitcoat that was at once her comfort and her torment. She held the garment tightly, her face pressed to the fabric. The scent of Jonathan filled her spirit as well as her nostrils.

If she told Janet the incredible story and then showed her the coat—

Elisabeth stopped in midthought and shook her head. Janet would never believe she'd brought the jacket back from another era. Most of the time, Elisabeth didn't believe that herself. And yet the coat was real and her memories were so vivid, so piquant.

After a long time, Elisabeth put the suitcoat back in its place and exchanged her blouse and black corduroy slacks for another football jersey. Her fingers strayed to the pendant she took off only to shower.

"Jonathan," she said softly, and just saying his name was a sweet relief, like taking a breath of fresh air after being closed up in a stuffy house.

Elisabeth performed the usual ablutions, then switched off her lamp and crawled into bed. Ever since that morning when she'd recovered the necklace, a current of excitement had coursed just beneath the surface of her thoughts and feelings. She ached for the magic to take her back to that dream place, even though she was afraid to go there.

It didn't happen.

Elisabeth awakened the next morning to the sound of her clock radio. She put the pendant on the dresser, stripped off her jersey and took a long, hot shower. When she'd dressed in pink slacks and a rose-colored sweater, she hurried downstairs to find Janet in the kitchen, sipping coffee.

Janet was wearing shorts, sneakers and a hooded sweatshirt, and it was clear that she'd already been out for her customary run. She smiled. "Good morning."

"Don't speak to me until I've had a jolt of caffeine," Elisabeth replied with pretended indignation.

Her friend laughed. "I saw a notice for a craft show at the fairgrounds," she said as Elisabeth poured coffee. "Sounds like fun."

Elisabeth only shrugged. She was busy sipping.

"We could have lunch afterward."

"Fine," Elisabeth said. "Fine." She was almost her normal self by the time they'd had breakfast and set out for the fairgrounds in Elisabeth's car.

Blossom petals littered the road like pinkish-white snow, and Janet sighed. "I can see why you like the country," she said. "It has a certain serenity."

Elisabeth smiled, waving at Miss Cecily, who was standing at her mailbox. Miss Cecily waved back. "You wouldn't last a week," Elisabeth said with friendly contempt. "Not enough action."

Janet leaned her head back and closed her eyes. "I suppose you're right," she conceded dreamily. "But that doesn't mean I can't enjoy the moment."

They spent happy hours at the craft show, then dined on Vietnamese food from one of the many concession booths. It was when they paused in front of a quilting display that Elisabeth was forcibly reminded of the Jonathan episode.

The slender, dark-haired woman behind the plankboard counter stared at her necklace with rounded eyes and actually retreated a step, as though she thought it would zap her with an invisible ray. "Where did you get that?" she breathed.

Janet's brow crinkled as she frowned in bewilderment, but she just looked on in silence.

Elisabeth's heart was beating unaccountably fast, and she felt defensive, like a child caught stealing. "The necklace?" At the woman's nervous nod, she went on. "I inherited it from my aunt. Why?"

The woman was beginning to regain her composure. She smiled anxiously, but came no closer to the front of the booth. "Your aunt wouldn't be Verity Claridge?"

A finger of ice traced the length of Elisabeth's backbone. "Yes."

Expressive brown eyes linked with Elisabeth's blue-green ones. "Be careful," the dark-haired woman said.

Elisabeth had dozens of questions, but she sensed Janet's discomfort and didn't want to make the situation worse.

"What was that all about?" Janet asked when she and Elisabeth were in the car again, their various purchases loaded into the back. "I thought that woman was going to faint."

Chastity Pringle. Elisabeth hadn't made an effort to remember the name she'd read on the woman's laminated badge; she'd known it would still burn bright in her mind after nine minutes or nine decades. Whoever Ms. Pringle was, she knew Aunt Verity's necklace was no ordinary piece of jewelry, and Elisabeth meant to find out the whole truth about it.

"Elisabeth?"

She jumped slightly. "Hmm?"

"Didn't you think it was weird the way that woman acted?"

Elisabeth was navigating the early afternoon traffic, which was never all that heavy in Pine River. "The world is full of weird people," she answered.

Having gotten the concession she wanted, Janet turned her mind to the afternoon's entertainment. She and Elisabeth rented a stack of movies at the convenience store, put in an order for a pizza to be delivered later and returned to the house.

By the time breakfast was over on Sunday morning, Janet was getting restless. When noon came, she loaded up her things, said goodbye and hastened back to the city, where her boyfriend and her job awaited.

The moment Janet's car turned onto the highway, Elisabeth dashed to the kitchen and began digging through drawers. Finding a battered phone book, she flipped to the *P*'s. There was a Paul Pringle listed, but no Chastity.

After taking a deep breath, Elisabeth called the man and asked if he had a relative by the name of Chastity. He barked that nobody in his family would be fool enough to give an innocent little girl a name like that and hung up.

Elisabeth got her purse and drove back to the fairgrounds. The quilting booth was manned by a chunky, gray-haired grandmother this time, and sunlight was reflected in the rhinestone-trimmed frames of her glasses as she smiled at Elisabeth.

"Chastity Pringle? Seems like a body couldn't forget a name like that one, but it appears as if I have, because it sure doesn't ring a bell with me. If you'll give me your phone number, I'll have Wynne Singleton call you. She coordinated all of us, and she'd know where to find this woman you're looking for."

"Thank you," Elisabeth said, scrawling the name and phone number on the back of a receipt from the cash machine at her Seattle bank.

Back at home, Elisabeth changed into old clothes again, but this time she tackled the yard, since the house was in good shape. She found an old lawn mower in the shed and fired it up, after making a run to the service station for gas, and spent a productive afternoon mowing the huge yard.

When that was done, she weeded the flower beds. At sunset, weariness and hunger overcame her and she went inside.

The little red light on the answering machine she'd hooked up to Aunt Verity's old phone in the hallway was blinking. She pushed the button and held her breath when she heard Rue's voice.

"Hi, Cousin, sorry I missed you. Unless you get back to me within the next ten minutes, I'll be gone again. Wish I could be there with you, but I've got another assignment. Talk to you soon. Bye."

Hastily, Elisabeth dialed Rue's number, but the prescribed ten minutes had apparently passed. Rue's machine picked up, and Elisabeth didn't bother to leave a message. She felt like crying as she went wearily up the stairs to strip off her dirty jeans and T-shirt and take a bath.

When she came downstairs again, she heated a piece

of leftover pizza in the microwave and sat down for a solitary supper. Beyond the breakfast nook windows, the sky had a sullen, heavy look to it. Elisabeth hoped there wouldn't be another storm.

She ate, rinsed her dishes and went upstairs to bed, bringing along a candle and matches in case the power were to go out. Stretched out in bed, her body aching with exhaustion from the afternoon's work, Elisabeth thoroughly expected to fall into a fathomless sleep.

Instead, she was wide awake. She tossed from her left side to her right, from her stomach to her back. Finally, she got up, shoved her feet into her slippers and reached for her bathrobe.

She made herself a cup her herbal tea downstairs, then settled at the desk in her room, reaching for a few sheets of Aunt Verity's vellum writing paper and a pen.

"Dear Rue," she wrote. And then she poured out the whole experience of meeting Jonathan and Trista, starting with the first time she'd heard Trista's piano. She put in every detail of the story, including the strange attraction she'd felt for Jonathan, ending with the fact that she'd awakened the next morning to find herself wearing his coat.

She spent several hours going over the letter, rewriting parts of it, making it as accurate an account of her experience as she possibly could. Then she folded the missive, tucked it into an envelope, scrawled Rue's name and address and applied a stamp.

In the morning, she would put it in the mailbox down by the road, pull up the little metal flag and let the chips fall where they may. Rue was the best friend Elisabeth had, but she was also a pragmatic newswoman. She was just as likely to suggest professional help as Elisabeth's father would be. Still, Elisabeth felt she had to tell somebody what was going on or she was going to burst.

She was just coming upstairs, having carried the letter down and set it in the middle of the kitchen table so she wouldn't forget to mail it the next morning, when she heard the giggles and saw the glow of light on the hallway floor.

Elisabeth stopped, her hand on the necklace, her heart racing with scary exhilaration. They were back, Jonathan and Trista—she had only to open that door and step over the threshold.

She went to the portal and put her ear against the wood, smiling as Trista's voice chimed, "And then I said to him, Zeek Filbin, if you pull my hair again, I'll send my papa over to take your tonsils out!"

Elisabeth's hand froze on the doorknob when another little girl responded with a burst of laughter and, "Zeek Filbin needed his wagon fixed, and you did it right and proper." Vera, she thought. Trista's best friend. How would the child explain it if Elisabeth simply walked into the room, appearing from out of nowhere?

She knew she couldn't do that, and yet she felt a longing for that world and for the presence of those people that went beyond curiosity or even nostalgia.

The low, rich sound of Jonathan's voice brought her eyes flying open. "Trista, you and Vera should have been asleep hours ago. Now settle down."

There was more giggling, but then the sound faded and the light gleaming beneath the door dimmed until the darkness had swallowed it completely. Elisabeth had missed her chance to step over the threshold into Jonathan's world, and the knowledge left her feeling oddly bereft. She went to bed and slept soundly, awakening to the jangle of the telephone early the next morning.

Since the device was sitting on the vanity table on the other side of the room, Elisabeth was forced to get out of bed and stumble across the rug to snatch up the receiver.

"Yes?" she managed sleepily.

"Is this Elisabeth McCartney?"

Something about the female voice brought her fully awake. "Yes."

"My name is Wynne Singleton, and I'm president of the Pine River County Quilting Society. One of our members told me you were anxious to get in touch with Ms. Pringle."

Elisabeth sat up very straight and waited silently.

"I can give you her address and telephone number, dear," Mrs. Singleton said pleasantly, "but I'm afraid it won't do you much good. She and her husband left just this morning on an extended business trip."

Disappointed, Elisabeth nonetheless wrote down the number and street address—Chastity Pringle apparently lived in the neighboring town of Cotton Creek—and thanked the caller for her help.

After she hung up, Elisabeth dressed in a cotton skirt and matching top, even though the sky was still threatening rain, and made herself a poached egg and a piece of wheat toast for breakfast.

When she'd eaten, she got into her car and drove to town. If Rue were here, she thought, she'd go to the newspaper office and to the library to see what facts she could gather pertaining to Aunt Verity's house in general and Jonathan and Trista Fortner in particular.

Only it was early and neither establishment was open yet. Undaunted, Elisabeth bought a bouquet of simple flowers at the supermarket and went on to the well-kept, fenced graveyard at the edge of town.

She left the flowers on Aunt Verity's grave and then

began reading the names carved into the tilting, discolored stones in the oldest part of the cemetery. Jonathan and Trista were buried side by side, their graves surrounded by a low iron fence.

Carefully, Elisabeth opened the gate and stepped through it, kneeling to push away the spring grass that nearly covered the aging stones. "Jonathan Stevens Fortner," read the chiseled words. "Born August 5, 1856. Perished June 1892."

"What day?" Elisabeth whispered, turning to Trista's grave. Like her father's, the little girl's headstone bore only her name, the date of her birth and the sad inscription, "Perished June 1892."

There were tears in Elisabeth's eyes as she got to her feet again and left the cemetery.

4

After leaving the Pine River graveyard, Elisabeth stopped by the post office to mail the letter she'd written to Rue the night before. Even though she loved and trusted her cousin, it was hard to drop the envelope through the scrolled brass slot, and the instant she had, she wanted to retrieve it.

All she'd need to do was ask the sullen-looking man behind the grilled window to fetch the letter for her, and no one would ever know she was having delusions.

Squaring her shoulders, Elisabeth made herself walk out of the post office with nothing more than a polite, "Good morning," to the clerk.

The library was open, but Elisabeth soon learned that there were virtually no records of the town's history. There was, however, a thin, self-published autobiography called, *My Life in Old Pine River*, written by a Mrs. Carolina Meavers.

While the librarian, a disinterested young lady with spiky blond hair and a mouthful of gum, issued a borrower's card and entered Elisabeth's name in the computer system, Elisabeth skimmed the book. Mrs. Meavers herself was surely dead, but it was possible she had family in the area.

"Do you know anyone named Meavers?" she asked, holding up the book.

The child librarian popped her gum and shrugged. "I don't pay a lot of attention to old people."

Elisabeth suppressed a sigh of exasperation, took the book and her plastic library card and left the small, musty building. She and Rue had visited the place often during their summer visits to Pine River, devouring books they secretly thought they should have been too sophisticated to like. Elisabeth had loved Cherry Ames, student nurse, and Rue had consumed every volume of the Tarzan series.

Feeling lonely again, Elisabeth crossed the wide street to the newspaper office, where the weekly *Pine River Bugle* was published.

This time she was greeted by a competent-looking middle-aged man with a bald spot, wire-rimmed glasses and a friendly smile. "How can I help you?" he asked.

Elisabeth returned his smile. "I'm doing research," she said, having rehearsed her story as she crossed the street. "How long has the *Bugle* been in publication?"

"One of the oldest newspapers in the state," the man replied proudly. "Goes back to 1876."

Elisabeth's eyes widened. "Do you have the old issues on microfilm?"

"Most of them. If you'll just step this way, Ms....?"

"McCartney," she answered. "Elisabeth McCartney."

"I'm Ben Robbins. Are you writing a book, Ms. McCartney?"

Elisabeth smiled, shook her head and followed him through a small but very noisy press room and down a steep set of stairs into a dimly lit cellar.

"They don't call these places morgues for nothing," Mr. Robbins said with a sigh. Then he gestured toward rows of file cases. "Help yourself," he said. "The microfilm machine is over there, behind those cabinets."

Elisabeth nodded, feeling a little overwhelmed, and

found the long table where the machine waited. After putting down her purse and the library book, she went to work.

The four issues of the *Bugle* published in June of 1892 were on one spool of film, and once Elisabeth found that and figured out how to work the elaborate projection apparatus, the job didn't seem so difficult.

During the first week of that long-ago year, Elisabeth read, Anna Jean Maples, daughter of Albert and Hester Eustice Maples, had been married to Frank Peterson on the lawn of the First Presbyterian church. Kelsey's Grocery had offered specials on canned salmon and "baseball goods."

The *Bugle* was not void of national news. It was rumored that Grover Cleveland would wrest the presidency back from Benjamin Harrison come November, and the people of Chicago were busy preparing for the World Columbian Exposition, to open in October.

Elisabeth skimmed the second week, then the third. A painful sense of expectation was building in the pit of her stomach when she finally came upon the headline she'd been searching for.

DR. FORTNER AND DAUGHTER PERISH IN HOUSE FIRE

She closed her eyes for a moment, feeling sick. Then she anxiously read the brief account of the incident.

No exact date was given—the article merely said, "This week, the people of Pine River suffered a tragic double loss." The reporter went on to state that no bodies or remains of any kind had been found, "so hot did the hellish blazes burn."

Practically holding her breath, Elisabeth read on, feeling just a flicker of hope. She'd watched enough reruns of *Quincy* to know just how stubbornly indestructible human bones could be. If Jonathan's and Trista's remains had not been found, they probably hadn't died in the fire.

She paused to sigh and rub her eyes. If that was true, where had they gone? And why were there two graves with headstones that bore their names?

Elisabeth went back to the article, hoping to find a specific date. Near the end she read, "Surviving the inferno is a young and apparently indigent relative of the Fortners, known only as Lizzie. Marshal Farley Haynes has detained her for questioning."

After scanning the rest of that issue and finding nothing but quilting-bee notices and offers to sell bulls, buggies and nursery furniture, Elisabeth went on to late July of that fateful year.

MYSTERIOUS LIZZIE TO BE TRIED FOR MURDER OF PINE RIVER FAMILY

Pity twisted Elisabeth's insides. Her head was pounding, and she was badly in need of some fresh air. After finding several coins in the bottom of her purse, she made copies of the last newspaper of June 1892, to read later. Then she carefully put the microfilm reel back in its cabinet and turned off the machine.

Upstairs, she found Ben Robbins in a cubicle of an office, going over a stack of computer printouts.

"I want to thank you for being so helpful," Elisabeth said. Her mind was filled with dizzying thoughts. Had Trista and Jonathan died in that blasted fire or hadn't they? And who the heck was this Lizzie person?

Ben smiled and took off his glasses. "Find what you were looking for?"

"Yes and no," Elisabeth answered distractedly, frowning as she shuffled the stack of microfilm copies and the library book resting in the curve of her arm. "Did you know this woman—Carolina Meavers?"

"Died when I was a boy," Ben said with a shake of his head. "But she was good friends with the Buzbee sisters. If you have any questions about Carolina, they'd be the ones to ask."

The Buzbee sisters. Of course. She guessed this was a case of overlooking the obvious. Elisabeth thanked him again and went out.

Belying the glowering sky of the night before, the weather was sunny and scented with spring. Elisabeth got into her car and drove home.

By the time she arrived, it was well past noon and she was hungry. She made a chicken-salad sandwich, took a diet cola from the refrigerator, found an old blanket and set out through the orchard behind the house in search of a picnic spot.

She chose the grassy banks of Birch Creek, within sight of the old covered bridge that was now strictly off limits to any traffic. Elisabeth and Rue had come to this place often with Aunt Verity to wade in the sparkling, icy stream and listen to those endless and singularly remarkable stories.

Elisabeth spread the blanket out on the ground and sat down to eat her sandwich and drink her soda. When she'd finished her lunch, she stretched out on her stomach to read about Lizzie's arrest. Unfortunately, the piece had been written by the same verbose and flowery reporter who had covered the fire, and beyond the obvious facts, there was no real information.

Glumly, Elisabeth set aside the photographs and flipped through the library book. There were pictures in the center, and she stopped to look at them. The author, with her family, posing on the porch—if those few rough planks of pine could be described as a porch—of a ramshackle shanty with a tarpaper roof. The author, standing on the steps of a country schoolhouse that had been gone long before Elisabeth's birth, clutching her slate and spelling primer to her flat little chest.

Elisabeth turned another page and her heart leapt up into her sinus passages to pound behind her cheeks. Practically the entire town must have been in that picture, and Elisabeth could see one side of the covered bridge. But it wasn't that structure that caught her eye and caused her insides to go crazy with a strange, sweet anxiety.

It was Jonathan's image, smiling back at her from the photograph. He was wearing trousers and a vest, and his dark hair was attractively rumpled. Trista stood beside him, a basket brimming with wildflowers in one hand, regarding the camera solemnly.

Elisabeth closed her eyes. She had to get a hold on her emotions. These people had been dead for a century. And whatever fantasies she might have woven around them, they could not be a part of her life.

She gathered the book and the photocopies and the debris of her lunch, then folded the blanket. Despite the self-lecture, Elisabeth knew she would cross that threshold into the past again if she could. She wanted to see Jonathan and warn him about the third week in June.

In fact, she just plain wanted to see Jonathan.

Back at the house, Elisabeth found she couldn't settle down to the needlework or reading she usually found so therapeutic. There were no messages on the answering machine.

Restless, she took the Buzbees' covered casserole dish,

now empty and scrubbed clean, and set out for the house across the road.

An orchard blocked the graceful old brick place from plain view, and the driveway was strewed with fragrant velvety petals. Elisabeth smiled to herself, holding the casserole dish firmly, and wondered how she had ever been able to leave Pine River for the noise and concrete of Seattle.

Miss Cecily came out onto the porch and waved, looking pleased to have a visitor. "I *told* Sister you'd be dropping in by and by, but she said you'd rather spend your time with young folks."

Elisabeth chuckled. "I hope I'm not interrupting anything," she said. "I really should have called first."

"Nonsense." Cecily came down the walk to link Elisabeth's arm with hers. "Nobody calls in the country. They just stop by. Did you enjoy the casserole, dear?"

Elisabeth didn't have the heart to say she'd put most of it down the disposal because there had been so much more than she could eat. "Yes," she said. "Every bite was delicious."

They proceeded up fieldstone steps to the porch, where an old-fashioned swing swayed in the mid-afternoon breeze. The ponderous grandfather clock in the entryway sounded the Westminster chimes, three o'clock, and Elisabeth was surprised that it was so late.

"Sister!" Cecily called, leading Elisabeth past the staircase and down a hallway. There was a note of triumph in her voice, an unspoken "I told you she would come to visit!" "Oh, Sister! We have company!"

Roberta appeared, looking just a little put out. Obviously, she preferred being right to being visited. "Well," she huffed, in the tone of one conceding grudging defeat, "I'll get the lemonade and the molasses cookies."

Soon the three women were settled at the white iron ice-cream table on the stone-floored sun porch, glasses of the Buzbee sisters' incomparable fresh-squeezed lemonade brimming before them.

"Elisabeth thought the casserole was delicious," Cecily announced with a touch of smugness, and Elisabeth resisted a smile, wondering what rivalries existed between these aging sisters.

"Wait until she tastes my vegetable lasagne," said Roberta, pursing her lips slightly as she reached for the sampler she was embroidering.

"I'd like to," Elisabeth said, to be polite. She took a molasses cookie, hoping that would balance things out somehow. "Mr. Robbins at the newspaper told me you probably knew Mrs. Carolina Meavers."

"My, yes," said Roberta. "She was our Sunday-school teacher."

"The old crow," muttered Cecily.

Elisabeth nibbled at her cookie. "She wrote a book about Pine River, you know. I checked it out of the library this morning."

Roberta narrowed her eyes at Elisabeth. "It's that crazy house. That's what's got you so interested in Pine River history, isn't it?"

"Yes," Elisabeth answered, feeling as though she'd been accused of something.

"There are some things in this world, young woman, that are better left alone. And the mysteries of that old house are among them."

"Don't be so fractious, Sister," Cecily scolded. "It's natural to be curious."

"It's also dangerous," replied Roberta.

Elisabeth could see that this visit was going to get her nowhere in unraveling a century of knotted truths, so she finished her cookie and her lemonade and made chitchat until she could politely leave. As Cecily was escorting her through the parlor, Elisabeth was jolted out of her reveries by a brown and hairy shrunken head proudly displayed on the back of the upright piano.

"Chief Zwilu of the Ubangis," Cecily confided, having followed Elisabeth's horrified gaze. "Since the dastardly deed had already been done, Sister and I could see no reason not to bring the poor fellow home as a souvenir."

Elisabeth shivered. "The customs people must have been thrilled."

Cecily shook her head and answered in a serious tone, "Oh, no, dear. They were quite upset. But Sister was uncommonly persuasive and they allowed us to bring the chief into the country."

Just before the two women parted at the Buzbee gate, Cecily patted Elisabeth's arm and muttered, "Don't mind Sister, now. She was just put out because she's always considered my beef casserole inferior to her vegetable lasagna."

"I won't give it another thought," Elisabeth promised. She didn't smile until she was facing away from Cecily, walking down the long driveway.

Reaching the downstairs hallway of her own house, Elisabeth found the light blinking on the answering machine and eagerly pushed the play button.

"Hello, Elisabeth." The voice belonged to Traci, her father's wife. "Marcus asked me to call and find out if you need any money and if there's anything we can do to convince you to come and spend the summer in Tahoe with us. If I don't hear from you, I'll assume you're all right. Bye-ee."

"Bye-ee," Elisabeth chimed sweetly, just as another message began to play.

"Elisabeth? It's Janet. Just wanted to say I had a great time visiting. How about coming to Seattle next weekend? Give me a call."

Elisabeth turned off the machine and went slowly up the stairs. On a whim, she continued up a second flight to the attic.

There was one way to find out if she'd walked in her sleep that night and found a man's coat to use as proof of the unprovable.

The attic door squeaked loudly on its hinges, and Elisabeth thought to herself that the shrill sound should have awakened the dead, let alone a sleepwalker. A flip of the switch located just inside the door illuminated the dust-covered trunks, bureaus, boxes and chairs.

Even from where she stood, Elisabeth could see that neither she nor anyone else had visited this chamber in a very long time. There were no tracks in the thick dust on the floor.

Taking the necklace out from under her sweater, Elisabeth returned to the second floor and stood opposite the sealed door. Her heart was beating painfully fast, and the pit of her stomach was jittery. "Be there," she whispered. "Please, Jonathan. Be there."

Elisabeth tried the knob, but even before she touched it, she knew it wasn't going to turn. Obviously, she could not enter the world on the other side of that door at will, even wearing the necklace. Other forces, all well beyond Elisabeth's comprehension, had to be present.

"I have to tell you about the fire," she said sadly, sliding down the wooden framework to sit on the hallway floor, her knees drawn up, her forehead resting on her folded arms. "Please, Jonathan. Let me in."

She must have dozed off right there on the floor. She came to herself with a start when she heard her name being whispered.

"Elisabeth! Elisabeth, come back! I *need* to talk to you!"

Elisabeth glanced wildly toward the fanlight at the end of the hall and saw that it was still light outside. Then she scrambled to her feet.

"Trista?" She reached for the doorknob, and it turned easily in her hand. On the other side of the door, she found the child who was a lifetime her senior.

Trista was sitting on the floor of her room, next to the big dollhouse, and her lower lip protruded. "I'm being punished," she said.

Elisabeth knelt beside the little girl and gave her a heartfelt hug, hoping she wouldn't feel the trembling. "What did you do?"

"Nothing." Jonathan's daughter handed Elisabeth a tiny china doll as she sat beside her on the rag rug, and Elisabeth smiled at its little taffeta dress and painted hair.

"Come on, Trista," she said. "Your father wouldn't restrict you to your room for no reason."

"Well, it wasn't a very *good* reason."

Elisabeth raised her eyebrows, waiting, and Trista's little shoulders rose and fell in a heavy sigh.

"I couldn't help it," she said. "I told my friend Vera about you, and she told everybody in the county that Papa had a naked woman here. Now I have to come straight to my room after school every day for a solid month!"

Elisabeth touched the child's glossy dark pigtail. "I'm sorry, sweetheart. I didn't mean to get you in trouble. I do, however, feel duty bound to point out that I wasn't naked—I was wearing a football jersey."

"You didn't get me into trouble," Trista said. "Vera did. And what's a football jersey?"

"A very fancy undershirt. Is your papa at home, Trista?" Elisabeth couldn't help the little shiver of excitement that passed through her at the prospect of encountering Jonathan again, though God knew he probably wouldn't be thrilled to see *her*.

Glumly, Trista nodded. "He's out in the barn, I think. Maybe you could tell him that a month is too long to restrict a girl to her bedroom."

Elisabeth chuckled and kissed the child's forehead. "Sorry, short person. It isn't my place to tell your father how to raise his daughter."

With care, Elisabeth unclasped the necklace and put it in a little glass bowl on Trista's bureau. "You'll keep this safe for me, won't you?"

Trista nodded, watching Elisabeth with curious eyes. "I've never seen a lady wear pants before," she said. "And I'll bet you haven't got a corset on, neither."

Elisabeth grinned over one shoulder as she opened the door. "That's one bet you're bound to win," she said. And then she was moving down the hallway.

The pictures of glowering men in beards and steely eyed, calico-clad women were back, and so was the ghastly rose-patterned runner on the floor. Elisabeth felt exhilarated as she hurried toward the back stairway, also different from the one she knew, and walked through the kitchen.

There was a washtub hanging on the wall outside the back door, and chickens clucked and scratched in the yard. A woman was standing nearby, hanging little calico pinafores and collarless white shirts on a clothesline. She didn't seem to notice Elisabeth.

Wife? Housekeeper? Elisabeth decided on the latter. When Jonathan had snatched the necklace from Elisabeth's neck during her first visit, he'd spoken of his spouse in the past tense.

When she stepped through the wide doorway of the sturdy, unpainted barn—which was a teetering ruin in her time—she saw golden hay wafting down from a loft. A masculine voice was singing a bawdy song that made Elisabeth smile.

"Jonathan?" she called, waiting for her eyes to adjust to the dimmer light. The singing instantly stopped.

Jonathan looked down at her from the hayloft, his chest shirtless and glistening with sweat, a pitchfork in one hand. His dark hair was filled with bits of straw. Something tightened inside Elisabeth at the sight of him.

"You." His tone was so ominous, Elisabeth took a step backward, ready to flee if she had to. "Stay right there!" he barked the moment she moved, shaking an index finger at her.

He tossed the pitchfork expertly into the hay and climbed down rough-hewn rungs affixed to the wall beside the loft. Standing within six feet of Elisabeth, he dragged his stormy-sky eyes over her in angry wonderment, then dragged a handkerchief from his hip pocket and dried his brow.

Elisabeth found the sight and scent of him inexplicably erotic, even though if she could have described her primary emotion, she would have said it was pure terror.

"Trousers?" he marveled, stuffing the handkerchief back into his pocket. "Who are you, and where the devil did you disappear to the other night?"

Elisabeth entwined her fingers behind her back, hiding the crazy, nonsensical joy she felt at seeing him again. "Where I come from, lots of women wear—trousers," she said, stalling.

He went to a bucket on a bench beside the wall and

raised a dipperful of water to his mouth. Elisabeth watched the muscles of his back work, sweaty and hard, as he swallowed and returned the dipper to its place.

"You don't look Chinese," he finally said, dryly and at length.

"Listen, if I tried to tell you where I really came from, you'd never believe me. But I—I know the future."

He chuckled and shook his head, and Elisabeth was reminded of his medical degree. The typical man of science. Jonathan probably believed only in things he could reduce to logical components. "No one knows the future," he replied.

"I do," Elisabeth insisted, "because I've been there. And I'm here to warn you." She swallowed hard as he regarded her with those lethally intelligent eyes. Somehow she couldn't get the words out; they'd sound too insane.

"About what?"

Elisabeth closed her eyes and forced herself to answer. "A fire. There's going to be a terrible fire, the third week of June. Part of the house will be destroyed, and you and Trista will—will disappear."

Jonathan's hand shot out and closed around her elbow, tight as a steel manacle. "Who are you, and what asylum did you escape from?" he snapped.

"I told you before—my name is Elisabeth McCartney. And I'm *not* insane!" She paused, biting her lip and futilely trying to pull out of his grasp. "At least, I don't think I am."

He dragged her into the dusty, fading sunlight that filled the barn's doorway and examined her as though she were a creature from another planet. "Your hair," he muttered. "No woman I've ever seen wears her hair sheared off at the chin like that. And your clothes."

Elisabeth sighed. "Jonathan, I'm from the future," she said bluntly. "Women dress like this in the 1990s."

He touched her forehead, just as he had once before. "No fever," he murmured, as though she hadn't spoken at all. "This is the damnedest thing I've ever seen."

"I guess they didn't cover this in medical school, huh?" Elisabeth said, getting testy because he seemed to see her as more of a white mouse in a laboratory than a flesh-and-blood woman. "Well, here's another flash for you, Doc—they're not bleeding people with leeches anymore, but there's still no cure for psoriasis."

Jonathan's grip on her arm didn't slacken. "Who are you?" he repeated, and it was clear to Elisabeth that her host was running out of patience. If he'd ever possessed any in the first place.

"Margaret Thatcher," she snapped. "Damn it, Fortner, will you let go of my arm! You're about to squeeze it off at the elbow!"

He released her. "You said your name was Elisabeth," he said in all seriousness.

"Then why did you have to ask who I am? It isn't as though I haven't told you more than once!"

He crossed the barn, snatched a shirt from a peg on the wall and slipped his arms into it. "How did you manage to vanish from my house last week, Miss McCartney?"

Elisabeth waited for him in the doorway, knowing she'd never be able to outrun him. "I told you. There's a passageway between your time and mine. You and I are roommates, in a manner of speaking."

Jonathan placed a hand on the small of Elisabeth's back and propelled her toward the house. There was no sign of the woman who had been hanging clothes on the line. The set of his jaw told Elisabeth he was annoyed with her answers to his questions.

Which wasn't surprising, considering.

He steered her up the back steps and through the door into the kitchen. "They must have cut your hair off while you were in the asylum," he said.

"I've never been in an asylum," Elisabeth informed him. "Except in college, once. We visited a mental hospital as part of a psychology program."

Jonathan's teeth were startlingly white against his dirty face. "Sit down," he said.

Elisabeth obeyed, watching as he took a kettle from the stove and poured hot water into a basin. He added cold from the pump over the sink and then began to wash himself with pungent yellow soap. She found she couldn't look away, even though there was something painfully intimate in the watching.

By the time he turned to her, drying himself with a damask towel, Elisabeth's entire body felt warm and achy, and she didn't trust herself to speak. The man was so uncompromisingly masculine, and his very presence made closed places open up inside her.

Jonathan took his medical bag from a shelf beside the door, set it on the table with a decisive thump and opened the catch. "The first order of business, Miss McCartney," he said, taking out a stethoscope and a tongue depressor, "is to examine you. Open your mouth and say awww."

"Oh, brother," Elisabeth said, but she opened her mouth.

5

"Are you satisfied?" Elisabeth demanded when Dr. Jonathan Fortner had finished the impromptu examination. "I'm perfectly healthy—physically *and* mentally."

There were freshly ironed shirts hanging from a hook on the wall behind a wooden ironing board, and Jonathan took one down and shrugged into it. Elisabeth tried to ignore the innately male grace in the movements of his muscles.

He didn't look convinced of her good health. "I suppose it's possible you really believe that," he speculated, frowning.

Elisabeth sighed. "If all doctors are as narrow-minded as you are, it's a real wonder they ever managed to wipe out diphtheria and polio."

She had Jonathan's undivided attention. "What did you say?"

"Diphtheria and polio," Elisabeth said seriously. But inside, she was enjoying having the upper hand for once. "They're gone. No one gets them anymore."

The desire to believe such a miracle could be accomplished was plain in Jonathan's face, but so was his skepticism and puzzlement. He dragged back a chair at the table and sat in it, staring at Elisabeth.

She was encouraged. "You were born in the wrong century, Doc," she said pleasantly. "They say more medical advances were made in the twentieth century than in all the rest of time put together.''

He was watching her as if he expected her head to spin around on her shoulders.

Elisabeth was enjoying the rare sense of being privy to startling information. "Not only that, but people actually walked on the moon in 1969, and—''

"Walked on the moon?'' He shoved back his chair, strode across the room and brought back a dipperful of cold well water. "Drink this very slowly.''

Disappointment swept over Elisabeth when she realized she wasn't convincing him after all. It was followed by a sense of hopelessness so profound, it threatened to crush her. If she didn't find some way to influence Jonathan, he and Trista might not survive the fire. And she would never be able to bear knowing they'd died so horribly, because they were real people to her and not just figures in an old lady's autobiography.

She tasted the water, mostly because she knew he wouldn't leave her alone until she had, and then turned her head away. "Jonathan, you must listen to me,'' she whispered, forgetting the formalities. "Your life depends on it, and so does Trista's.''

He returned the dipper to the bucket, paying no attention to her words. "You need to lie down.''

"I don't....''

"If you refuse, I can always give you a dose of laudanum,'' Jonathan interrupted.

Elisabeth's temper flared. "Now just a minute. *Nobody* is giving me laudanum. The stuff was—is—made from opium, and that's addictive!''

Jonathan sighed. "I know full well what it's made of, Miss McCartney. And I wasn't proposing to make you dependent and sell you into white slavery. It's just that you're obviously agitated—"

"I am *not* agitated!"

His slow, leisurely smile made something shift painfully inside her. "Of course, you're not," he said in a patronizing tone.

Now it was Elisabeth who sighed. She'd known Jonathan Fortner, M.D., for a very short time, but one thing she had learned right off was that he could be mule stubborn when he'd set his mind on a certain course of action. Arguing with him was useless. "All right," she said sweetly, even managing a little yawn. "I guess I would like to rest for a while. But you've got to promise not to send for the marshal and have me arrested."

She saw a flicker of amusement in his charcoal eyes. "You have my word, Elisabeth," he told her, and she loved the way he said her name. He took her arm and led her toward the back stairs, and she allowed that, thinking how different Dr. Fortner was from Ian, from *any* man she knew in her own time. There was a courtly strength about him that had evidently been lost to the male population as the decades progressed.

He deposited her in the same room she'd had during her last visit, settling her expertly on the narrow iron bed, slipping off her shoes, covering her with a colorful quilt. His gentle, callused hand smoothed her hair back from her forehead.

"Rest," he said hoarsely, and then he was gone, closing the door quietly behind him.

Elisabeth tensed, listening for the click of a key in the lock, but it never came. She relaxed, soaking up the atmosphere of this world that apparently ran parallel to her own. Everything was more substantial, somehow, more vivid and richly textured. The ordinary sound of an errant bee buzzing and bumping against the window, the support of the feather-filled mattress beneath her, the poignant blue of the patch of sky visible through the lace curtains at the window—all of it blended together to create an undeniable reality.

She was definitely not dreaming and, strangely, she was in no particular hurry to get back to her own century. There was no one there waiting for her, while here, she had Trista and Jonathan. She would stay a few days, if Jonathan would let her, and perhaps find some way to avert the disaster that lay ahead.

When the door of her room opened, she was only a little startled. Trista peered around the edge, her Jonathan-gray eyes wide with concerned curiosity. "Are you sick?" she asked.

Elisabeth sat up and patted the mattress. "No, but your father thinks I am. Come and sit here."

Shyly, Trista approached the bed and sat on the edge of the mattress, her small, plump hands folded in her lap.

"I've heard you practicing your piano lessons," Elisabeth said, settling back against her pillows and folding her arms.

Trista's eyes reflected wonder rather than the disbelief Elisabeth had seen in Jonathan's gaze. "You have?"

"I don't think you like it much," Elisabeth observed.

The child made a comical face. "I'd rather be outside. But Papa wants me to grow up to be a lady, and a lady plays piano."

"I see."

Trista smiled tentatively. "Do you like music?"

"Very much," Elisabeth answered. "I studied piano when I was about your age, and I can still play a little."

The eight-year-old's gapped smile faded to a look of somber resignation. "Miss Calderberry will be here soon to give me my lesson. I'm allowed to leave my room for that, of course."

"Of course," Elisabeth agreed seriously.

"Would you care to come down and listen?"

"I'd better not. Something tells me your father wouldn't want me to be quite so—visible. I'm something of a secret, I think."

Trista sighed, then nodded and rose to go downstairs and face her music teacher. She had the air of Anne Boleyn proceeding to the Tower. "Your necklace is in the dish on my bureau, just where you left it," she whispered confidentially, from the doorway. "You won't leave without saying goodbye, will you?"

Elisabeth felt her throat tighten slightly. "No, sweetheart. I promise I won't go without seeing you first."

"Good," Trista answered. And then she left the room.

After a few minutes, Elisabeth got out of bed and wandered into the hallway. At the front of the house was a large, arched window looking down on the yard, and she couldn't resist peering around the curtains to watch a slender woman dressed in brown sateen climb delicately down from the seat of a buggy.

Miss Calderberry wore a feathered hat that hid her face from Elisabeth, but when Jonathan approached from the direction of the barn, smiling slightly, delight seemed to radiate from the piano teacher's countenance. Her trilling voice reached Elisabeth's ears through the thick, bubbled glass.

"Dr. Fortner! What a pleasure to see you."

In the next instant, Jonathan's gaze rose and seemed to lock with Elisabeth's, and she remembered that she was supposed to be lying down, recovering from her odious malady.

She stepped back from the window, but only because

she didn't want Miss Calderberry to see her and carry a lot of gossip back to the fine folks of Pine River. It wouldn't do to ruin whatever might be left of the good doctor's reputation following Vera's accounts of a naked lady in residence.

When Trista's discordant efforts at piano playing started to rise through the floorboards, Elisabeth grew restless and began to wander the upstairs, though she carefully avoided Jonathan's room.

She made sure the necklace was still in Trista's crystal dish, then peeked into each of the other bedrooms, where she saw brass beds, chamberpots, pitchers and basins resting on lovely hardwood washstands. From there, she proceeded to the attic.

The place gave her a quivery feeling in the pit of her stomach, being a mirror image of its counterpart in her own time. Of course, the contents were different.

She opened a trunk and immediately met with the scent of lavender. Setting aside layers of tissue paper, she found a delicate ivory dress, carefully folded, with ecru-lace trim on the cuffs and the high, round collar.

Normally, Elisabeth would not have done what she did next, but this was, in a way, her house. And besides, all her actions had a dreamlike quality to them, as though they would be only half-remembered in the morning.

She took the dress out of the trunk, held it against her and saw that it would probably fit, then she stripped off her slacks and sweater. Tiny buttons covered in watered silk graced the front of the gown, fastening through little loops of cloth.

When she had finished hooking each one, Elisabeth looked around for a mirror, but there was none in sight. She dipped into the trunk again and found a large, elegantly shaped box, which contained a confection of a hat

bursting with silk flowers—all the color of rich cream—
and tied beneath the chin with a wide, ivory ribbon.

Elisabeth couldn't resist adding the hat to her costume.

Holding up her rustling skirts with one hand, she made
her way cautiously down the attic steps and along the
hallway to her room. She was inside, beaming with pleasure and turning this way and that in front of the standing
mirror, when she sensed an ominous presence and turned
to see Jonathan in the doorway.

He leaned against the jamb, the sleeves of his white
shirt rolled up to reveal muscle-corded forearms folded
across his chest.

"Make yourself right at home, Miss McCartney," he
urged in an ill-tempered tone. An entirely different emotion was smoldering in his eyes, however.

Elisabeth had been like a child, playing dressup. Now
her pleasure faded and her hands trembled as she reached
up to untie the ribbon that held the hat in place. "I'm so
sorry," she whispered, mortified, realizing that the clothes
had surely belonged to his wife and that seeing someone
else wearing them must be painful for him. "I don't know
what came over me...."

Jonathan stepped into the room and closed the door
against the distant tinkle of piano keys, probably not wanting their voices to carry to Trista and Miss Calderberry.
His eyes were narrowed. "When I first met you, you were
wearing my wife's necklace, and when it disappeared, so
did you. Tell me, Elisabeth...do you know Barbara?"

Elisabeth shook her head. "H-how could I, Jonathan?
She—I live in another century, remember?"

He arched one dark eyebrow and hooked his thumbs in
the pockets of his black woolen vest. "Yet, somehow, my
wife's necklace came to be here. Without Barbara. She

never let it out of her sight, you know. She claimed it had powers."

A hard lump formed in Elisabeth's throat, and she swallowed. If Barbara Fortner had known about the necklace's special energy and had used it, she could have crossed the threshold into the modern world....

"This is all getting pretty farfetched," Elisabeth said, squaring her shoulders. "I didn't know your wife, Jonathan." She looked down at the lovely dress. "I truly am sorry for presuming on your hospitality this way, though."

"Keep the dress," he told her with a dismissive gesture of one hand. "It will raise a lot fewer questions than those trousers of yours."

Elisabeth felt as though she'd just been given a wonderful gift. "Thank you," she breathed softly, running her hands down the satiny skirt.

"You'd better hunt up some calico and sateen for everyday," he finished, moving toward the door. "Naturally, women don't cook and clean in such fancy getup."

"Jonathan?" Elisabeth approached him as he waited, his hand on the doorknob. She stood on tiptoe to kiss his now-stubbly cheek, and again she felt a powerful charge of some mystical electricity. "Thank you. But I won't need special clothes if I go back to my own time."

He rolled his eyes, but there was a look of tenderness in their depths. "Something tells me you're going to be here for a while," he said, and then his gaze moved slowly over Elisabeth, from her face to the incongruous toes of her sneakers and back again. His hands rested lightly on the sides of her waist, and she felt a spiritual jolt as he looked deeply into her eyes, as though to find her soul behind them.

It seemed natural when his lips descended toward hers

and brushed lightly against them, soft and warm and moist. A moment later, however, he was kissing her in earnest.

With a whimper, Elisabeth put her arms around his neck and held on, afraid she would sink to the floor. The gentle assault on her senses continued; her mouth was open to his, and even through the dress and the bra beneath, her nipples hardened against the wall of his chest. A sweet, grinding ache twisted in the depths of her femininity, a wild need she had never felt with Ian, and if Jonathan had asked her, she would have surrendered then and there.

Instead, he set her roughly away from him and avoided her eyes. Trista's labored piano playing filled their ears.

"There's obviously no point in keeping you locked up in your room," he said hoarsely. "If you encounter Miss Calderberry, kindly introduce yourself as my wife's sister."

With that, he was gone. Elisabeth stood there in the center of her room, her cheeks flaring with color because he'd kissed her as no other man ever had—and because he was ashamed to have her under his roof. She wanted to laugh and cry, both at the same time, but in the end she did neither.

She crept down the back stairway and out the kitchen door and headed in the direction of the stream where she had picnicked by herself almost a hundred years in the future. The scent of apple blossoms filled her spirit as she walked through the recently planted orchard. Birds sang in the treetops, and in the near distance, she could hear the rustling song of the creek.

It occurred to her then that she could be blissfully happy in this era, for all its shortcomings. On some level, she had always yearned for a simpler, though certainly not easier, life and a man like Jonathan.

Elisabeth hurried along, the soft petals billowing around her like fog in a dream, and finally reached the grassy bank.

The place was different and yet the same, and she stood in exactly the spot where she'd spread her blanket to eat lunch and read. The covered bridge towered nearby, but its plank walls were new, and the smell of freshly sawed wood mingled with the aromas of spring grass and the fertile earth.

In order to protect her dress from green smudges, Elisabeth sat on a boulder overlooking the stream instead of on the ground. She removed the hat and set it beside her, then lifted her arms to her hair, winding it into a French knot at the back of her head even though she had no pins to hold it. Her reflection smiled back at her from the crystal-bright waters of the creek, looking delightfully Victorian.

A clatter on the road made her lift her head, her hands still cupped at her nape, and she watched wide-eyed as a large stagecoach, drawn by eight mismatched horses, rattled onto the bridge. The driver touched his hat brim in a friendly way when the coach reappeared, and Elisabeth waved, laughing. It was like playing a part in a movie.

And then the wind picked up suddenly, making the leaves of the birch and willow trees whisper and lifting Elisabeth's borrowed hat right off the rock. She made a lunge, and both she and the bonnet went straight into the creek.

With a howl of dismay, Elisabeth felt the slippery pebbles on the bottom of the icy stream give way beneath the soles of her sneakers. As the luscious hat floated merrily away, she tumbled forward and landed in the water with a splash.

Jonathan was standing on the bank when she floundered her way back to shore, her lovely dress clinging revealingly to her form, and though he offered his hand, Elisabeth ignored it.

"What are you doing?" she sputtered furiously, her teeth already chattering, her hair hanging in dripping tendrils around her face. "Following me?"

He grinned and shrugged. "I saw you walking this way, and I thought you might be planning to hitch a ride on the afternoon stage. It seems you've been swimming instead."

Elisabeth glared at him and crossed her arms over her breasts. Because of the unexpected dip in the creek, her nipples were plainly visible beneath the fabric. "It isn't funny," she retorted, near tears. "This is the prettiest dress I've ever had, and now it's ruined!"

He removed his suitcoat and laid it over her shoulders. "I suppose it is," he allowed. "But there are other dresses in the world."

"Not like this one," Elisabeth said despairingly.

Jonathan's arm tightened briefly around her before falling to his side. "That's what you think," he countered. "Go through the trunks again. If you don't find anything you like, I'll *buy* you another dress."

Elisabeth gave him a sidelong look, shivering inside his coat as they walked toward the orchard and the house beyond. No one needed to tell her that nineteenth-century country doctors didn't make a lot of money; many of Jonathan's patients probably paid him in chickens and squash from the garden. "Did this dress belong to your wife?" she ventured to ask, already knowing the answer, never guessing how much she would regret the question until it was too late to call it back.

Jonathan's jawline tightened, then relaxed again. He did not look at her, but at the orchard burgeoning with flowers. "Yes," he finally replied.

"Doesn't it bother you to see another woman wearing her things?"

He rubbed his chin, then thrust both hands into the pockets of his plain, practical black trousers. "No," he answered flatly.

Elisabeth thought of the two graves inside the little fence, back in modern-day Pine River, and her heart ached with genuine grief to think of Jonathan and Trista lying there. At the same time, she wondered why Jonathan's mate wasn't buried in the family plot. "Did she die, Jonathan? Your wife?"

They had reached the grove of apple trees, and petals clung to the hem of Elisabeth's spoiled dress. Jonathan's hands knotted into fists in his trouser pockets. "As far as Trista and I are concerned," he replied some moments later, "yes."

Pressing him took all Elisabeth's courage, for she could sense the controlled rage inside him. And yet she had to know if she was feeling all these crazy emotions for another woman's husband. "She left you?"

"Yes."

"Then, technically, you're a married man."

Jonathan's eyes sliced to Elisabeth's face and the expression she saw in them brought color pulsing to her cheeks. "Technically?" He chuckled, but there wasn't a trace of humor in the sound. "An odd word. No, Elisabeth, I'm not the rogue you think I am. When it became clear that Barbara didn't plan to return, I went to Olympia and petitioned the legislature for a divorce. It was granted.''

''All of this must have been very difficult for Trista,'' Elisabeth observed, wondering why Barbara Fortner hadn't taken her daughter along when she left. Perhaps Jonathan had prevented that by some legal means, or maybe the woman had doubted her own ability to support a child in such a predominantly male world.

The house was within sight now, and twilight was beginning to fall over the fragrant orchard. Elisabeth felt a tug in her heart as they walked toward the glow of lantern light in the kitchen windows. She knew she'd been homesick for this time, this place, this man at her side, all of her life.

He shocked her with his reply to her remark about the effect the divorce had had on Trista. ''My daughter believes her mother died in an accident in Boston, while visiting her family, and I don't want anyone telling her differently. Since the Everses have disinherited their daughter, I don't think there's any danger that they'll betray the secret.''

Elisabeth stopped to stare at him, even though it was chilly and her wet dress was clinging to her skin. ''But it's a lie.''

''Sometimes a lie is kinder than the truth.'' Having spoken these words, Jonathan picked up his stride and Elisabeth was forced to follow him into the kitchen or stand in the yard until she caught her death.

Inside, Jonathan turned the wicks up in the lamps so that the flames burned brightly, then he opened a door in the stove and began shoving in wood from the box beside it. Elisabeth huddled nearby, gratefully soaking up the warmth.

''A lie is never better than the truth,'' she said, having

finally worked up the courage to contradict him so bluntly. He was bull stubborn in his opinions; Rue would have said he was surely a Republican.

He wrenched a blue enamel pot from the back of the stove, carried it to the sink and used the hand pump to fill it with water. Then he set the pot on to heat. "You'll be wanting tea," he remarked, completely ignoring her statement. "I'll go and find you a dressing gown."

Elisabeth drew closer to the stove, wanting the heat to reach the marrow of her bones. She had stopped shivering, at least, when Jonathan returned with a long flannel night-gown and a heavy blue corduroy robe to go over it.

"You can change in the pantry," he said, shoving the garments at Elisabeth without meeting her eyes.

She took them and went into the little room—where the washer and drier were kept in her time—and stripped in the darkness. The virginal nightgown felt blissfully warm against her clammy, goose-pimpled skin.

She was tying the belt on the robe when she came out of the pantry to find Jonathan pouring hot water into a squat, practical-looking brown teapot. "I'd be happy to cook supper," she said, wanting to be useful and, more than that, to belong in this kitchen, if only for an hour.

"Good," he said with a sigh, going to the wall of cupboards for mugs, which he carried back to the table. "Trista doesn't cook, and Ellen—that's our house-keeper—tends to be undependable on occasion. She was here earlier, but she wandered off and probably won't be back until tomorrow."

Elisabeth opened the icebox she'd discovered the first night and squatted to look inside it. Two large brook trout stared at her from a platter, and she carried them to the counter nearest the stove. "Did you catch these fish?"

she asked, mostly because it gave her a soft, bittersweet sensation to be cooking and chatting idly with Jonathan.

He poured tea into the cups and went to the base of the back stairs to call Trista down. Evidently, she'd dutifully returned to her room after Miss Calderberry left.

"They were given to me," he answered presently, "in payment for a nerve tonic."

Elisabeth found a skillet in the pantry, along with jars of preserved vegetables and fruit. She selected a pint of sliced carrots and one of stewed pears, and carried them into the kitchen. By this time, Trista was setting the table with Blue Willow dishes, and Jonathan was nowhere in sight.

"He went out to the barn to feed the animals," Trista offered without being asked.

Elisabeth smiled. "Did you enjoy your piano lesson?"

"No," Trista answered. "How come your hair is all wet and straggly like that?"

Elisabeth put the trout into the skillet, minus their heads. "I fell into the creek," she replied. "Is there any bread?"

Trista went to a maple box on the far counter and removed a loaf wrapped in a checkered dish towel. She set it on a plate, then brought a bowl of butter from the icebox. "I fell in the creek once," she confided. "I was only two, and I think maybe I would have drowned if my mama hadn't pulled me right out."

Elisabeth felt a small pull in the tenderest part of her soul. "It's a good thing she was around," she said gently, remembering a small tombstone with Trista's name carved into it. She had to look away to hide sudden tears that burned hot along her lashes.

"Maybe you could play the piano for us, after supper," Trista said.

Subtly, Elisabeth dried her eyes with the soft sleeve of the wrapper Jonathan had brought to her. Like the spoiled dress, it smelled faintly of lavender. "I haven't touched a keyboard in weeks, so I'm probably out of practice," she said with a cheerful sniffle. She took her first sip of the tea Jonathan had made for her and found it strong and sweet.

Trista laughed. "You couldn't sound worse than I do, no matter how long it's been since you've practiced."

Elisabeth laughed, too, and hugged the little girl. Through the window, she saw Jonathan moving toward the house in the last dim light of day. In that moment, she was as warm as if the noontime sun had been shining unrestrained on her bare skin.

She dished up the fish and the preserved carrots while Jonathan washed at the sink, then they all sat down at the table.

Elisabeth was touched when Trista offered a short grace, asking God to take special care that her mama was happy in heaven. At this, Elisabeth opened her eyes for an accusing peek at Jonathan and found him staring defiantly back at her, his jawline set.

When the prayer was over, Jonathan immediately cut three perfect slices from the loaf of bread and moved one to his plate.

"Don't you have any cows?" Elisabeth asked. She'd noticed that Jonathan hadn't carried in a bucket of fresh milk, the way farmers did in books and movies.

He shook his head. "Don't need one," he replied. "I get all the butter and cream we can use from my patients."

"Do any of them give you money?" Elisabeth inquired, careful not to let so much as a trace of irony slip into her tone.

Still, Jonathan's look was quick and sharp. "We manage," he replied crisply.

After that, Trista carried the conversation, chattering cheerfully about the upcoming spelling bee at school and how she'd be sure to win it because she had so much time to practice her words. When supper was over, she and Elisabeth washed the dishes while Jonathan put on his suitcoat—it had been drying on the back of a chair near the stove—and reached for his medical bag.

"I won't be long," he said, addressing his words to Trista. "I want to check and see if Mrs. Taber is any closer to delivering that baby."

Trista nodded and hung up the dish towel neatly over the handle on the oven door, but Elisabeth followed Jonathan outside.

"You mean you're leaving your daughter all alone here, with a total stranger?" she demanded, her hands on her hips.

Jonathan took a lantern from the wall of the back porch and lit it after striking a wooden match. "You're not a stranger," he said. "You and I are old friends, though I admit I don't remember exactly where we met." He bent to kiss her lightly on the cheek. "In case I don't see you before morning, good night, Lizzie."

6

Lizzie.

Being called by that name made Elisabeth sway on her feet. She grasped at the railing beside the porch steps to steady herself.

Jonathan didn't notice her reaction, which was probably just as well because Elisabeth was in no condition to offer more explanations. She watched, stricken, as he strode toward the barn, the lantern in one hand, his medical bag in the other.

The moment he disappeared from sight, Elisabeth sank to the steps and just sat there, trembling, her hands over her face. Dear God in heaven, why hadn't she guessed? Why hadn't she known that *she* was the woman accused of setting the fire that probably killed Jonathan and Trista?

"Elisabeth?" Trista's voice was small and full of concern. "Is something the matter?"

Elisabeth drew in a deep breath and made herself speak in a normal tone of voice. "No, sweetheart," she lied, "everything is just fine."

The child hovered in the doorway behind her. "Are you going to play for me?" she asked hopefully. "I'm still in trouble, but I know Papa wouldn't mind my staying downstairs for just one song."

Elisabeth rose from the step, feeling chilly even in the warm robe and nightgown Jonathan had brought her.

What a scandal her state of dress would cause in Victorian Pine River, she thought in a wild effort to distract herself. But there was no forgetting—if she didn't do something to change history, two people she already cherished would die tragically and she would be blamed for their deaths.

"One song," she answered sadly, taking Trista's hand and holding it tightly in her own.

"Elisabeth played a boogie," Trista told her father the next morning as she ate the oatmeal Ellen had made for her. Jonathan frowned, and the housekeeper stiffened slightly in disapproval, her shoulders going rigid under her cambric dress.

"A what?" His head ached; deception did not come naturally to him. And he knew Ellen hadn't believed his story about his late wife's sister arriving suddenly for a visit.

"Land sakes," muttered Ellen, slamming the fire door after shoving another stick of wood into the stove.

"A boogie-woogie," Trista clarified, and it was clear from her shining face that she enjoyed just saying the word.

Just then, Elisabeth came somewhat shyly down the back stairs and Jonathan's sensible heart skittered over two full beats when he saw her. She'd pinned her hair up in back, but it still made soft, taffy-colored curls around her face, and she was wearing a blue-and-white-flowered dress he didn't remember seeing on Barbara.

She smiled as she advanced toward the kitchen table, where Trista had set a place for her. "Good morning."

Remembering his manners, Jonathan rose and stood until Elisabeth was seated. "Ellen," he said, "This is my— sister-in-law, Miss Elisabeth McCartney. Elisabeth, our housekeeper, Ellen Harwood."

Ellen, a plain girl with a freckled face and frizzy red-brown hair, nodded grudgingly but didn't return Elisabeth's soft hello.

Jonathan waited until Ellen had gone upstairs to clean to ask, "What in the devil is a boogie-woogie?"

Elisabeth and Trista looked at each other and laughed. "Just a lively song," Elisabeth answered.

"A *very* lively song," Trista confirmed.

Jonathan sighed, pushed back his plate and pulled his watch from his vest pocket to flip open the case. He should have been gone an hour already, but he'd waited for a glimpse of Elisabeth, needing the swelling warmth that filled his bruised, stubborn heart when he looked at her. He could admit that to himself, if not out loud to her. "If you're ready, Trista, I'll drop you off at the schoolhouse on my way into town."

His daughter cast a sidelong glance at their strange but undeniably lovely guest. "I thought I'd walk this morning, Papa," Trista answered. "Elisabeth wants to see where I go to school."

Jonathan narrowed his eyes as he regarded Elisabeth, silently issuing warnings he could not say in front of Trista. "I'm sure she wouldn't be foolish enough to wander too far afield and get herself lost."

"I'm sure she wouldn't," Elisabeth said wryly, watching him with those blue-green eyes of hers. Their beauty always startled him, caught him off guard.

Jonathan left the table, then, and took his suitcoat from the peg beside the back door. Trista was ready with his medical bag, looking up at him earnestly. "Don't worry, Papa," she confided in a stage whisper. "I'll take very good care of Elisabeth."

He bent to kiss the top of her head, then tugged lightly at one of her dark pigtails. "I'm sure you will," he replied. After one more lingering look at Elisabeth, he left the house to begin his rounds.

Elisabeth marveled as she walked along, Trista's hand in hers. In the twentieth century, this road was a paved highway, following a slightly different course and lined with telephone poles. It was so quiet that she could hear the whisper of the creek on the other side of the birch, cedar and Douglas fir trees that crowded its edges.

A wagon loaded with hay clattered by, drawn by two weary-looking horses, and Elisabeth stared after it. By then, she'd given up the idea that this experience was any kind of hallucination, but she still hadn't gotten used to the sights and sounds of a century she'd thought was gone forever.

Trista gazed up at her speculatively. "Where did you go when you went away before?"

"Back to my own house," Elisabeth replied after careful thought.

"Are you going to stay with Papa and me from now on?"

Elisabeth had to avert her eyes, thinking of the fire. She'd spent most of the night tossing and turning, trying to come up with some way to evade fate. For all she knew, it could not be changed.

Again, she took her time answering. "Not forever," she said softly.

Trista's strong little fingers tightened around Elisabeth's. "I don't want you to go."

In that moment, Elisabeth realized that she didn't want to leave...ever. For all its hard realities, she felt that she belonged in this time, with these people. Indeed, it was her other life, back in twentieth-century Washington state, that seemed like a dream now. "Let's just take things one day at a time, Trista," she told the child.

They rounded a wide bend in the road and there was the brick schoolhouse—nothing but a ruin in Elisabeth's day—with glistening windows and a sturdy shake roof. The bell rang in the tower while a slender woman with dark hair and bright blue eyes pulled exuberantly on the rope.

Elisabeth stood stock-still. "It's wonderful," she whispered.

Trista laughed. "It's only a schoolhouse," she said indulgently. "Do you want to meet my teacher, Miss Bishop?" The child gazed up at Elisabeth, gray eyes dancing, and dropped her voice to a confidential whisper. "She's sweet on the blacksmith, and Ellen says she probably won't last out the term!"

Elisabeth smiled and shook her head. "It's time for class to start, so I'll meet Miss Bishop later."

Trista nodded and hurried off to join the other children surging up the steps and through the open doorway of the schoolhouse. A few of them looked back over their shoulders at Elisabeth, freckled faces puzzled.

She stood outside, listening, until the laughter and noise faded away. Being a teacher herself, she relished the familiar sounds.

The weather was bright and sunny, and Elisabeth had no particular desire to go back to Jonathan's house and face that sullen housekeeper, so she continued on toward town. As she neared the outskirts, the metallic squeal of a steam-powered saw met her ears and her step quickened. Even though she was scared—her situation gave new meaning to the hackneyed term "a fish out of water"—she was driven by a crazy kind of curiosity that wouldn't allow her to turn back.

Her first glimpse of the town stunned her, even though she'd thought she was prepared. The main street seemed to be composed of equal measures of mud and manure, and the weathered buildings clustered alongside were like something out of a *Bonanza* rerun. Any minute now, Hoss and Little Joe were sure to come ambling out through the swinging doors of the Silver Lady Saloon....

There were horses and wagons everywhere, and the noisy machinery in the sawmill screeched as logs from the timber-choked countryside were fed through its blades. Elisabeth wandered past a forge worked by a man wearing a heavy black apron. and she sidestepped two lumberjacks who came out of the general store to stand in the middle of the sidewalk, leering.

When she saw Jonathan's shingle up ahead, jutting out from the wall of a small, unpainted building, she hurried toward it. There was a blackboard on the wall beside the door, with the word *In* scrawled on it in white chalk. Elisabeth smiled as she opened the door.

A giant man in oiled trousers and a bloody flannel shirt sat on the end of an old-fashioned examining table. Jonathan was winding a clean bandage around the patient's arm, but he paused, seeing Elisabeth, took off his gold-rimmed spectacles and tucked them into his shirt pocket.

A tender whirlwind spun in her heart and then her stomach.

"Is there a problem?" he asked.

Elisabeth was feeling a little queasy, due to the sight and smell of blood. She groped for a chair and sank into the only seat available—the hard wooden one behind Jonathan's cluttered desk. "No," she answered. "I was just exploring Pine River."

The lumberjack smiled at her, revealing gaps between

his crooked, tobacco-stained teeth. "This must be the lady you've been hidin' away out at your place, Doc," he said.

Jonathan gave his patient an annoyed glance and finished tying off the bandage. "I haven't been hiding anything," he replied. "And don't go telling the whole damn town I have, Ivan, or I'll sew your mouth shut, just like I did your arm."

Ivan stood and produced a coin from the pocket of his filthy trousers, but even as he paid Jonathan, he kept his eyes on Elisabeth. "Good day to you, ma'am," he said, and then he reluctantly left the office.

Jonathan began cleaning up the mess Ivan and his blood had made. "Coming here was probably not the most intelligent thing you ever did," he observed presently.

Elisabeth's attention had strayed to the calendar page on the wall. April 17, 1892. It was incredible. "I was curious," she said distractedly, thinking of a documentary she'd watched on public television recently. "In a few more months—August, if I remember correctly—a woman in Fall River, Massachusetts, will be accused of murdering her father and stepmother with an ax. Her name is Lizzie Borden. She'll be acquitted of the crime because of a lack of evidence."

His gaze held both pity and irritation. "Is that supposed to have some kind of significance—the fact that she has the same first name as you do?"

A chill went through Elisabeth; she hadn't thought of that. "No. Besides, nobody ever calls me Lizzie."

"I do," Jonathan answered flatly, pouring water into a clean basin and beginning to wash his hands.

"I'm glad to see that you're taking antisepsis seriously," Elisabeth said, as much to change the subject as anything. She still had that jittery feeling that being around Jonathan invariably gave her. "Most disease is caused by germs, you know."

Jonathan leaned forward slightly and rounded his eyes. "No," he said, pretending to be surprised.

"I guess maybe you've figured that out already," Elisabeth conceded, folding her hands in her lap.

"Thank you for that," he answered, drying his hands on a thin, white towel and laying it aside.

Just then, the door opened and a tall man wearing a cowboy hat and a battered, lightweight woolen coat strode in. He needed a shave, and carried a rifle in his right hand, holding it with such ease that it seemed a part of him. When he glanced curiously at Elisabeth, she saw that his eyes were a piercing turquoise blue. Pinned to his coat was a shiny nickel-plated badge in the shape of a star.

Wow, Elisabeth thought. *A real, live lawman.*

"'Morning, Farley," Jonathan said. "That boil still bothering you?"

Farley actually flushed underneath that macho five-o'clock shadow of his. "Now, Jon," he complained in his low drawl, "there was no need to mention that in front of the lady. It's personal-like."

Elisabeth averted her face for a moment so the marshal wouldn't see that she was smiling.

"Sorry," Jonathan said, but Elisabeth heard the amusement in his voice even if Farley didn't. He gave her a pointed look. "The lady is just leaving. Let's get on with it."

Elisabeth nodded and bolted out of her chair. They wouldn't have to tell her twice—the last thing she wanted to do was watch Jonathan lance a boil on some private part of the marshal's body. "Goodbye," she said from the doorway. "And it was very nice to meet you, Mr. Farley."

"Just Farley," rumbled the marshal.

"Whatever," Elisabeth answered, ducking out and closing the door. There was something summarial in the way Jonathan pulled the shades on both windows.

Since her senses were strained from all the new things she was trying to take in, Elisabeth was getting tired. She walked back through town, nodding politely to the women who stared at her from the wooden sidewalks and pointed, and she hoped she hadn't ruined Jonathan's practice by marching so boldly into town and walking right into his office.

Reaching Jonathan's house, she found Ellen in the backyard. She'd hung a rug over the clothesline and was beating it with a broom.

Elisabeth smiled in a friendly way. "Hello," she called.

"If you want anything to eat," the housekeeper retorted, "you'll just have to fix it yourself!"

With a shrug, Elisabeth went inside and helped herself to a piece of bread, spreading it liberally with butter and strawberry jam. Then she found a blanket, helped herself to a book from Jonathan's collection in the parlor and set out for her favorite spot beside the creek.

She supposed Janet was probably getting worried, if she'd tried to call, and the Buzbee sisters would be concerned, too, if they went more than a few days without seeing her. She spread the blanket on the ground and sat down, tucking her skirts carefully around her.

A sigh escaped Elisabeth as she watched the sunlight making moving patterns on the waters of the creek. She was going to have to go back soon, back where she belonged. Her throat went tight. Before she could do that, she had to find some way to convince Jonathan that he and Trista were in very real danger.

The book forgotten at her side, Elisabeth curled up on

the blanket and watched the water flow by, shimmering like a million liquid diamonds in the bright sunshine. And her sleepless night caught up with her.

When she awakened, it was to the sound of children's laughter echoing through the trees. Elisabeth rose, automatically smoothing her hair and skirts, and left the blanket and book behind to follow the path of the stream, walking beneath the covered bridge.

Presently, she could see the schoolhouse across the narrow ribbon of water. The children were all outside at recess. While the boys had divided up into teams for baseball, the girls pushed each other in the rustic swings and played hopscotch. She spotted Trista and wondered if the plain little girl at her side was Vera, who would eventually give birth to Cecily and Roberta Buzbee.

Deciding that her presence would just raise a lot of awkward questions for Trista, Elisabeth slipped away and, after fetching the blanket and Jonathan's book, went back to the house.

By this time, there was a nice stew simmering on the stove and fresh bread cooling on the counter under a spotless dishtowel. Ellen had apparently left for the day.

Relieved, Elisabeth opened the icebox and peered inside. There was a bowl of canned pears left over from breakfast, so she dished up a serving and went out onto the back step to eat them. She was enjoying the glorious spring afternoon when Jonathan pulled up alongside the barn, driving his horse and buggy. He sprang nimbly down from the seat and walked toward her, his medical bag in one hand.

Elisabeth felt a sweet tightening in the most feminine part of her as he approached. "Must have been an easy day," she said when he sat down beside her.

He chuckled ruefully. "'Easy' isn't the word I would

use to describe it," he said. "I couldn't stop thinking about you, Elisabeth."

Elisabeth drew a deep breath, and suddenly her heart and her spirit and all of her body were full of springtime. She lifted one eyebrow and forced herself to speak in a normal tone. "I suppose you were wondering if I was chasing poor Ellen all over the farm with an ax."

Jonathan laughed and shook his head. "No, I've considered doing that myself." His expression turned solemn in the next moment, however, and his sure, callused hand closed over one of Elisabeth's. "Who are you?" he rasped out. "And what spell have you cast over me?"

Never before had Elisabeth guessed that tenderness toward another person could run so deep as to be painful. "I'm just a woman," she said softly. "And I wouldn't have the first idea how to cast a spell."

He stood slowly, drawing Elisabeth with him, discounting her words with a shake of his head. She knew where he meant to take her, but she couldn't protest because it seemed to her that she'd been moving toward this moment all of her life. Maybe even for all of eternity.

She closed her eyes as he held her hand to his mouth and placed featherlight kisses on her knuckles.

Once they were inside the house, he lifted her easily into his arms and started up the back stairs. Elisabeth buried her face in his muscular neck, loving the smell and the strength and the substance of him. She looked up when she heard the creak of a door and found herself in a version of her room back in the world she knew.

The bed, made of aged, intricately carved oak, stood between the windows facing the fireplace. The walls were unpapered, painted a plain white, and Elisabeth didn't recognize any of the furniture.

Jonathan set her on her feet and just as she would have

found the wit to argue that what they were about to do was wrong, he kissed her. So great was his skill and his innate magnetism that Elisabeth forgot her objections and lost herself in his mastery.

He unpinned her hair, combing it through with his fingers, and then very slowly began unbuttoning the front of her dress. Uncovering the lacy bra beneath, he frowned, and Elisabeth reached up to unfasten the front catch, revealing her full breasts to him.

Jonathan drew in his breath, then lifted one hand to caress her lightly. The pad of his thumb moved over her nipple, turning it button hard and wrenching a little cry of pleasure and surrender from Elisabeth.

She tilted her head back in glorious submission as he bent his head to her breast, pushing the dress down over her hips as he suckled. Elisabeth entwined her fingers in his thick, dark hair, her breathing shallow and quick.

When both her nipples were wet from his tongue, Jonathan laid her gently on the bed, taking no notice of her sneakers as he pulled them off and tossed them away. She crooned and arched her back as he slipped her panties down over her legs and threw them aside, too. He caressed her until she was damp, her body twisting with readiness.

His clothes seemed to disappear as easily as hers had, and soon he was stretched out on the mattress beside her. The April breeze ruffled the curtains at the windows and passed over their nakedness, stirring their passion to even greater heights rather than cooling it.

Elisabeth moaned as Jonathan claimed her mouth in another consuming kiss, his tongue sparring with hers. Her fingers dug into the moist flesh on his back as he moved his lips down over her breasts and her belly. Then he gripped her ankles and pressed her heels to the firm flesh of her bottom. Boldly, he burrowed through the silken barrier and tasted her.

Elisabeth's head moved from side to side on the pillow. "Oh, Jonathan—please—it's too much—"

"I want you to be ready for me," he told her gruffly, and then he enjoyed her in earnest, as greedy as if she were covered in honey.

The exercise moistened Elisabeth's skin, making small tendrils of hair cling to her face, and her breath came hard as she rose and fell in time with the rhythm Jonathan set for her. A low, guttural cry escaped her when he set her legs over his shoulders and teased her into the last stages of response.

She called his name when a sweet volcano erupted within her, her body arched like a bow drawn tight to launch an arrow. He spoke gently as he laid her, quivering, upon the bed and poised himself over her. She was still floating when he began kissing her collarbone.

"Shall I make love to you, Elisabeth?" he asked quietly, and a new tenderness swept over her in that moment because she knew he would respect her decision, whatever it might be.

"Yes," she whispered, twisting one finger in a lock of his hair. "Oh, yes."

He touched her with his manhood, and Elisabeth trembled with anticipation and a touch of fear. After all, there had only been one other man in her life and her experience was limited.

"I promise I won't hurt you," Jonathan said, and she was diffused with heat when he teased her by giving her just the tip of his shaft.

She clutched at his back. "Jonathan!"

He gave her a little more, and she marveled that he filled her so tightly. "What?"

"I want you—I need you—"

In a long, smooth glide, he gave her his length, and Elisabeth uttered a muffled shout of triumph. An instant later, she was in the throes of release, buckling helplessly beneath Jonathan, sobbing as her body worked out its sweet salvation.

She was embarrassed when she could finally lie still, and she would have turned her head away if Jonathan hadn't caught her chin in his hand and made her look at him.

"You were beautiful," he said. "So—beautiful."

Elisabeth's eyes brimmed with tears. Jonathan had given her a kind of pleasure she'd never dreamed existed, and she wanted to do the same for him. She cupped his face in her hands, moving her thumbs slowly over his jawbones, and she began to move beneath him.

He uttered a strangled moan and his powerful frame tensed, then he began to meet her thrusts with more and more force, until he finally exploded within her, filling her with his warmth. When it was over, he collapsed beside her, his head on her chest, one leg sprawled across her thighs, and Elisabeth held him.

After a long time, he asked quietly, "Who was he?"

Elisabeth braced herself, knowing men of Jonathan's generation expected women to come to their beds as virgins. "My husband," she said.

Instantly, Jonathan raised his head to stare into her eyes. "Your what?"

Her face felt hot. "Your honor is safe, Doctor," she assured him. "Ian and I were divorced a year ago."

He cleared his throat and sat up, reaching for his clothes. The distance in his manner wounded Elisabeth; she felt defensive. "Now I suppose I'm some kind of social pariah, just because my marriage didn't last," she said. "Well, things are different where I come from, Jonathan. Divorced women aren't branded as sinners for the rest of their lives."

Jonathan didn't answer, he just kept dressing.

There was a black-and-blue-plaid lap robe folded across the foot of the bed. Elisabeth snatched it up to cover herself. "Jonathan Fortner, if you walk out of here without speaking to me, I swear I'll never forgive you!"

He watched as she tried to dress without letting the lap robe slip. "Why did he divorce you?"

Elisabeth was furious; her cheeks ached with color. "He *didn't*—the choice was mine!"

Jonathan's shoulders slackened slightly, as though pressed under some great weight, and he sat down on the edge of the bed with a sigh. When he extended a hand to Elisabeth, she took it without thinking, and he settled her gently beside him, buttoning the front of her dress as he spoke.

"I'm sorry. I was judging what you did in terms of my own experience, and that's unreasonable."

Elisabeth couldn't resist touching the dark, rumpled hair at his nape. "Did she hurt you so badly, Jonathan?" she whispered.

"Yes," he answered simply. And then he stood and started toward the door. "Trista will be home soon," he said, without looking back. And he was gone.

Barely fifteen minutes later, when Elisabeth was in the kitchen brewing tea, Trista came in, carrying her slate and a spelling primer. The child set her school things down and went to the icebox for the crockery pitcher.

"How was school?" Elisabeth asked.

Trista's gray eyes sparkled as she poured milk into a glass and then helped herself to cookies from a squat china jar. "When Miss Bishop opened her lunch pail, there was a love letter inside—from Harvey Kates."

"The blacksmith?" Elisabeth took a cookie and joined Trista at the table.

The little girl nodded importantly, and there was now a milk mustache on her upper lip. "His sister Phyllis is in the seventh grade, and he gave her a penny to put the note where Miss Bishop would be sure to find it."

"And, of course, Phyllis told all of you exactly what her brother had written," Elisabeth guessed.

Trista nodded. "He said he was crazy for her."

Before Elisabeth could respond to that, Jonathan came into the kitchen. He gave Trista a distracted kiss on the top of her head, without so much as glancing at the houseguest he'd taken to bed only a short time before. "You've paid your debt to society," he said to the child. "You don't have to spend any more afternoons in your room."

Trista's face glowed with delight and gratitude. "Thank you, Papa."

Elisabeth might have been invisible for all the attention Jonathan was paying her.

"I'll be on rounds. Would you like to go along?"

The child shook her head. "I want to practice my piano lessons," she said virtuously.

Jonathan looked amused, but he made no comment. His gray eyes touched Elisabeth briefly, questioningly, and then he was gone. Sadness gripped her as she realized he now regretted what had happened between them.

While Trista trudged bravely through her music, Elisabeth made her way slowly up the back stairs and into the little girl's room. She was becoming too enmeshed in a way of life that could never be hers, and she had to put some space between herself and Jonathan before she fell hopelessly in love with him.

The decision was made. She would say goodbye to Trista, go back to her own time and try to make herself believe that all of this had been a dream.

7

The necklace was gone.

Elisabeth dried her eyes with the back of one hand as relief and panic battled within her. After drawing a very deep breath and letting it out slowly, she made her way downstairs to the parlor, where Trista was struggling through *Ode to Joy* at the piano.

Elisabeth paused in the doorway, watching the little girl practice and marveling that she'd come to love this child so deeply in such a short time. "Trista?"

Innocent gray eyes linked with Elisabeth's and the notes reverberated into silence. "Yes?"

"I can't find my necklace. Have you seen it?"

Trista's gaze didn't waver, though her lower lip trembled slightly. "Papa has it. He said the pendant was valuable and might get lost if we left it lying around."

"I see," Elisabeth replied as righteous indignation welled up inside her. The fact that they'd been so gloriously intimate made Jonathan's action an even worse betrayal than it would ordinarily have been. "Do you know where he put it?"

Moisture brimmed along Trista's lower lashes; somehow, Trista had guessed that Elisabeth meant to leave and that the necklace had to go with her. She shook her head. "I don't," she sniffled. "Honest."

Elisabeth's heart ached, and she went to sit beside

Trista on the piano bench, draping one arm around the little girl's shoulders. "There are people in another place who will be worrying about me," Elisabeth said gently. "I have to go and let them know I'm all right."

A tear trickled down Trista's plump cheek. "Will you be back?"

Elisabeth leaned over and lightly kissed the child's temple. "I don't know, sweetheart. Something very strange is happening to me, and I don't dare make a lot of promises, because I'm not sure I can keep them." She thought about the impending fire and a sense of hopelessness swept over her. "I'll tell you this, though—if I have any choice in the matter, I *will* see you again."

Trista nodded and rested her head against Elisabeth's shoulder. "Most times, when grown-up people go away, they don't come back."

Knowing the child was referring to her lost mother, Elisabeth hugged her again. "If I don't return, Trista, I want you to remember that it was only because I couldn't, and not because I didn't want to." She stood. "Now, you go and finish your practicing while I look for the necklace."

Elisabeth searched Jonathan's study, which was the small parlor in modern times, and found nothing except a lot of cryptic notes, medical books jammed with bits of paper and a cabinet full of vials and bottles and bandage gauze. From there, she progressed to the bedroom where he had made such thorough love to her only that afternoon.

She was still angry, but just being in that room again brought all the delicious, achy sensations rushing back, and she was almost overwhelmed with the need of him. She began with the top drawer of his bureau, finding nothing but starched handkerchiefs and stiff celluloid collars.

"Did you lose something?"

Jonathan's voice startled Elisabeth; like a hard fall, it left her breathless. She turned, her cheeks flaming, to face him.

"My necklace," she said, keeping her shoulders squared. "Where is it, Jonathan?"

He went to the night table beside his bed, opened the drawer and took out a small leather box. Lifting the lid, he looped the pendant over his fingers and extended it to Elisabeth.

"I'm going back," she said, unable to meet his eyes. For the moment, it was all she could do to cope with the wild emotions this man had brought to life inside her. He had taught her one thing for certain: she had never truly loved Ian or any other man. Jonathan Fortner had first claim on both her body and her soul.

He kept his distance, perhaps sensing that she would fall apart if he touched her. "Why?"

"We made love, Jonathan," she whispered brokenly, her hands trembling as she opened the catch on the pendant and draped the chain around her neck. "That changed things between us. And I can't afford to care for you."

Jonathan sighed. "Elisabeth—"

"No," she said, interrupting, holding up one hand to silence him. "I know you think I'm eccentric or deluded or something, and maybe you're right. Maybe this is all some kind of elaborate fantasy and I'm wandering farther and farther from reality."

He came to her then and took her into his arms. She felt the hard strength of his thighs and midsection. "I'm real, Elisabeth," he told her with gentle wryness. "You're not imagining me, I promise you."

She pushed herself back from the warm solace of him.

"Jonathan, I came here to warn you," she said urgently. "There was—will be—a fire. You've got to do something, if not for your own sake, then for Trista's."

He kissed her forehead. "I know you believe what you're saying," he replied, his tone gentle and a little hoarse. "But it's simply not possible for a human being to predict the future. Surely you understand that I cannot throw my daughter's life into an uproar on the basis of your...premonitions."

Elisabeth stiffened as a desperate idea struck her. "Suppose I could prove that I'm from the future, Jonathan—suppose I could show you the article that will be printed in the *Pine River Bugle*?"

Jonathan was frowning at her, as though he feared she'd gone mad. "That would be impossible."

She gave a brief, strangled laugh. "Impossible. You know, Jonathan, until just a short while ago, I would have said it was *impossible* to travel from my century to yours. I thought time was an orderly thing, rolling endlessly onward, like a river. Instead, it seems that the past, present and future are all of a piece, like some giant celestial tapestry."

All the while she was talking, Jonathan was maneuvering her toward the bed, though this time it was for a very different reason. "Just lie down for a little while," he said reasonably. His bag was close at hand, like always, and he snapped it open.

"Jonathan, I'm quite all right...."

He took out a syringe and began filling it from a vial.

Elisabeth's eyes went wide and she tried to bolt off the bed. "Don't you dare give me a shot!" she cried, but Jonathan put his free hand on her shoulder and pressed her easily back to the mattress. "Ouch!" she yelled when the needle punctured her upper arm. "Damn you, Jonathan, I'm not sick!"

He withdrew the needle and reached for the plaid lab robe Elisabeth had tried to hide behind after their lovemaking that afternoon. "Just rest. You'll feel better in a few hours," he urged, laying the blanket over her.

Elisabeth sat up again, only to find that all her muscles had turned to water. She sagged back against the pillows. "Jonathan Fortner, what did you give me? Do you realize that there are laws against injecting things into people's veins?"

"Be quiet," he ordered sternly.

The door creaked open and Trista peered around the edge. "What's wrong with Elisabeth?" she asked in a thin, worried voice.

Jonathan sighed and closed his medical bag with a snap. "She's overwrought, that's all," he answered. "Run along and do your spelling lesson."

"Pusher!" Elisabeth spat out once the door had closed behind the little girl. The room was starting to undulate, and she felt incredibly weak. "I should get that Farley person out here and have you arrested."

"Don't you think you're being a little childish?" Jonathan asked, bending over the bed. "I admit I shouldn't have shoved you down that way, but you didn't give much choice, did you?"

Elisabeth rolled her eyes. "A pusher is… Oh, never mind! But you mark my words, *Doctor*—I'm filing a complaint against you!"

"And I'm sure Marshal Haynes will track me down and throw me in the hoosegow the minute his boil is healed and he can sit a horse again." In the next moment, Jonathan was gone.

Struggling to stay awake, Elisabeth wondered how she

could ever expect to get through to this man if he was going hold her down and drug her every time she talked about her experience. She drifted off into a restless sleep, waking once to find Trista standing beside the bed, gently bathing her forehead with a cool cloth.

Elisabeth felt a surge of tenderness and, catching hold of Trista's hand, she gave it a little squeeze. Then she was floating again.

The house was dark when the medication finally wore off, and the realization that this was Jonathan's bed came to her instantly. She laid very still until she was sure he wasn't beside her.

Her hand rose to her throat, and she was relieved to find the necklace was still there. Another ten minutes passed before she had the wit to get out of bed and grope her way through the blackness to the door.

In the hallway, she carefully took the pendant off and tossed it over Trista's threshold. Only when she was on the other side did she put it on again.

There was pale moonlight shining in through the little girl's window, and Elisabeth went to her bedside and gently awakened her.

"You're leaving," Trista whispered, holding very tightly to her rag doll.

Elisabeth bent to kiss her forehead. "Yes, darling, I'm going to try. Remember my promise—if I can come back to you, I will."

Trista sighed. "All right," she said forlornly. "Good-bye, Elisabeth."

"Goodbye, sweetheart." Elisabeth put her arms around Trista and gave her a final hug. "No matter what happens, don't forget that I love you."

Trista's eyes were bright with tears as she sank her teeth into her lower lip and nodded.

Elisabeth drew a deep breath and went back to the door, closing her eyes as she reached for the knob, turned it and stepped through.

She was back in the twentieth century. Elisabeth opened her eyes to find herself in a carpeted hallway, then reached out for a switch and found one. Suddenly the electric wall sconces glared.

She opened the door to her room and peeked in. A poignant, bitter loneliness possessed her because there was no trace, no hint of Jonathan's presence. After lingering for a moment, she turned and went downstairs to the telephone table in the hallway.

Not surprisingly, the little red light on her answering machine was blinking.

There were three messages from Janet, each more anxious than the last, and several other friends had called from Seattle. Elisabeth shoved her fingers through her hair, sighed and padded into the kitchen, barefoot. She was still wearing the cambric dress Jonathan had given her, and she smiled, thinking what a sensation it would cause if she wore it to the supermarket.

Since she hadn't had dinner, Elisabeth heated a can of soup before finding the microfilm copies she'd made in the *Bugle* offices. It gave her a chill to think of showing Jonathan a newspaper account of his own death and that of his daughter.

While she huddled at the kitchen table, eating, Elisabeth read over the articles. It still troubled her that no bodies had been found, but then, such investigations hadn't been very thorough or scientific in the nineteenth century. Maybe the discovery had even been hushed up, out of some misguided Victorian sense of delicacy.

Flipping ahead in the sheaf of copies, Elisabeth came

to her own trial for the murder of Jonathan and Trista Fortner. With a growing sense of unreality, she read that Lizzie McCartney, who "claimed to be" the sister of the late Barbara McCartney Fortner, had been found guilty of the crime of arson, and thus murder, and sentenced to hang.

Elisabeth pushed away the last of her soup, feeling nauseous. Destiny had apparently decreed her death, as well as Jonathan's and Trista's, and she had no way of knowing whether or not their singular fates could be circumvented.

She took her bowl to the sink and rinsed it, then went upstairs to take a long, hot shower. When that was finished Elisabeth brushed her teeth, put on a lightweight cotton nightgown and crawled into bed.

Unable to sleep, she lay staring up at the ceiling. It would be easy to avoid being tried and hanged—all she would have to do was drop the necklace down a well somewhere and never go back to Jonathan's time. But even as she considered this idea, Elisabeth knew she would discard it. She loved Trista and, God help her, Jonathan, too. And she could not let two human beings die without trying to save them.

Throughout the rest of the night, Elisabeth slept only in fits and starts. The telephone brought her summarily into a morning she wasn't prepared to face.

"Hello?" she grumbled into the ornate receiver of the French telephone on the vanity table. Having stubbed her toe on a chest while crossing the room, Elisabeth made the decision to move the instrument closer to the bed.

"There you are!" Janet cried, sounding both annoyed and relieved. "Good heavens, Elisabeth—*where have you been?*"

Elisabeth sighed an sank down onto the vanity bench.

"Relax," she said. "I was only gone for a couple of days."

"A couple of days? Give me a break, Elisabeth, I've been trying to reach you for *two weeks!* You were supposed to come to Seattle and spend a weekend with me, remember?"

Two weeks? Elisabeth gripped the edge of the vanity table. The question was out of her mouth before she could properly weigh the effect it would have. "Janet, what day is it?"

Her friend's response was a short, stunned silence, followed by, "It's the first of May. I'm on my way. Don't you set foot out of that house, Elisabeth McCartney, until I get there."

Elisabeth's mind was still reeling. If there was no logical correlation between her time and Jonathan's, she might return to find that the fire had already happened. The idea set her trembling, but she knew she had to keep Janet from coming to visit and get back to 1892.

She ran the tip of her tongue quickly over her dry lips. "Listen, Janet, I'm all right, really. It's just that I met this fascinating man." That much, at least, was true. Bullheaded though he might be, Jonathan *was* fascinating. "I guess I just got so caught up in the relationship that I wasn't paying attention to the calendar."

Janet sounded both intrigued and suspicious. "Who is this guy? You haven't mentioned any man to me."

"That's because I just met him." She thought quickly, desperately. "We were away for a while."

"Something about this doesn't ring true," Janet said, but she was weakening. Elisabeth could hear it in her voice.

"I—I really fell hard for him," she said.

"Who is he? What does he do?"

Elisabeth took a deep breath. "His name is Jonathan Fortner, and he's a doctor."

"I'd like to meet him."

Elisabeth stifled an hysterical giggle. "Yes—well, he and I are taking off for a vacation. But maybe I can arrange something after I—we get back."

"Where are you going?" Janet asked quickly, sounding worried again.

"San Francisco." It was the first place that came to mind.

"Oh. Well, I'll just come to the airport and see you off. That way, you could introduce Jonathan and me."

"Umm," Elisabeth stalled, biting her lower lip. "We're going by car," she finally answered. "I promise faithfully that I'll call you the instant I step through the doorway."

Janet sighed. "All right but, well, there isn't anything wrong with this guy, is there? I mean, it's almost like you're hiding something."

"You've pried it out of me," Elisabeth teased. "He's a vampire. Even as we speak, he's lying in a coffin in the basement, sleeping away the daylight hours."

The joke must have reassured Janet, because she laughed. A moment later, though, her tone was serious again. "You'd tell me if you weren't all right, wouldn't you?"

Elisabeth hesitated. As much as she loved Janet, Rue was the only person in the world she could have talked to about what was happening to her. "If I thought there was anything you could do to help, yes," she answered softly. "Please don't worry about me, Janet. I'll call you when I get back." *If I get back.* "And we'll make plans for my visit to Seattle."

Mollified at least for the moment, Janet accepted Elisabeth's promise, warned her to be careful and said good-bye.

She showered and put on white corduroy pants and a sea green tank top, along with a pair of plastic thongs. Then after a hasty trip to the mailbox—there were two postcards from Rue, one mailed from Istanbul, the other from Cairo, along with a forwarded bank statement and a sales flier addressed to "occupant"—Elisabeth made preparations to return to Jonathan and Trista.

As she looked at the copies of the June 1892 issue of the *Bugle,* however, she began to doubt that Jonathan would see them as proof of anything. He was bound to say that, while the printing admittedly looked strange, she could have had the articles made up.

Elisabeth laid the papers down on the kitchen table and went up the back stairs and along the hallway to her room. In the bathroom medicine cabinet, she found the half-filled bottle of penicillin tablets she'd taken for a throat infection a few months before.

The label bore a typewritten date, along with Elisabeth's name, but it was the medicine itself that would convince Jonathan. After all, he was a doctor. She dropped the bottle into the pocket of her slacks and went back out to the vanity.

Aunt Verity's necklace was lying there, where she'd left it before taking her shower that morning. Her fingers trembled with mingled resolution and fear as she put the chain around her neck and fastened the clasp.

Reaching the hallway, Elisabeth went directly to the sealed door and clasped the knob in her hand.

Nothing happened.

"Please," Elisabeth whispered, shutting her eyes. "Please."

Still, that other world was closed to her. Fighting down

panic, she told herself she had only to wait for the "window" to open again. In the meantime, there was something else she wanted to do.

After riffling through a variety of scribbled notes beside the hallway phone, she found the name and number she wanted. She dialed immediately, to keep herself from having time to back out.

"Hello?" a woman's voice answered.

Elisabeth had a clear picture of Chastity Pringle in her mind, standing in that quilting booth at the craft show, looking at the necklace as though it was something that had slithered out of hell. "Ms. Pringle? This is Elisabeth McCartney. You probably don't remember me, but we met briefly at the craft fair, when you were showing your quilts—"

"You were wearing Verity's necklace," Chastity interrupted in a wooden tone.

"Yes," Elisabeth answered. "Ms. Pringle, I wonder if I could see you sometime today—it's important."

"I won't set foot in that house" was the instant response.

"All right," Elisabeth agreed quietly, "I'll be happy to come to you. If that's convenient, of course."

"I'll meet you at the Riverview Café," Chastity offered, though not eagerly.

"Twelve-thirty?"

"Twelve-thirty," the woman promised.

The Riverview Café was about halfway between Pine River and Cotton Creek, the even smaller town where Chastity lived. Elisabeth couldn't help wondering, as she stared blankly at a morning talk show to pass the time, why Ms. Pringle was being so cloak-and-dagger about the whole thing.

At twelve-fifteen, Elisabeth pulled into the restaurant

parking lot, got out of her car and went inside. Chastity hadn't arrived yet, but Elisabeth allowed a waitress to escort her to a table with a magnificent view of the river and ordered herbal tea to sip while she waited.

Chastity appeared, looking anxious and rushed, at exactly twelve-thirty. She was trim and very tanned, and her long, dark hair was wound into a single, heavy braid that rested over one shoulder. She focused her gaze on Elisabeth's necklace and shuddered visibly.

Elisabeth waited until the waitress had taken their orders before bracing her forearms against the table edge and leaning forward to ask bluntly, "What was your connection with my Aunt Verity, and why are you afraid of this necklace?"

"Verity was my friend," Chastity answered, "at a time when I needed one very badly." The waitress brought their spinach and smoked salmon salads, then went away again. "As for the pendant..."

"It was yours once," Elisabeth ventured, operating purely on instinct. "Wasn't it...Barbara?"

The woman's dark eyes were suddenly enormous, and the color drained from her face. "You know? About the doorway, I mean?"

Elisabeth nodded.

Barbara Fortner reached for her water glass with an unsteady hand. "You've met Jonathan, then, I suppose, and Trista." She paused to search Elisabeth's face anxiously. "How is my little girl?"

"She believes you're dead," Elisabeth answered, not unkindly.

Barbara flinched. Misery was visible in every line of her body. "Jonathan would have told her something like that. He'd be too proud to admit to the truth, that he drove me away."

Elisabeth's hands tightened on the arms of her chair. Her entire universe had been upended, but here was a woman who understood. Whatever Elisabeth's personal feelings about Barbara might be, she was relieved to find a person who knew about the world beyond that threshold.

"Did he divorce me?" Barbara asked quietly, after a long moment.

Elisabeth hesitated. "Yes."

Jonathan's ex-wife took several sips of water and then shrugged, although Elisabeth could see that she was shaken. "How is Trista?"

Elisabeth opened her purse and took out the folded copies of the newspaper articles. "She's in a lot of danger, Barbara, and so is Jonathan. They need your help."

Barbara's face blanched as she scanned the newspaper accounts. "Oh, my God, my baby...I knew I should have found a way to bring her with me."

A quivering sensation in the pit of her stomach kept Elisabeth constantly on edge. She was aware of every tick of the clock, and the idea that it might already be too late to help Jonathan and Trista tormented her. "Sometimes I can make the trip back and sometimes I can't," she said in a low voice. "Do you know if there's some way to be sure of connecting?"

Tears glimmered in Barbara's eyes as she met Elisabeth's gaze. "I—I don't know—I only did it a couple of times—but I think there has to be some sort of strong emotion. Are you going back?"

Elisabeth nodded. "As soon as I can manage it, yes."

Barbara sat up very straight in her chair, her salad forgotten. "You're in love with Jonathan, aren't you?"

The answer came immediately; Elisabeth didn't even need to think about it. "Yes."

"Fine. Then the two of you will have each other." She

leaned forward, her eyes pleading. "Elisabeth, I want you to send Trista over the threshold to me. It might be the only way to save her."

Barbara's statement was undeniable, but it caused Elisabeth tremendous pain. If she put the necklace on Trista and sent her through the doorway, she would disappear forever. Jonathan would be heartbroken, and he'd never believe the truth. No, he'd think Elisabeth had harmed the child, and he'd hate her for it.

And that wasn't all. Without the necklace, Elisabeth would be trapped in the nineteenth century, friendless and despised. Why, she might even be blamed for Trista's disappearance and hanged or sent to prison.

She swallowed hard. "Jonathan loves Trista, and he's a good father. Besides, your daughter believes you died in Boston, while visiting your family."

Barbara's perfectly manicured index finger stabbed at the stack of photocopies lying on the tabletop. "If you don't send her to me, she'll burn to death!"

Elisabeth looked away, toward the river flowing past. "I'll do what I can," she said. Presently, she met Barbara's eyes again, and she was calmer. "How could you have left her in the first place?" she asked, no longer able to hold the question back.

The other woman lowered her eyes for a moment. "I was desperately unhappy, and I'd had a glimpse of this world. I couldn't stop thinking about it. It was like a magnet." She sighed. "I wasn't cut out to live there, to be the wife of a country doctor. I had a lover, and Jonathan found out. He was furious, even though Matthew and I had broken off. I was afraid he was going to kill me, so I came here to stay. Verity took me in and helped me establish an identity, and I left the necklace with her because I knew I'd never want to go back."

"Not even to help your daughter?"

Color glowed in Barbara's cheeks. "I don't dare step over that threshold," she said, almost in a whisper. "I'm too afraid of Jonathan."

Although Elisabeth would never have denied that Jonathan was imposing, even arrogant and opinionated, she didn't believe for a moment that he would ever deliberately hurt another person. He was a doctor, after all, and an honorable man. She changed the subject.

"How long have you been here, in the twentieth century?"

Barbara dried her eyes carefully with a cloth napkin. "Fifteen years," she answered. "And I've been happy."

Elisabeth felt another chill. Fifteen years. And yet Trista was only eight—or she had been, when Elisabeth had seen her last. She gave up trying to figure out these strange wrinkles in time and concentrated on what was important: saving Trista and Jonathan.

"If I can find a way to protect Trista while still keeping her there, that's what I'm going to do," she warned, rising and reaching for her purse and the check. "Jonathan adores his daughter, and it would crush him to lose her."

Barbara lifted one eyebrow, but made no move to stand. "Are you really thinking of Jonathan, Elisabeth? Or is it yourself you're worried about?"

It was a question Elisabeth couldn't bear to answer. She paid for the lunches neither she nor Barbara had eaten and hurried out of the restaurant.

8

By the time Elisabeth arrived at home, she was in a state of rising panic. She *had* to reach Jonathan and Trista, had to know that they were all right. She glanced fitfully at the telephone and answering machine on the hallway table, not pausing even though the message light was blinking.

Could you please connect me with someone in 1892? she imagined herself asking a bewildered operator.

Shaking her head, Elisabeth went on into the kitchen and tossed her purse onto the table. Then she crossed the room to switch the calendar page from April to May. She was still standing there staring, her teeth sunk into her lower lip, when a loud pounding at the back door startled her out of her wonderment.

Miss Cecily Buzbee peered at her through the frosted oval glass, and Elisabeth smiled as she went to admit her neighbor, who had apparently come calling alone.

"I don't mind telling you," the sweet-natured spinster commented after Elisabeth had let her in and offered a glass of ice tea, "that Sister and I have been concerned about you, since we don't see hide nor hair of you for days at a time."

Elisabeth busied herself with the tasks of running cold water into a pitcher and adding ice and powdery tea. "I'm sorry you were worried," she said quietly. She carried the pitcher to the table, along with two glasses. "I don't mean to be a recluse—I just need a lot of solitude right now."

Cecily smiled forgivingly. "I don't suppose there's any lemon, is there, dear?"

Elisabeth shook her head regretfully. Even if she'd remembered to buy lemons the last time she'd shopped, which she hadn't, that had been two weeks before and they would probably have spoiled by now. "Miss Cecily," she began, clasping her hands together on her lap so her visitor wouldn't see that they were trembling, "how well did you know my Aunt Verity?"

"Oh, very well," Cecily trilled. "Very well, indeed."

"Did she tell you stories about this house?"

Cecily averted her cornflower blue eyes for a moment, then forced herself to look at Elisabeth again. "You know how Verity liked to talk. And she *was* a rather fanciful sort."

Elisabeth smiled, remembering. "Yes, she was. She told Rue and me lots of things about this house, about people simply appearing, seemingly out of nowhere, and other things like that."

The neighbor nodded solemnly. "Sister and I believe that young Trista Fortner haunts this house, poor soul. Her spirit never rested because she died so horribly."

Unable to help herself, Elisabeth shuddered. If she did nothing else, she had to see that Trista wasn't trapped in that fire. "I can't buy the ghost theory," she said, sipping the tea and barely noticing that it tasted awful. "I mean, here are these souls, supposedly lost in the scheme of things, wandering about, unable to find their way into whatever comes after this life. Why would God permit that, when there is so much order in everything else, like the seasons and the courses of the planets?"

"My dear," Cecily debated politely, "reputable people

have seen apparitions. They cannot all be dismissed as crackpots.''

Elisabeth sighed, wondering which category she would fall into: crackpot or reputable person. ''Isn't it just possible that the images were every bit as real as the people seeing them? Perhaps there are places where time wears thin and a person can see through it, into the past or the future, if only for a moment.''

Miss Buzbee gave the idea due consideration. ''Well, Elisabeth, as the bard said, there are more things in heaven and earth...''

Anxiety filled Elisabeth as her mind turned back to Jonathan and Trista. Would she return to 1892 only to find them gone—if she was able to reach them at all? ''More tea?'' she asked, even though she was desperate to be alone again so that she could make another attempt at crossing the threshold.

Trista's friend, Vera, had apparently trained her daughters not to overstay their welcome. ''I really must be running along,'' Cecily said. ''It's almost time for Sister and I to take our walk. Two miles, rain or shine,'' she said with resignation, frowning grimly as she looked out through the windows. Storm clouds were gathering on the horizon.

''I've enjoyed our visit,'' Elisabeth replied honestly, following Miss Cecily to the door. She wondered what Cecily would say if told Elisabeth had had a glimpse of Vera, the Buzbee sisters' mother, as a little girl playing on the school grounds.

A light rain started to fall after Cecily had gone, and Elisabeth stood at the back door for a long moment, her heart hammering as she gazed at the orchard. The beautiful petals of spring were all gone now, replaced by healthy green leaves—another reminder that two weeks of her life had passed without her knowing.

When thunder rolled down from the mountains and lightning splintered the sky, Elisabeth shuddered and closed the door. Then she hurried up the back stairs and along the hallway.

"Trista!" she shouted, pounding with both fists at the panel of wood that separated her from that other world. "Trista, can you hear me?"

There was no sound from the other side, except for the whistle of the wind, and Elisabeth sagged against the wood in frustrated despair. "Oh, God," she whispered, "don't let them be dead. *Please* don't let them be dead."

After a long time, she turned away and went back down the stairs to the kitchen. She put on a rain coat and dashed out to the shed for an armload of kindling and aged apple wood, which she carried to the hearth in the main parlor.

There, she built a fire to bring some warmth and cheer to that large, empty room. When the wood was crackling and popping in the grate, she put the screen in place and went to the piano, lifting the keyboard cover and idly striking middle C with her index finger.

"Hear me, Trista," she pleaded softly, flexing her fingers. "Hear and wish just as hard as you can for me to come back."

She began to play the energetic tune she'd described to Trista as a boogie-woogie, putting all her passion, all her hopes and fears into the crazy, racing, tinkling notes of the song. When she finally stopped, her fingers exhausted, the sound of another pianist attempting to play the song met her ears.

Elisabeth nearly overturned the piano bench in her eagerness to run upstairs to the door that barred her from the place where she truly belonged. She wrenched hard on the knob, and breathtaking exultation rushed into her when it turned.

Trista's awkward efforts at the piano tune grew louder and louder as Elisabeth raced through the little girl's bedroom and down the steps. When she burst into the parlor, Trista's face lit up.

She ran to Elisabeth and threw her arms around her.

Elisabeth embraced her, silently thanking God that she wasn't too late, that the fire hadn't already happened, then knelt to look into Trista's eyes. "Sweetheart, this is important. How long have I been gone?"

Trista bit her lip, seeming puzzled by the question. "Since last night, when you came in and kissed me goodbye. It's afternoon now—school let out about an hour ago."

"Good," Elisabeth whispered, relieved to learn that days or weeks hadn't raced by in her absence. "Was your father upset to find that I wasn't here?"

"He cussed," Trista replied with a solemn nod. "It reminded me of the day Mama went away to Boston. Papa got angry then, too, because she didn't say goodbye to us."

Elisabeth sat down on the piano bench and took Trista onto her lap, recalling her talk with Barbara Fortner in the Riverview Café. Sending Trista over the threshold to her mother might be the only way to save her, but Jonathan would never understand that. "Where is he now?"

Trista sighed. "In town. There was a fight at one of the saloons, and some people needed to be stitched up."

Elisabeth winced and said, "Ouch!" and Trista laughed.

"Papa's going to be happy when he sees you're back," the child said after an interval. "But he probably won't admit he's pleased."

"Probably not," Elisabeth agreed, giving Trista's pig-tail a playful tug. She looked down at her slacks and tank top. "I guess I'd better change into something more fit-ting," she confided.

Trista nodded and took Elisabeth's hand. They went upstairs together, and the little girl's expression was thoughtful. "I wish Papa would let *me* wear trousers," she said. "It would be so much better for riding a horse. I hate sitting sideways in the saddle, like a priss."

"Do you have a horse?" Elisabeth asked as they reached the second floor, but continued on to the attic, where Barbara's clothes were stored.

"Yes," Trista answered, somewhat forlornly. "Her name is Estella, she's about a thousand years old, and she's a ninny."

Elisabeth laughed. "What a way to talk about the poor thing!" The attic door creaked a little as they went in, and the bright afternoon sunlight was flecked with a gal-axy of tiny dust particles. "Most little girls love their horses, if they're lucky enough to have one."

Trista dusted off a short stool and sat down, smoothing the skirts of her flowered poplin pinafore as she did so. "Estella just wants to wander around the pasture and chew grass, and she won't come when I call because she doesn't like to be ridden. Do you have your own horse, Elisabeth?"

Opening the heavy doors of the cedar-lined armoire, Elisabeth ran her hand over colorful, still-crisp skirts of lawn and cambric and poplin and satin and even velvet. "I don't," she said distractedly, "but my Cousin Rue does. When her grandfather died, she inherited a ranch in Montana, and I understand there are lots of horses there." She took a frothy pink lawn gown from the wardrobe and

GET **3** BOOKS FREE!

To get your 3 free books, affix this peel-off sticker to the reply card and mail it today!

MIRA BOOKS, the brightest star in women's fiction, presents

the Best of the Best

Superb collector's editions of the very best romance novels by the world's best-known authors!

* **Free Books!** Get one free book by Debbie Macomber, one by Linda Lael Miller and one by CharlotteVale Allen!

* **Free Gift!** Get a stylish picture frame absolutely free!

* **Best Books!** "The Best of the Best" brings you the best books by the world's hottest romance authors!

GET ALL 3

We'd like to send you three free books to introduce you to "The Best of the Best." Your three books have a combined cover price of $16.48, but they are yours free! We'll even send you a lovely "thank-you" gift—the attractive picture frame shown below. You can't lose!

DARING MOVES
by Linda Lael Miller
"One of the hottest romance authors writing today." — *Romantic Times*

SOMEBODY'S BABY
by Charlotte Vale Allen
"A powerful and compelling story ." — *Rapport*

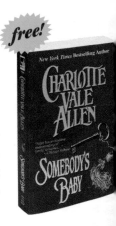

PROMISE ME FOREVER
by Debbie Macomber
"Debbie Macomber's stories sparkle with love and laughter."
— *Bestselling author Jayne Ann Krentz*

BOOKS FREE!

THE BEST OF THE BEST™: HERE'S HOW IT WORKS —

Accepting free books places you under no obligation to buy anything. You may keep the books and gift and return the shipping statement marked "cancel." If you do not cancel, about a month later we will send you 3 additional novels and bill you just $3.99 each, plus 25¢ delivery per book and applicable sales tax, if any.* That's the complete price, and—compared to cover prices of $5.50 each—quite a bargain! You may cancel at any time, but if you choose to continue, every month we'll send you 3 more books, which you may either purchase at the discount price…or return to us and cancel your subscription.

*Terms and prices subject to change without notice. Sales tax applicable in N.Y.

held it against her, waltzing a little because it was so shamelessly frilly.

"Wasn't he your grandfather, too, if you and Rue are cousins?"

Elisabeth bent to kiss the child's forehead, while still enjoying the feel of the lovely dress under her hands. "Our fathers were brothers," she explained. "The ranch belonged to Rue's mother's family."

"Could we visit there sometime?" The hopeful note in Trista's voice tugged at Elisabeth's heart, and unexpected tears burned in her eyes.

She shook her head, turning her back so Trista wouldn't see that she was crying. "It's very faraway," she said after a long time had passed.

"Montana isn't so far," Jonathan's daughter argued politely. "We could be there in three days if we took the train."

But we wouldn't see Rue, Elisabeth thought sadly. *She hasn't even been born yet.* She stepped behind a dusty folding screen and slipped off her tank top and slacks, then pulled the pink dress on over her head. "I don't think your papa would want you to go traveling without him," she said, having finally found words, however inadequate, to answer Trista.

When Elisabeth came out from behind the screen, Trista drew in her breath. "Thunderation, Elisabeth—you look beautiful!"

Elisabeth laughed, put her hands on her hips and narrowed her eyes. "Thanks a heap, kid, but did you just swear?"

Trista giggled and scurried around behind Elisabeth to begin fastening the buttons and hooks that would hold the dress closed in back. "*Thunderation* isn't a swear word," she said indulgently. "But I don't suppose it's very lady-like, either."

The light was fading, receding across the dirty floor toward the windows like an ebbing tide, so the two went down the attic steps together, Elisabeth carrying her slacks and tank top over one arm. She felt a sense of excitement and anticipation, knowing she would see Jonathan again soon.

In her room, Elisabeth brushed her hair and pinned it up, while Trista sat on the edge of the bed, watching with her head tilted to one side and her small feet swinging back and forth.

Downstairs, Elisabeth checked the pot roast Ellen had left to cook in the oven. She found an apron to protect her gown, then set to work washing china from the cabinet in the dining room. In a drawer of the highboy, she found white tapers and silver candle sticks, and she set these on the formal table.

"We never eat in here," Trista said.

Outside, twilight was falling, and with it came a light spring rain. "We're going to tonight," Elisabeth replied.

"Why? It isn't Christmas or Easter, and it's not anybody's birthday."

Elisabeth smiled. "I want to celebrate being home," she said, and only when the words were out of her mouth did she realize how presumptuous they sounded. Jonathan had made love to her, but it wasn't as though he'd expressed a desire for a lifelong commitment or anything like that. This wasn't her home, it was Barbara's, as was the china she was setting out and the dress she was wearing.

As were the child and the man she loved so fiercely.

"Don't be sad," Trista said, coming to stand close to Elisabeth in a show of support.

Elisabeth gave her a distracted squeeze, and said brightly, "I think we'd better get some fires going, since it's so dreary out."

"I'll do it," Trista announced. "So you don't ruin your pretty dress." With that, she fetched wood from the shed out back and laid fires in the grates in the parlor and the dining room. Rain was pattering at the windows and blazes were burning cheerily on the hearths when Elisabeth saw Jonathan drive his buggy through the wide doorway of the barn.

It was all she could do not to run outside, ignoring the weather entirely, and fling herself into his arms. But she forced herself to remain in the kitchen, where she and Trista had been sipping tea and playing Go Fish while they waited for Jonathan.

When he came in, some twenty minutes later, he was wet to the skin. The look in his gray eyes was grim, and Elisabeth felt a wrench deep inside when she saw him.

"You," he said, tossing his medical bag onto the shelf beside the door and peeling off his coat. He wasn't wearing a hat, and his dark hair streamed with rain water. His shirt was so wet, it had turned transparent.

Elisabeth refused to be intimidated by his callous welcome. "Yes, Dr. Fortner," she said, "I'm back."

He glared at her once, then stormed up the stairs. When he came down again, he was wearing plain black trousers and an off white shirt, open at the throat to reveal a wealth of dark chest hair. But then, Elisabeth knew all about that wonderful chest...

"Go stand by the fire," she told him as she lifted the roasting pan from the oven. Inside was a succulent blend of choice beef, a thin but aromatic gravy and perfectly cooked potatoes and carrots. "You'll catch your death."

Trista was in the dining room, lighting the candles.

"Where were you?" Jonathan demanded in a furious undertone. "I searched every inch of this house and the barn and the woodshed...."

Elisabeth shrugged. "I've explained it all before, Jonathan, and you never seem to believe me. And, frankly, I'd rather not risk having you throw me down on a bed and inject some primitive sedative into my veins because you think I'm hysterical."

He rolled his wonderful gray eyes in exasperation. *"Where did you go?"*

"Believe it or not, most of the time I was right here in this house." She wanted to tell him about seeing Barbara, but the moment wasn't right, and she couldn't risk having Trista overhear what she said. "For now, Jonathan, I'm afraid you're going to have to be satisfied with that answer."

He glared at her, but there was a softening in his manner, and Elisabeth knew he was glad she'd come back— a fact that made her exultant.

The three of them ate dinner in the dining room, then Trista volunteered to clear the table and wash the dishes. While she was doing that, Elisabeth sat at the piano, playing a medley of the Beatles ballads.

Jonathan stood beside the fireplace, one arm braced against the mantelpiece, listening with a frown. "I've never heard that before," he said.

Elisabeth smiled but made no comment.

He came to stand behind her, lightly resting his hands on her shoulders, which the dress left partially bare. "Lizzie," he said gruffly, "please tell me who you are. Tell me how you managed to vanish that way."

She stopped playing and turned slightly to look up at him. Her eyes were bright with tears because the name Lizzie had brought the full gravity of the situation down on her again, though she'd managed to put it out of her mind for a little while.

"There's something I want to show you," she said. "Something I brought back from—from where I live. We'll talk about it after Trista goes to bed."

He bent reluctantly and gave her a brief, soft kiss. He'd barely straightened up again when his daughter appeared, her round little cheeks flushed with pride.

"I did the dishes," she announced.

Jonathan smiled and patted her small shoulder. "You're a marvel," he said.

"Can we go to the Founder's Day picnic tomorrow, Papa?" she asked hopefully. "Since Elisabeth would be there to take me home, it wouldn't matter if you had to leave early to set a broken bone or deliver a baby."

Jonathan's gaze shifted uncertainly to Elisabeth, and she felt a pang, knowing he was probably concerned about the questions her presence would raise. "Would you like to go?" he asked.

Elisabeth thrived on this man's company, and his daughter's. She wanted to be wherever they were, be it heaven or hell. "Yes," she said in an oddly choked voice.

Pleasure lighted Jonathan's weary eyes for just a moment, but then the spell was broken. He announced that he had things to do in the barn and went out.

Elisabeth exchanged the pink gown for her slacks and tank top and began heating water on the stove for Trista's bath. Once the little girl had scrubbed from head to foot, dried herself and put on a warm flannel nightgown, she and Elisabeth sat near the stove, and Elisabeth gently combed the tangles from Trista's hair.

"I wish you were my mama," Trista confessed later, when Elisabeth was tucking her into bed, after reading her a chapter of *Huckleberry Finn*.

Touched, Elisabeth kissed the little girl's cheek. "I wish that, too," she admitted. "But I'm not, and it's no good pretending. However, we can be the very best of friends."

Trista beamed. "I'd like that," she said.

Elisabeth blew out Trista's lamp, then sat on the edge of the bed until the child's breathing was even with sleep. Her eyes adjusted now to the darkness, Elisabeth made her way to the inner door that led down to the kitchen.

Jonathan was seated at the table, drinking coffee. His expression and his bearing conveyed a weariness that made Elisabeth want to put her arms around him.

"What were you going to show me?"

Elisabeth put one hand into the pocket of her slacks and brought out the prescription bottle. "Nothing much," she said, setting it on the table in front of him. "Just your ordinary, everyday, garden-variety wonder drug."

He picked up the little vial and squinted at the print on the label. "Penicillin." His eyes widened, and Elisabeth thought he was probably reading the date. As she sat down next to him, he looked at her in skeptical curiosity.

"In proper doses," she said, "this stuff can cure some heavy hitters, like pneumonia. They call it an antibiotic."

Jonathan tried to remove the child-proof cap and failed, until Elisabeth showed him the trick. He poured the white tablets into his palm and sniffed them, then picked one up and touched it to his tongue.

Elisabeth watched with delight as he made a face and dropped all the pills back into the bottle. "Well? Are you convinced?"

Still scowling, the country doctor tapped the side of the bottle with his finger nail. "What is this made of?"

"Plastic," Elisabeth answered. "Another miracle. Take

it from me, Jonathan, the twentieth century is full of them. I just wish I could show you everything."

He studied her for a moment, then shoved the bottle toward her. It was obvious that, while he didn't know what to think, he'd chosen not to believe Elisabeth. "The twentieth century," he scoffed.

"Almost the twenty-first," Elisabeth insisted implacably. No matter what this guy said or did, she wasn't going to let him rile her again. There was simply too much at stake. She let her eyes rest on the penicillin. "When you use that, do it judiciously. The drug causes violent reactions, even death, in some people."

Jonathan shook his head scornfully, but Elisabeth noticed that his gaze kept straying back to the little vial. It was obvious that he was itching to pick it up and examine it again.

She sighed, allowing herself a touch of exasperation. "All right, so you can dismiss the pills as some kind of trick. But what about the bottle? You admitted it yourself—you've never seen anything like it. And do you know why, Jonathan? Because it doesn't exist in your world. It hasn't been invented yet."

Clearly, he could resist no longer. He reached out and snatched up the penicillin as if he thought Elisabeth would try to beat him to it, dropping the bottle into the pocket of his shirt.

"Where did you go?" he demanded in an impatient whisper.

Elisabeth smiled. "Why on earth would I want to tell you that?" she asked. "You'll just think I'm having a fit and pump my veins full of dope."

"Full of what?"

"Never mind." She reached across the table and patted his hand in a deliberately patronizing fashion. "From here on out, just think of me as a...guardian angel. Actually, that should be no more difficult to absorb than the truth. I have the power to help you and Trista, even save your lives, if you'll only let me."

Jonathan surprised her with a slow smile. "A guardian angel? More likely, you're a witch. And I've got to admit, I'm under your spell."

Elisabeth glanced nervously toward the rear stairway, half expecting to find Trista there, listening. "Jonathan, while I was—er—where I was, I talked with Barbara."

The smile faded, as Elisabeth had known it would. "Where? Damn it, if that woman has come back here, meaning to upset my daughter—"

"She's a century away," Elisabeth said. "And Trista is her daughter, too."

"Are you telling me that Barbara..."

"Went to the future?" Elisabeth finished for him. "Yes. She was wearing my necklace at the time, though, of course, it was *her* necklace then."

Jonathan erupted from his chair with such force that it clattered to the floor. Elisabeth watched as he went to the stove to refill his coffee mug, and even through the fabric of his shirt, she could see that the muscles in his shoulders were rigid. "You're insane," he accused without facing Elisabeth.

"I saw her. She said she had a lover, and you'd found out about him. She was afraid of what you might do to her."

Jonathan went to the stairway and looked up to make sure his daughter wasn't listening. "Is that why you're here?" he snapped cruelly when he was certain they were alone. "Did Barbara send you to spy on me?"

It was getting harder and harder to keep her temper. Elisabeth managed, although her hands trembled slightly as she lifted her cup to her mouth and took a sip. "No. I stumbled onto this place quite by accident, I assure you— rather like Alice tumbling into the rabbit hole. That story has been written, I presume?"

He gave her a look of scalding sarcasm. "Every school-child knows it," he said. "Where are those newspaper accounts you mentioned? The ones that cover my death?"

Elisabeth ran the tip of her tongue over dry lips. "Well, I had them, but in the end I decided you would only say I'd had them printed up somewhere myself. What I can't understand is why you think I would want to pull such an elaborate hoax in the first place. Tell me exactly what you think I would have to gain by making up such a story."

He took her cup, rather summarily, and refilled it. "You probably believe what you're saying."

She threw her hands out from her sides in a burst of annoyance. "If you think I'm a raving lunatic, why do you allow me to stay here? Why do you trust me with your daughter?"

Jonathan smiled and sat down again. "Because I think you're a *harmless* lunatic."

Elisabeth shoved her fingers through her hair, completely ruining the modified Gibson Girl style. "Thank you, Sigmund Freud."

"Sigmund Who?"

"Forget it. It's too hard to explain."

Her host rolled his eyes and then leaned forward ominously, in effect ordering her to try.

"Listen, you're bound to read about Dr. Freud soon, and all your questions will be answered. Though you shouldn't take his theories concerning mothers and sons too seriously."

Jonathan rubbed his temples with a thumb and forefinger and sighed in a long-suffering way.

"How are you going to explain me to the good citizens of Pine River at that picnic tomorrow?" Elisabeth asked, not only because she wanted to change the dead-end subject, but because she was curious. "By telling them I'm your wife's sister?"

"I'm not about to change my story now," he said. "Of course, Ellen's told half the county you're a witch, popping in and out whenever it strikes your fancy."

Close, Elisabeth thought with grim humor, *but no cigar.* "Maybe it would be simpler if I just stayed here."

"We can't hide you away forever, especially after that visit you paid to my office."

Elisabeth fluttered her eyelashes. "I think I have an admirer in the big fella," she teased. "What was his name again? Moose? Svend?"

Jonathan laughed. "Ivan." He pushed back his chair and carried his cup and Elisabeth's to the sink, leaving them for Ellen to wash in the morning. Then he waited, in that courtly way of his, while Elisabeth stood. "Will you disappear again tonight?" he asked.

"You wouldn't tease if you knew how uncertain it is," she answered. "I could get stuck on the other side and never find my way back."

He escorted her to the door of the spare room and gave her a light, teasing kiss that left her wanting more. Much more. "Good night, Lizzie," he said. "I'll see you in the morning—I hope."

9

Elisabeth was pleasantly surprised to learn that the Founder's Day picnic was to be held in one of her favorite places—the grassy area beside the creek, next to the covered bridge. All that sunny Saturday morning, while she and Trista were frying chicken and making a version of potato salad, wagons and buggies rattled past on the road.

When Jonathan returned from his morning rounds, the three of them walked through the orchard to the creek, Jonathan carrying the food in a big wicker basket. Elisabeth, wearing a demure blue-and-white checked gingham she'd found in one of the attic trunks, was at his side. Though her chin was at a slightly obstinate angle, there was no hiding her nervousness.

There were rigs lining the road on both sides of the bridge, and dozens of blankets had been spread out on the ground alongside the creek. Boys in caps and short pants chased each other, pursued in turn by little girls with huge bows in their hair. The ladies sat gracefully on their spreads, their skirts arranged in modest fashion. Some used ruffle-trimmed parasols to shelter their complexions from the sun, while others, clad in calico, seemed to relish the light as much as the children did.

Most of the men wore plain trousers and either flannel or cotton shirts, and Jonathan was the only one without a hat. They stood in clusters, talking among themselves and smoking, but when the Fortner household arrived, it seemed they all turned to look, as did the women.

Elisabeth was profoundly aware of the differences between herself and these people and, for one terrible moment, she had to struggle to keep from turning and running back to the shelter of the house.

Vera came over, a tiny emissary with flowing brown hair and freckles, and looked solemnly up into Elisabeth's face. "You don't look like a witch to me," she remarked forthrightly.

"Does this mean they won't burn me at the stake?" Elisabeth whispered to Jonathan, who chuckled.

"She's not a witch," Trista said, arms akimbo, her gray gaze sweeping the crowd and daring any detractor to step forward. Her youthful voice rang with conviction. "Elisabeth is my friend."

Jonathan set the picnic basket down and began unfolding the blanket he'd been carrying under one arm, while Elisabeth waited, staring tensely at the population of Pine River, her smile wobbling on her mouth.

Finally, one of the women in calico came forward, returning Elisabeth's smile and offering her hand. "I'm Clara Piedmont," she said. "Vera's mother."

"Lizzie McCartney," Jonathan said, making the false introduction smoothly, just a moment after Trista and Vera had run off to join the other kids, "my wife's sister."

"How do you do?" Clara asked as a shiver went down Elisabeth's back. As long as she lived, which might not be very long at all, she would never get used to being called Lizzie.

This show of acceptance reassured her, though, and her smile was firm on her lips, no longer threatening to come unpinned and fall off. She murmured a polite response.

"Will you be staying in Pine River?" Clara inquired.

Elisabeth glanced in Jonathan's direction, not certain how to respond. "I—haven't decided," she said lamely.

Although Clara was not a pretty woman, her smile was warm and open. She patted Elisabeth's upper arm in a friendly way. "Well, you come over for tea one day this week. Trista will show you where we live." She turned to Jonathan. "Would it be all right if Trista stayed at our house tonight? Vera's been plaguing me about it all day."

Jonathan didn't look at Elisabeth, which was a good thing, because even a glance from him would have brought the color rushing to her cheeks. With Trista away, the two of them would be alone in the house.

"That would be fine," he said.

Elisabeth felt a rush of anticipation so intense that it threatened to lift her off the ground and spin her around a few times, and she was mortified at herself. She didn't even want to think what modern self-help books had to say about women who wanted a particular man's love-making that much.

Over the course of the afternoon, she managed to blend in with the other women, and after eating, everyone posed for the town photographer, the wooden bridge looming in the background. Later, while the boys fished in the creek, girls waded in, deliberately scaring away the trout. The men puffed on their cigars and played horseshoes, and the ladies gossiped.

Toward sunset, when people were packing up their children, blankets and picnic baskets, the hooves of a single horse hammered over the plank floor of the bridge. The rider paused on the road above the creek bank and called, "Is Doc Fortner here? There's been a man cut up pretty bad, over at the mill."

Jonathan waved to the rider. "I'll get my bag and meet

you there in ten minutes,'' he said. Then, after giving Elisabeth one unreadable look, he disappeared into the orchard, headed toward the house.

Elisabeth finished gathering the picnic things, feeling much less a part of the community now that Jonathan was gone. She was touched when Trista came to say goodbye before leaving with Vera's family. "I'll see you tomorrow, in church," she promised. "Could I have a kiss, please?"

With a smile, Elisabeth bent to kiss the child's smudged, sun-warmed cheek. "You certainly may." She was painfully conscious of how short her time with this child might be and of how precious it was. "I love you, Trista," she added.

Trista gave her a quicksilver, spontaneous hug, then raced off to scramble into the Piedmonts' wagon with Vera. Carrying the picnic basket, now considerably lighter, and the blanket, Elisabeth turned and started for home.

Although Jonathan had left a lamp burning in the kitchen, its glow pushing back the twilight, he had, of course, already left for the sawmill. Elisabeth shivered to think what horrors might be awaiting him in that noisy, filthy place.

Taking pitchy chunks of pine from the woodbox beside the stove, Elisabeth built up the fire and put a kettle on for tea. Then, because she knew Jonathan would be tired and shaken when he returned, she filled the hot-water reservoir on the stove and put more wood in to make the flames burn hotter.

His clothes were covered with blood when he came in, nearly two hours later, and his gray eyes were haunted. "I couldn't save him," Jonathan muttered as Elisabeth took his bag and set it aside, then began helping him out of his coat. "He had a wife and four children."

Elisabeth stood on tiptoe to kiss Jonathan's cheek, which was rough with a new beard. "I'm so sorry," she said gently. She'd set the oblong tin bathtub in the center of the kitchen floor earlier, and scouted out soap and a couple of thin, coarse towels. While Jonathan watched her bleakly, she began filling the tub with water from the reservoir and from various kettles on the stove. "Take off your clothes, Jon," she urged quietly when he didn't seem to make the connection. "I'll get you a drink while you're settling in."

He was unbuttoning his shirt with the slow, distracted motions of a sleepwalker when Elisabeth went into the dining room. Earlier, she'd found virtually untouched bottles of whiskey and brandy behind one of the doors in the china cabinet, and she took her time deciding which would be most soothing.

When she returned to the kitchen with the brandy, Jonathan was in the bathtub, his head back, his eyes closed. His bloody shirt and trousers were draped neatly over the back of a chair.

"You were telling the truth," he said when she knelt beside the tub and handed him a glass, "when you claimed to be a guardian angel."

Elisabeth wasn't feeling or thinking much like an angel. She was painfully, poignantly conscious of Jonathan's powerful body, naked beneath the clear surface of the water. "We all need someone to take care of us once in a while—no matter how strong we are."

"I half expected you to be gone when I got back," Jonathan confessed, lifting the glass to his lips. He took a healthy swallow and then set the liquor aside on the floor. "I figured you might not want to be here, without Trista to act as an unofficial chaperone."

Elisabeth couldn't quite meet his eyes. "I don't think I want to be chaperoned," she said.

Jonathan's chuckle was a raw sound, conveying despair and weariness, as well as amusement. "Ladies must be very forward where you come from," he teased. Elisabeth could feel him watching her, caressing her with his gaze.

She made herself look at him. "I guess compared to Victorian women, they are." She reached for soap and a wash cloth and made a lather. Jonathan looked pleasantly bewildered when she began washing his back. "The term 'Victorian,'" she offered, before he could ask, "refers to the time of Queen Victoria's reign."

"I deduced that," Jonathan said with a sigh, relaxing slightly under Elisabeth's hand.

Bathing him was so sensual an experience that Elisabeth's head was spinning, and the warm ache between her legs had already reached such a pitch that it was nearly painful.

"You know, of course," Jonathan told her, leaning back as she began to wash his chest, "that I mean to take you directly from here to my bed and make love to you until you've given me everything?"

Elisabeth swallowed. Her heart was beating so hard, she could hear it. "Yes, Jon," she replied. "I know."

He took the soap and cloth from her hand and, after watching her face for a long moment, set about finishing his bath. Elisabeth left the kitchen, climbing the stairs to his bedroom.

As soon as the door closed behind her, she began undressing. She had barely managed to wash and put on a thin white eyelet chemise she'd found when Jonathan entered the room.

His dark hair was rumpled, and he was naked except for the inadequate towel wrapped around his waist. Thunder rattled the windows suddenly, like some kind of celestial warning, and Jonathan went to the fireplace and struck a match to the shavings that waited in the grate. On top of them, he laid several sticks of dry wood.

Elisabeth trembled, shy as a virgin, when he turned down the kerosene lamps on the mantelpiece, leaving the room dark except for the primitive crimson glow of the fire. He came to her, resting his strong, skilled hands on the sides of her waist.

"Thank you," he said.

Heat was surging through Elisabeth's system, and she could barely keep from swaying on her feet. "For what?" she managed to choke out as Jonathan began to caress her breasts through the fabric of the chemise.

He bent, nibbling at her neck even as his thumbs chafed her covered nipples into hard readiness for his mouth. "For being here, now, tonight, when I need you so much."

Elisabeth gave a little moan and ran her hands up and down his muscled, still-damp back. He smelled of soap and brandy and manhood. "I need you, too, Jonathan," she admitted in a whisper.

Jonathan drew back far enough to raise the chemise over her head and toss it aside. His charcoal eyes seemed to smolder as he took in the curves and valleys of her body, bare except for the rhythmic flicker of the firelight. He let the towel fall away.

She hadn't meant to be bold, but he was so magnificent that she couldn't resist touching him. When her fingers closed around his heated shaft, he tilted his head back and gave a low growl of fierce surrender. With one hand, she pressed him gently backward into a chair, while still caressing him with the other.

"Dear God, *Elisabeth*..." he moaned as she knelt between his knees and began kissing the bare skin of his upper thighs. "Stop..."

"I'm not going to stop," she told him stubbornly between flicks of her tongue that made his flesh quiver. "I haven't even begun to pleasure you."

He uttered a raspy shout of shock and delight when she took him, his fingers entangling themselves in her hair. "Lizzie," he gasped. "Oh...Lizzie...my God..."

Elisabeth lightly stroked the insides of his thighs as she enjoyed him.

Finally, with a ragged cry, he clasped her head in his hands and forced her to release him. In a matter of seconds, he'd lifted her from the floor so that she was standing in the chair itself, her feet on either side of his hips. He parted her with the fingers of one hand and then brought her down onto his mouth.

There was no need to be quiet, since they were alone in the house, and that was a good thing, because such pleasure knifed through Elisabeth that she burst out with a throaty yell. Her hands gripped the back of the chair in a desperate bid for balance as Jonathan continued to have her.

She began to pant as her hips moved back and forth of their own accord, and a thin film of perspiration broke out over every inch of her. She could feel tendrils of her hair clinging to her cheeks as she blindly moved against Jonathan's mouth.

When she felt release approaching, she tried to pull away, wanting her full surrender to happen when Jonathan was inside her, but he wouldn't let her go. Gripping her hips in his work-roughened hands, he held her to him even as the violent shudders began, making her fling her head back and moan without restraint.

He was greedy, granting her absolutely no quarter, and Elisabeth's captured body began to convulse with pleasure. The firelight and the darkness blurred as she gave up her essence and then collapsed against the back of the chair, exhausted.

But Jonathan wasn't about to let her rest. Within five minutes her cries of delighted fury again rang through the empty house.

"Now you're ready for me," he informed her in a husky voice as he lowered her to his lap and then stood, carrying her to the bed.

Elisabeth's two releases had been so violent, so all-consuming, that she was left with no breath in her lungs. She lay gasping, gazing up at Jonathan as he arranged her in the center of the bed and put two fluffy pillows under her bottom.

He lay down beside her on the mattress, slightly lower so that he could take her nipple into his mouth while his hand stroked her tender mound.

"Jonathan," she managed to whisper. "Please—*oh*—please..."

Jonathan spread her legs and knelt between them, parting her to give her one more teasing stroke. Then he poised himself over her. He had played her body so skillfully that in the instant his shaft glided inside her, she came apart.

While she buckled under the slow, deliberate strokes of his manhood, her head tossed back and forth on the mattress and she sobbed his name over and over again.

Her vindication came when the last little whimper of satisfied surrender had been wrung from her, because that was when Jonathan's release began. She toyed with his nipples and talked breathlessly of all the ways she meant to pleasure him in the future. With a fevered groan and a curse, he quickened his pace.

"I'll put you back in that chair again," she told him as he moved more and more rapidly upon her, his head thrust back. "Only next time, I won't let you stop me...."

Jonathan gave a strangled shout and stiffened, his eyes glazed, his teeth bared as he filled Elisabeth with his warmth. She stroked his back and buttocks until he'd given up everything. He sank to the bed beside her, resting his head on her breasts.

A blissful hour passed and the fire was burning low before Jonathan rose on one elbow to look into her face. "Stay with me, Elisabeth," he whispered. "Be my wife, so that I can bring you to this room, this bed, in good conscience."

She plunged her fingers into his dark, freshly washed hair. "Jon," she sighed, "I'm a stranger. You have no idea what marrying me would mean."

He parted her thighs and touched her brazenly in that moist, silken place where small tremors of passion were already starting to stir again. "It would mean," he drawled, his eyes twinkling, "that I would either have to put a gag over your mouth or move Trista to a room downstairs."

Elisabeth blushed hotly, glad of the darkness. It wasn't like her to carry on the way she had; with Ian, she'd hardly made a sound. But then, there had been no reason to cry out. "You're a very vain man, Jon Fortner."

He laughed and kissed her. "Maybe so," he answered, "but you make me feel like something more than a man."

She blinked and tried to turn her head, but Jonathan clasped her chin in his hand and prevented that.

"Don't you think I'm—I'm cheap?" she whispered, only too aware of Victorian attitudes toward sex.

Jonathan got up and fed the fire, and then Elisabeth heard the chink of china. Only when he brought a basin of tepid water back to the bed and began gently washing her did he reply. "Because you enjoy having a man make love to you?" He continued to cleanse her, using a soft cloth. "Lizzie, it was refreshing to see you respond like that." He set the cloth and basin aside on the floor, but would not let her close her legs. "Did you mean what you said about the next time I sit in that chair?"

Elisabeth's face pulsed with heat, but she nodded, unable to break the link between his eyes and hers. "I meant it," she said hoarsely.

At that, he kissed her, his tongue teasing her lips until they parted to take him in. "I meant what I said, too," he told her presently, moving his lips downward, toward her waiting breasts. "I want you to be my wife. And I won't let you put me off forever."

God help us, Elisabeth thought, just before she succumbed to the sweet demands of her body, *we don't have forever.*

Elisabeth felt like a fraud, sitting there in church beside Jonathan the next morning, pretending to be his sister-in-law. Maybe these good people didn't know she'd spent most of the night tossing in his bed, but God did, and He was bound to demand an accounting.

All she could do was hope it made a difference, her loving Jonathan the way she did.

After the service, she and Jonathan and Trista went home, the three of them crowded into Jonathan's buggy. He saw to the horses while Elisabeth and Trista went inside to put a fresh ham in the oven.

When Jonathan appeared, just as the women finished peeling potatoes to go with the pork, he was carrying two simple bamboo fishing poles. Trista's eyes lit up at the prospect of a Sunday afternoon beside the creek, and Elisabeth's heart was touched. Jonathan led a busy, demanding life, and he and Trista probably didn't have a lot of time together.

"You'll come with us, won't you?" the little girl cried, whirling to look up into Elisabeth's face with an imploring expression.

Elisabeth glanced at Jonathan, who winked almost imperceptibly, then nodded. "If you don't think I'll be interrupting," she agreed.

The creek bank was theirs again, now that yesterday's picnickers had all gone home, taking their blankets and scraps with them. Elisabeth sat contentedly on her favorite rock while Jonathan and Trista dug worms from the loamy ground and then threw their lines into the water.

Trista's laughter was liquid crystal, like the creek sparkling in the sunshine, and Elisabeth's heart climbed into her throat. It wasn't fair that this beautiful child was destined to die in just a few short weeks—she'd never had a chance to live!

Neither Jon nor Trista noticed when Elisabeth got down from the boulder and walked away, trying to distract herself by gathering the wild daisies and tiger lilies that hadn't been crushed by the picnickers the day before. She was under the bridge, watching the water flow by, when Jonathan suddenly materialized at her side.

"Where's Trista?" she asked, looking away quickly in hopes that he wouldn't read too much from her eyes.

"She went back to the house to make a pitcher of lemonade," Jonathan answered sleepily, taking one of the tiger lilies from Elisabeth's bouquet and brushing its fragrant orange petals against the underside of her chin. When she turned her head, he kissed her and the tangle of flowers tumbled to the smooth pebbles at her feet. "I want to bring you here," he told her when he'd finally released her mouth, "and make love to you in the moonlight."

Elisabeth trembled as his fingers found the pins in her hair and removed them, letting the soft blond tresses fall around her face. His name was all the protest she managed before he kissed her again.

By the time Trista returned with the lemonade, Elisabeth was badly in need of something that would cool her off. She sat in the grass with the man and the child, sipping the tart drink and hoping she wasn't flushed. Trista chattered the whole time about how they'd have the trout they'd caught for breakfast, firmly maintaining that Vera and *her* father had certainly never caught so many fine fish in one single day.

They returned to the house in midafternoon to eat the lovely ham dinner, and Jonathan was called away before he could have dessert. He seemed to be contemplating whether to leave or stay with them as he kissed Trista on top of the head and gave Elisabeth's shoulder a subtle squeeze.

Just that innocent contact sent heated shards through her, and she couldn't help recalling what Jonathan had said about making love to her in the moonlight under the covered bridge.

She and Trista cleared the table when they were finished eating, then they went out to the orchard and sat on the same thick, low branch of a gnarled old tree. Elisabeth listened and occasionally prompted while Trista practiced her spelling.

They were back in the house, seated together on the

piano bench and playing a duet that wouldn't be composed for another seventy years or so, when Jonathan returned. He was in much better spirits than he had been the night before.

"Susan Crenshaw had a baby girl," he said, his eyes clear.

Elisabeth wanted to kiss him for the happiness she saw in his face, but she didn't dare because Trista was there and because she wasn't entirely sure the air wouldn't crackle. "I guess delivering a healthy baby makes up for a lot of bad things, doesn't it?"

"That it does," he agreed, and his fingers touched her shoulder again, making her breasts ache. Elisabeth watched Jonathan as he walked away, disappearing into his study, and she dared to consider what it would be like to be his wife and share his bed every night.

"Your face is red," Trista commented, jolting her back to matters at hand. "Are you getting a fever?"

Elisabeth smiled. "Maybe," she replied, "but it isn't the kind you have to worry about. Now, let's trade places, and you can play harmony while I do the melody."

Trista nodded eagerly and moved to the spot Elisabeth had occupied.

Because Trista had had an exciting weekend—the picnic, spending the night with Vera and going fishing with her father and Elisabeth—she went to bed early. Jonathan read to his daughter, then came downstairs to join Elisabeth in the parlor.

Standing behind her chair in front of the fireplace, he bent and kissed the crown of her head. "Play something for me," he urged, and Elisabeth went immediately to the piano. Strange as it seemed, making music for his ears was a part of their lovemaking; it warmed Elisabeth's blood and made her heart beat faster and her breathing quicken.

She played soft, soothing Mozart, and she was almost able to believe that she belonged there in that untamed century, where life was so much more difficult and intense. When she'd finished, she turned on the piano bench to gaze at Jonathan, who was standing at the window.

"Have you decided?" he asked after a long interval of comfortable silence had passed.

Elisabeth didn't need to ask what he meant; she knew. Although Jonathan had never once said he loved her, he wanted her to marry him. She smoothed her skirts. "I've decided," she said.

He arched one eyebrow, waiting.

"I'll marry you," Elisabeth said, meeting his eyes. "But only on one condition—you have to promise that we'll go away on a wedding trip. We'll be gone a full month, and Trista will be with us."

Jonathan's expression was grim. "Elisabeth, I'm the only doctor between here and Seattle—I can't leave these people without medical care for a month."

"Then I have to refuse," Elisabeth said, although it nearly killed her.

Dr. Fortner held out a hand to her. "It seems you need a little convincing," he told her in a low voice that set her senses to jumping.

Elisabeth couldn't help herself; she went to him, let him enfold her fingers in his. "May I remind you," she said in a last-ditch effort at behaving herself, "that there's a child only a few rooms away?"

"That's why I'm taking you to the bridge." Jonathan led her through the dining room and the kitchen and out into the cool spring night. There was a bright silver wash of moonlight glimmering in the grass.

She had to hurry to keep up with his long, determined strides. She thought fast. "Jonathan, what if someone needs you…?"

"You need me," he answered without missing a beat, pulling her through the orchard, where leaves rustled overhead and crushed petals made a soft carpet under her feet. "I'm about to remind you how much."

In the shadow of the covered bridge, Jonathan dragged Elisabeth against his chest and kissed her soundly, and the mastery of his lips and tongue made her knees go weak beneath her. He pressed her gently into the fragrant grass, his fingers opening the tiny buttons of her high-collared blouse. He groaned when he found her breasts bare underneath, waiting for him, their sweet tips reaching.

Elisabeth surrendered as he closed his mouth around one nipple, sucking eagerly, and she flung her arms back over her head to make herself even more vulnerable. While he made free with her breasts, Jonathan raised Elisabeth's skirts and, once again, found no barrier between him and what he wanted so much to touch.

"Little witch," he moaned, clasping her in his hand so that the heel of his palm ground against her. "Show me your magic."

He'd long since aroused Elisabeth with words and looks and touches, and she tugged feverishly at his clothes until he helped her and she could feel bare flesh under her palms. Finally, he lay between her legs, and she guided him into her, soothing Jonathan even as she became his conqueror.

10

"**P**rove it," Jonathan challenged in a whisper when he and Elisabeth had finally returned to the house. They were standing in the upstairs hallway, their clothes rumpled from making love on the ground beside the creek. Jonathan had lit the lamp on the narrow table against the wall. A light spring rain was just beginning to fall. "If you can leave this century at will, then show me."

Elisabeth paused, her hand resting on the knob of the door to the spare bedroom. "It's not a parlor trick, Jon," she told him with sad annoyance. "I don't have the first idea how or why it works, and there's always the chance that I won't be able to get back."

His eyes seemed to darken, just for a moment, but his gaze was level and steady. "If you want me to believe what you've been saying, Lizzie, then you'll have to give me some evidence."

"All right," she agreed with a forlorn shrug. She didn't like the idea of leaving Jonathan, even if it was only a matter of stepping over a threshold and back. "But first I want a promise from you. If I don't return, you have to take Trista away from this house and not set foot in it again until after the first of July."

Jonathan watched her for a moment, his arms folded, and then nodded. "You have my word," he said with wry skepticism in his eyes.

Elisabeth went silently into her room to collect the necklace from its hiding place. Then she went into Trista's room. After casting one anxious look at the sleeping, unsuspecting child, Elisabeth put the chain around her neck. She could see Jonathan clearly, standing in the hallway.

She took a deep breath, closed her eyes, and stepped over the threshold.

In one instant, Elisabeth had been there, closing her eyes and wishing on that damned necklace as though it were some sort of talisman. In the next, she was gone.

Shock consumed Jonathan like a brushfire, and he sank against the wall, squinting at the darkened doorway, hardly daring to trust his own vision.

"Lizzie," he whispered, running one hand down his face. Then reason overcame him. It had to be a trick.

He thrust himself away from the wall and plunged through Trista's quiet room. The inner door was fastened tightly. Jonathan wrenched it open and bounded down the steep steps to the kitchen.

"Elisabeth!" he rasped, his patience wearing thin, his heart thrumming a kind of crazy dread.

Jonathan searched every inch of the downstairs, then carrying a lantern, he went out into the drizzling rain to look in all the sheds and check the barn. Finding nothing, he strode through the orchard and even went as far as the bank of the creek.

There was no sign of her, and fear pressed down on him as he made his way slowly back to the house, his hair dripping, his shirt clinging wetly to his skin. "Elisabeth," he said. Despair echoed in the sound.

Elisabeth stood smugly on the back porch of Jonathan's house, watching him cross the rainy yard with the lantern and waiting for him to look up and see her standing there on the step.

When he raised his eyes, he stopped and stared at her through the downpour.

"Get in here," she said, scurrying out to take Jonathan's free hand and drag him toward the door. "You'll catch something!"

"How did you do that?" he demanded, setting the lantern on the kitchen table and gaping at Elisabeth while she fed wood into the stove and urged him closer to the heat.

She tapped the side of the blue enamel coffeepot with her fingertips to see if it was still hot and gave an exasperated sigh. "Your guess is as good as mine," she said, fetching a mug from the cabinets and filling it with the stout coffee. "You must have seen *something*, Jonathan. Did I fade out, or was I gone in a blink?"

Jonathan sank into a chair at the table and she set the mug before him. He didn't even seem to be aware of his sodden shirt and hair. "You simply—disappeared."

This was no time for triumph; Jonathan's teeth were already chattering. Elisabeth got a dry shirt from his room and a towel from the linen chest upstairs and returned to the kitchen.

He was standing close to the stove, bare chested, sipping his coffee. "I've had enough nonsense from you, Lizzie," he said, shaking a finger at her. "You fooled me, and I want to know how."

Elisabeth laughed and shook her head. "I always thought my father was stubborn," she replied, "but when it comes to bullheaded, you beat him all to hell." Her eyes danced as she approached Jonathan, laying her hands on his shoulders. "Face it, Jon. I vanished into thin air, and you saw it happen with your own eyes."

His color drained away and he rubbed his temples with a thumb and forefinger. "Yes. Good God, Lizzie, am I losing my mind?"

She slipped her arms around his waist. "No. It's just that there's a lot more going on in this universe than we poor mortals know."

Jonathan pressed her head against his bare shoulders, and she felt a shudder go through him. "I want to try it," he said. "I want to see the other side."

It was as though Elisabeth had stepped under a pounding, icy waterfall. "No," she whispered, stepping away from him.

He allowed her to go no farther than arm's length. "Yes," he replied, his gaze locked with hers. "If this world you've been telling me about is really there, I want a glimpse of it."

Elisabeth began to shake her head slowly from side to side. "Jonathan, no—you'd be taking a terrible chance...."

His deft, doctor's fingers reached beneath her tousled hair to unclasp the necklace. Then, holding it in one hand, he rounded Elisabeth and started up the short stairway that led to Trista's room.

"Jonathan!" Elisabeth cried, scrambling after him. "Jonathan, *wait* there are things I need to tell you...."

She reached the first door just as he got to the one leading out into the main hallway. Her eyes widened when he stepped across the threshold. Like a rippling reflection on the surface of a pond, he diffused into nothingness. Elisabeth clasped one hand over her mouth and went to stand in the empty doorway.

She sagged against the jamb, half-sick with the fear that she might never see him again. Heaven knew how she would explain his absence to Trista or to Marshal Haynes and the rest of the townspeople. And then there was the prospect of living without him.

It was the damnedest thing Jonathan had ever seen.

A second ago, he'd been standing in Trista's bedroom, on a rainy night. Now, a fierce spring sun was shining and the familiar hallway had changed drastically.

There were light fixtures on the walls, and beneath his feet was a thick rug the color of ripe wheat. For a few moments, he just stood there, gripping the necklace, trying to understand what was happening to him. He was scared, but not badly enough to turn around and go back without seeing what kind of world Elisabeth lived in.

Once he'd regained his equilibrium, he crossed the hall and opened the door to the master bedroom.

Like the hallway, it was structurally the same, but there the similarities ended. Jonathan's scientific heart began to beat faster with excitement.

When the shrill sound of a bell filled the air, he jumped and almost bolted. Then he realized the jangle was coming from a telephone.

He looked around, but there was no instrument affixed to the wall. Finally, he tracked the noise to a fussy-looking gadget resting on the vanity table and he lifted the earpiece.

"Hello!" he snapped, frowning. There were telephones in Seattle, of course, but the lines hadn't reached Pine River yet, and Jonathan hadn't had much practice talking into a wire.

"Who is this?" a woman's voice demanded.

"This is Jonathan Fortner," he answered, fascinated. "Who are you, and why are you telephoning?"

There was a pause. "I'm Janet Finch, Elisabeth's friend. Is she there?"

A slow grin spread across Jonathan's mouth. "I'm afraid not," he replied. And then he laid the receiver in its cradle and walked away.

Almost immediately, the jarring noise began again, but Jonathan ignored it. There were things he wanted to investigate.

Just as he was descending the front stairway, an old woman with fussy white hair and enormous blue eyes peered through one of the long windows that stood on either side of the door. At the sight of Jonathan, she gave a little shriek, dropped something to the porch floor with a clatter and turned to run away.

Jonathan went to the window, grinning, and watched her trot across the road, her legs showing beneath her short dress. If this was truly the future, the elderly lady probably thought he was a ghost.

He just hoped he hadn't scared her too badly.

With a sigh of resignation, Jonathan proceeded to the kitchen, where he made an amazed inspection. He figured out the icebox right away, and he identified the thing with metal coils on top as a stove by process of elimination. He turned one of the knobs and then moved on to the sink, frowning at the gleaming spigots. When he gave one a twist, water shot out of a small pipe, startling him.

One of the spirals on the stove was red hot when he looked back, and Jonathan held his palm over it, feeling the heat and marveling.

By far the most interesting thing in the room, however, was the box that sat on the counter. It had little dials, like the stove, and a window made out of the same stuff as Elisabeth's medicine bottle, only clear.

Jonathan tampered with the knobs and suddenly the window flashed with light and the face of an attractive African woman with stiff hair loomed before him.

"Are you tired of catering to your boss's every whim?" she demanded, and Jonathan took a step backward, speechless. The woman was staring at him, as if waiting for an answer, and he wondered if he should speak to her. "Today's guests will tell you how to stand up for yourself and still keep your job!" she finished.

"What guests?" Jonathan asked, looking around the kitchen. Music poured out of the box, and then a woman with hair the same color as Elisabeth's appeared, holding up a glass of orange juice.

"No, thank you," Jonathan said, touching the knob again. The window went dark.

He ambled outside to look at the barn—it had fallen into a shameful state of disrepair—and stood by the fence watching automobiles speed by. They were all colors now, instead of just the plain black he'd seen on the streets of Boston and New York.

When half an hour passed and he still hadn't seen a single horse, Jonathan shook his head and turned toward the house. He walked around it, noting the changes.

The section that contained Trista's room and the second rear stairway was gone, leaving no trace except for a door in the second-story wall. Remembering what Elisabeth had said about a fire, he shoved splayed fingers through his hair and strode inside.

He could hear her calling to him the moment he entered, and he smiled as he started up the rear stairs.

"Damn you, Jonathan Fortner, you get back here! Now!"

Jonathan took the necklace from his pocket and held it in one hand. Then he opened the door and stepped over the threshold.

Elisabeth was wearing different clothes—a black sateen skirt and a blue shirtwaist—and there were shadows under her eyes. "Oh, Jonathan," she cried, thrusting herself, shuddering, into his arms.

He kissed her temple, feeling pretty shaken himself. "It's all right, Lizzie," he said. "I'm here." He held her tightly.

She raised her eyes to his face. "People were starting to ask questions," she fretted. "And I had to lie to Trista and tell her you'd gone to Seattle on business."

Jonathan was stunned. "But I was only gone for an hour or so...."

Elisabeth shook her head. "Eight days, Jonathan," she said somberly. She pressed her cheek to his chest. "I was sure I'd never see you again."

He was distracted by the way she felt in his arms, all soft and warm. With a fingertip, he traced the outline of her trembling lips. "Eight days?" he echoed.

She nodded.

The mystery was more than he could assimilate all at once, so he put it to the back of his mind. "You must have missed me something fierce in that case," he teased.

A spark of the old fire flickered in her eyes, and a corner of her mouth quivered, as though she might forgive him for frightening her and favor him with a smile. "I didn't miss you at all," she said, raising her chin.

He spread his hands over her rib cage, letting the thumbs caress her full breasts, feeling the nipples just against the fabric in response. "You're lying, Lizzie," he scolded. His arousal struck like a physical blow; suddenly he was hard and heavy with the need of her. He bent and kissed the pulse point he saw throbbing under her right ear. "Are we alone?"

Her breath caught, and her satiny flesh seemed to tremble under his lips. "For the moment," she said, her voice breathless and muffled. "Trista isn't home from school yet, and Ellen is out in the vegetable garden, weeding."

"Good," Jonathan said, thinking what an extraordinarily long time an hour could be. And then he lost himself in Elisabeth's kiss.

Elisabeth knew her cheeks were glowing and, despite her best efforts, her hair didn't look quite the same as it had before Jonathan had taken it down from its pins.

"Imagine that," Ellen said, breaking open a pod and expertly scraping out the peas with her thumbnail. "The doctor came back from wherever he's been, but I didn't hear no wagon nor see a sign of a horse. Come to that, he never took his rig with him in the first place." She paused to cluck and shake her head. "Strange doin's."

Elisabeth was sitting on the front step, while Ellen occupied the rocking chair. Watching the road for Trista, Elisabeth brushed a tendril of pale hair back from her cheek. "There are some things in this life that just can't be explained," she informed the housekeeper in a moderate tone. She was tired of the woman's suspicious glances and obvious disapproval.

Ellen sniffed. "If you ask me—"

"I *didn't* ask you," Elisabeth interrupted, turning on the step to fix the housekeeper with a look.

Color seeped into Ellen's sallow cheeks, but she didn't say anything more. She just went on shelling peas.

When Elisabeth saw Trista coming slowly down the road from the schoolhouse, her head lowered, she smoothed her sateen skirts and stood. She met the child at the gate with a smile.

"Your papa is back from his travels," she said.

The transformation in Trista stirred Elisabeth's heart. The little girl fairly glowed, and a renewed energy seemed to make her taller and stronger in an instant. With a little cry of joy, Trista flung herself into Elisabeth's arms.

Elisabeth held the child, near tears. Over the past eight trying days, she'd seen the depths of the bond this child had with her father. To separate them permanently by sending Trista to Barbara, so far in the future, was no longer an option.

"I thought maybe he'd stay away forever, like Mama," Trista confided as the two of them went through the gate together.

Elisabeth had known what Trista was thinking, of course, but there hadn't been much she could do to reassure the uneasy child. She squeezed Trista's shoulders. "He'll be home for supper—if there isn't a baby ready to be born somewhere."

Ellen, in the meantime, had finished shelling the peas and returned to the kitchen, where she was just putting a chicken into the oven to roast. She sniffed again when she saw Elisabeth.

"I don't imagine I'll be needed around here much longer," she said to no one in particular.

So that was it, Elisabeth reflected. Ellen's tendency to be unkind probably stemmed from her fear of losing her job, now that the doctor's sister-in-law seemed to be a permanent fixture in the house. The problem was really so obvious, but Elisabeth had been too worried about Jonathan's disappearance into the twentieth century to notice.

Even now, Elisabeth couldn't reassure the woman because she didn't know what Jonathan thought about the whole matter. He had talked about marriage, and he could well expect Elisabeth to take on all the duties Ellen was handling then. He might have been more progressive than most men of his era, but he wouldn't be taking up the suffrage cause anytime soon.

"I'll let Jon—the doctor know you're concerned," Elisabeth finally said, and Ellen paused and looked back at her in mild surprise. "And for what it's worth, I think you do a very good job."

Ellen blinked at that. Clearly, she'd had Elisabeth tagged as an enemy and didn't know how to relate to her as a friend. "I'd be obliged," Ellen allowed at last. "The family depends on me, and if there ain't going to be a place for me here, I need to be finding another position."

Elisabeth nodded and went back into the house to look about. Lord knew, there weren't any labor-saving devices, and she'd never been all that crazy about housework, but the idea of being a wife to Jonathan filled her with a strange, sweet vigor. Maybe she *was* crazy, she thought with a crooked little smile, because she really wanted to live out this life fate had handed to her.

Twilight had already fallen when Jonathan returned, and the kitchen was filled with the succulent aroma of roasting chicken and the cheery glow of lantern light. Trista was working out her fractions while Elisabeth mashed the potatoes.

The moment she heard her father's buggy in the yard, Trista tossed down her schoolwork and bolted for the back door, her face flushed and wreathed in smiles.

Elisabeth watched with her heart in her throat as the child launched herself from the back step into Jonathan's arms, shrieking, "Papa!"

He laughed and caught her easily, planting a noisy kiss on her forehead. "Hello, sweetheart," he said. There was a suspicious glimmer in his eyes, and his voice was a little hoarse.

Trista's small arms tightened around his neck. "I missed you so much!" she cried, hugging him tightly.

Jonathan returned the child's embrace, told her he loved

her and set her back on the steps. Only then did Elisabeth notice how tired he looked.

"I imagine your patients missed you, too," she said as he followed Trista into the house and set his bag in the customary place. One of the greatest sources of Elisabeth's anxiety, during Jonathan's absence, was the fact that people had constantly come by looking for him. It hadn't been easy, knowing patients who needed his professional attention were being left to their own devices.

He sighed, and Elisabeth could see the strain in his face and in the set of his shoulders. "There are times," he said, "when I think being a coal miner would be easier."

Although she wanted to touch him, to take him into her arms and offer comfort, Elisabeth was painfully aware that she didn't have that option—not with Trista in the room.

It was bad enough that they'd lied to the child, telling her Elisabeth was Barbara's sister. For the past week, Trista had been begging for stories of the childhood Elisabeth had supposedly shared with her mother.

"Sit down, Jon," Elisabeth said quietly, letting her hands rest on his tense shoulders for a moment after he sank into a chair at the kitchen table.

Trista, delighted that her father was home, rushed to get his coffee mug, but it was Elisabeth who filled it from the heavy enamel pot on the stove.

The evening passed pleasantly—by some miracle, no one came to call Jonathan away—and after Trista had been settled in bed, he came into the kitchen and began drying dishes as Elisabeth washed them.

That reminded her of Ellen's concerns. "You need to have a talk with your housekeeper," she said. "She wants to look for another job if you're planning to let her go."

Jonathan frowned. "Isn't her work satisfactory?"

Elisabeth couldn't help smiling, seeing this rugged doctor standing there with an embroidered dishtowel in his hands. "Her work is fine. But you have given the community—and me, I might add—the impression that I might be staying around here permanently." She paused, blushing because the topic was a sensitive one. "I mean, if I'm to be your wife...."

He put down the towel and the cup he'd been drying and turned Elisabeth to face him. Her hands were dripping suds and water, and she dried them absently on her apron.

His expression was wry. "I'm not as destitute as you seem to think," he said. "I had an inheritance from my father and I invested it wisely, so I can afford to keep a housekeeper *and* a wife."

Elisabeth flushed anew; she hadn't meant to imply that he was a pauper.

Her reaction made Jonathan laugh, but she saw love in his eyes. "My sweet Lizzie—first and foremost, I want you to be a wife and partner to me. And I hope you'll be a mother to Trista. But running a house is a lot of work, and you're going to need Ellen to help you." He tilted his head to one side, studying her more soberly now. "Does this mean you're going to agree to marry me?"

Elisabeth sighed. The motion left her partially deflated, like a balloon the day after a party. There was still the specter of the fire looming over them, and the question had to be resolved. "That depends, Jonathan," she said, grieving when he took his hands away from her shoulders. "You've been over the threshold now, you've experienced what I have. I guess it all distills down to one question—do you believe me now?"

She saw his guard go up, and her disappointment was so keen and so sudden that it made her knees go weak.

Jonathan shoved one hand through his dark, rumpled hair. "Lizzie..."

"You *saw* it, Jonathan!" she cried in a ragged whisper as panic pooled around her like tidewater, threatening to suck her under. "Damn it, *you were there!*"

"I imagined it," he said, and his face was suddenly hard, his eyes cold and distant.

Elisabeth strode over to the sidetable where his medical bag awaited and snapped it open, taking out the prescription bottle and holding it up. "What about this, Jonathan? Did you imagine this?"

He approached her, took the vial from her hands and dropped it back into the bag. "I experienced *something*," he said, "but that's all I'm prepared to admit. The human mind is capable of incredible things—it could all have been some sort of elaborate illusion."

Elisabeth was shaking. Jonathan was the most important person in her topsy-turvy universe, and he didn't believe her. She felt she would go mad if she couldn't make him understand. "Are you saying we both had the same hallucination, Jon? Isn't that a little farfetched?"

Again, Jonathan raked the fingers of one hand through his hair. "No more than believing that people can actually travel back and forth between centuries," he argued, making an effort to keep his voice down for Trista's sake. "Lizzie, the past is gone, and the future doesn't exist yet. All we have is *this moment.*"

Elisabeth was in no mood for an esoteric discussion. For eight days she'd been mourning Jonathan, worrying about him, trying to reassure his daughter and his patients. She was emotionally exhausted and she wanted a hot bath and some sleep.

"I'd like the kitchen to myself now, if you don't mind," she said wearily, lifting the lid on the hot-water reservoir to check the supply inside. "I need a bath."

Jonathan's eyes lighted with humor and love. "I'd be happy to help you."

Elisabeth glared at him. "Yes, I imagine you would," she said, "but I don't happen to want your company just now, Dr. Fortner. As far as I'm concerned, you're an imbecile and I'd just as soon you kept your distance."

He smiled and lingered even after Elisabeth had dragged the big tin bathtub in from the combination pantry and storage room. His arms were folded across his chest. It was obvious that he was stifling a laugh.

Elisabeth brought out the biggest kettle in the kitchen, slammed it down in the sink and began pumping icy well water into it. It was amazing, she thought furiously, that she wanted to stay in this backward time with this backward man, when she could have hot and cold running water and probably a Democrat with an M.B.A. if she just returned to the 1990s. She lugged the heavy kettle to the stove and set it on the surface with a ringing thump.

When she turned to face Jonathan, her hands were on her hips and her jaw was jutting out obstinately. "I wouldn't give a flying *damn* whether you believed me or not," she breathed, "if it weren't for the fact that your life is hanging in the balance—and so is Trista's! Half of this house is going to burn in the third week in June, and they're not going to find a trace of you or your daughter. What they are going to do is try *me* for your murders!"

It hurt that the concern she saw in his face was so obviously for her sanity and not for his safety and Trista's. "Lizzie, there are doctors back in Boston and New York—men who know more than I do. They might be able to—"

"Just get out of here," Elisabeth spat out, tensing up like a cat doused in ice water, "and let me take my bath in peace."

Instead, Jonathan brought out more kettles and filled them at the pump, then set them on the stove. "You took care of me when I needed you," he said finally, his voice low, his expression brooking no opposition, "and I'm going to do what I have to do to take care of you, Lizzie. I love you."

Elisabeth had never been so confused. He'd said the words she most wanted to hear, but it also sounded as though he was planning to pack her off to the nearest loony bin the first chance he got. "If you love me," she said evenly, "then trust me, Jon. You didn't believe your own eyes and ears and...well...I'm all out of ways to convince you."

He sat her down in a chair, then fed more wood to the fire so her bathwater would heat faster. He didn't look at her when he spoke. "There isn't going to be a fire, Lizzie—you'll see. The third week of June will come and go, just like it always does."

She stared at his back. "You're going to pretend it didn't happen, aren't you?" she said in a thick whisper. "Jonathan, you were gone for *eight days*. How do you explain that—as a memory lapse?"

Heat began to surge audibly through the pots of water simmering on the stove. "Frankly," he answered, "I'm beginning to question *my* sanity."

11

Frantic pounding at the front door roused Elisabeth from a sound, dreamless sleep. She reached for the robe she'd left lying across the foot of the bed and hurried into the hallway, where she saw Jonathan leaving his room. He was buttoning his shirt as he descended the stairs.

She remembered the proprieties of the century and held back, sitting on one of the high steps and gripping a banister post with one hand.

"It's my little Alice," a man's voice burst out after Jonathan opened the door. "She can't breathe right, Doc!"

"Just let me get my bag," Jonathan answered with grim resignation. A few moments later, he was gone, rattling away into the night in the visitor's wagon.

Elisabeth remained on the stairway, even though it was chilly and her exhausted body yearned for sleep. She was still sitting there, huddled in her nightgown and robe when Jonathan returned several hours later.

He lit a lamp in the entryway and started upstairs, halting when he saw Elisabeth.

"What happened?" she asked, wondering if she was going to be in this kind of suspense every time Jonathan was summoned out on a night call. "Is the little girl..."

Jonathan sighed raggedly and shook his head. "Diphtheria," he said.

Elisabeth's knowledge of old-fashioned diseases was limited, but she'd heard and read enough about this one to know it was deadly. And very contagious. "Is there anything I can do to help?" she asked lamely, knowing there wasn't.

He advanced toward her, and his smile was rueful and sad. "Just be Lizzie," he said hoarsely.

They went back to their separate beds then, but it wasn't long before someone else came to fetch the doctor for *their* sick child. When Elisabeth finally gave up on sleeping somewhere around dawn and got up, Jonathan had still not returned.

She built up the kitchen fire and put coffee on to brew. And then she waited. This, she supposed, would be an integral part of being the wife of a nineteenth-century country doctor—if, indeed, destiny allowed her to marry Jonathan at all.

Sipping coffee, her feet resting on the warm, chrome footrail on the front of the stove, Elisabeth thought of her old life with Ian. It was like a half-remembered dream now, but once, that relationship had been the focal point of her existence.

Tilting her head back and closing her eyes, Elisabeth sighed and contemplated the hole her leaving would rend in that other world. Her disappearence would make one or two local newscasts, but after a while, she'd just be another nameless statistic, a person the police couldn't find.

Ian would cock an eyebrow, say it was all a pity and call his lawyer to see if he and the new wife had any claim on Elisabeth's belongings.

Her father would suffer, but he had his career and Traci and the new baby. In the long run, he'd be fine.

Janet and Elisabeth's other friends in Seattle would

probably be up in arms for a time, bugging the police and speculating among themselves, but they all had their own lives. Eventually, they'd go back to living them, and it would be as though Elisabeth had died.

Rue, of course, was an entirely different matter. She would come home from her travels, read the letter Elisabeth had written about her first experience with the threshold and be on the next plane for Seattle. Within an hour of landing, she'd be right here in this house, looking for any trace of her cousin, following up every lead, making the police wish they'd never heard of Elisabeth McCartney.

So close, Elisabeth thought, imagining Rue in these very rooms, her throat thickening with emotion, *and yet so far.*

The sound of Trista coming down the steps roused Elisabeth from her thoughts.

"What are you doing up so early?" Elisabeth asked, taking the child onto her lap.

Trista snuggled close. Although she was wearing a pinafore, black ribbed stockings and plain shoes with pointy toes, her dark hair hadn't been brushed or braided, and she was still warm and flushed from sleep. She yawned. "I kept hearing people knock on the door. Is Papa out?"

Elisabeth nodded, noting with a start that Trista's forehead felt hot against her cheek. *God, no,* she thought, pressing her palms to either side of the child's face. *No!* She made herself speak in an even tone of voice. "He's been gone for several hours," she said. "Trista—do you feel well?"

"My throat's sore," she said, "and my chest hurts."

Tears of alarm sprang to Elisabeth's eyes, but she forced them back. This was no time to lose her head. "Were you sick during the night?" She tightened her arms around the child, as if preparing to resist some giant, unseen hand that might wrench her away.

Trista looked up at Elisabeth. "I wanted to get into bed with you," she said shyly.

Elisabeth bit her lip and made herself speak calmly. "Well, I think we'd better forget about school and make you a nice, comfortable bed right here by the stove. We'll read stories and I'll play the piano for you. How would that be?"

A tremor ran through the small body in Elisabeth's arms. "I have to go to school," Trista protested. "There's a spelling bee today, and you know how hard I've been practicing."

There was an element of the frantic in the quick kiss Elisabeth planted on Trista's temple. "It would be my guess that there won't be any school today, sweetheart. And it's possible, you know, to practice too hard. Sometimes, you have to just do your best and then stand back and let things happen."

Trista sighed. "I *would* like to have a bed in the kitchen and hear stories," she confessed.

"Then let's get started," Elisabeth said with false cheer as she set Trista in a chair and automatically felt the child's face for fever again. "You stay right there," she ordered, waggling a finger. "And don't you dare think of even *one* spelling word!"

Trista laughed, but the sound was dispirited.

Elisabeth dragged a leather-upholstered Roman couch from Jonathan's study to the kitchen and set it as close to the stove as she dared. Then she hurried upstairs and collected Trista's nightgown and the linens from her bed.

By the time Jonathan came through the back door, looking hollow eyed and weary to the very center of his soul, his daughter was reclining on the couch, listening to

Elisabeth read from *Gulliver's Travels*. The expression on his face as he made the obvious deduction was terrible to see.

Immediately, he came to his daughter's bedside, touched her warm face, examined her ears and throat. Then his eyes linked with Elisabeth's, over Trista's head, and she knew it might not matter that there was going to be a fire the third week in June. Not to this little girl, anyway.

They went into Jonathan's study to talk.

"Diphtheria?" Elisabeth whispered, praying he'd say Trista just had the flu or common cold. But then, those maladies weren't so harmless in the nineteenth century, either. There were so many medical perils at this time that a child would never encounter in Elisabeth's.

Jonathan was standing at one of the windows, gazing past the lace curtain at the new, bright, blue-and-gold day. He shook his head. "It's a virus I've never seen before—and there seems to be an epidemic."

Elisabeth's fingers were entwined in the fabric of her skirts. "Isn't there anything we can do?"

He shrugged miserably. "Give them quinine, force liquids...."

She went and stood behind him, drawn by his pain and the need to ease it. She rested her hands on his tense shoulders. "And then?"

"And then they'll probably die," he said, walking away from her so swiftly that her hands fell to her sides.

"Jon, the penicillin—there wouldn't be enough for all the children, but Trista..." Her sentence fell away, unfinished, when Jonathan walked out of the study and let the door close crisply behind him. Without uttering a word, he'd told Elisabeth he had neither the time nor the patience for what he considered delusions.

He'd left his bag on his cluttered desk in the corner. Elisabeth opened it and rummaged through until she'd found the bottle of penicillin tablets. Removing the lid, she carefully tipped the pills into her palm and counted them.

Ten.

She scooped the medicine back into its bottle and dropped it into her pocket.

Jonathan was stoking the fire in the kitchen stove when Elisabeth joined him, while Trista watched listlessly from the improvised bed. Elisabeth could see the child's chest rise and fall unevenly as breathing became more difficult for her.

Elisabeth began pumping water into pots and kettles and carrying them to the stove, and soon the windows were frosted with steam and the air was dense and hot.

"Let me take her over the threshold, Jon," Elisabeth pleaded in a whisper when Trista had slipped into a fitful sleep an hour later. "There are hospitals and modern drugs..."

He glowered at her. "For God's sake, don't start that nonsense now!"

"You must have seen the cars going by on the road. It's a much more advanced society! Jonathan, I can help Trista—I know I can!"

"Not another word," he warned, and his gray eyes looked as cold as the creek in January.

"The medicine, then—"

The back door opened and Ellen came in, looking flushed and worried. When her gaze fell on Trista, however, the high color seeped from her face. "I'm sorry I couldn't come sooner, but it's the grippe—we've got it at our place, and Seenie's so hot, you can hardly stand to touch her!"

Jonathan's eyes strayed to Trista for a moment, but skirted Elisabeth completely. "I'll be there in few minutes," he said.

Ellen hovered near the door, looking as though she might faint with relief, but Elisabeth felt nothing but frustration and despair.

"I'll get your bag," she said to Jonathan, and disappeared into the study.

When she returned, the doctor had already gone outside to hitch up his horse and buggy. Elisabeth gave the bag to Ellen, but there seemed to be no reassuring words to offer. A look passed between the two women, and then Ellen hurried outside to ride back to her family's farm with Jonathan.

Throughout the afternoon, Elisabeth kept the stove going at full tilt, refilling the kettles and pots as their contents evaporated. The curtains, the tablecloth, Trista's bedclothes—everything in the room was moist.

Elisabeth found fresh sheets and blankets and a clean nightgown for Trista. The child hardly stirred as the changes were made. Her breathing was a labored rattle, and her flesh was hot as a stove lid.

Elisabeth knelt beside the couch, her head resting lightly on Trista's little chest, her eyes squeezed shut against tears of grief and helplessness. This, too, was part of being a Victorian woman—watching a beloved child slip toward death because there were no medicines, no real hospitals. Now, she realized that she'd taken the vaccinations and medical advances of her own time for granted, never guessing how deadly a simple virus could be.

Presently, Elisabeth felt the pharmacy bottle pressing against her hip and reached into her pocket for it, turning it in her fingers. She was no doctor—in fact, she had virtually no medical knowledge at all, except for the sketchy first-aid training she'd been required to take to get her teaching certificate. But she knew that penicillin was a two-edged sword.

For most people, it was perfectly safe and downright magical in its curative powers. For others, however, it was a deadly poison, and if Trista had an adverse reaction, there would be nothing Elisabeth could do to help. On the other hand, an infection was raging inside the child's body. She probably wouldn't live another forty-eight hours if someone didn't intercede.

Resolutely, Elisabeth got to her feet and went to the sink. A bucket of cold water sat beside it, pumped earlier, and Elisabeth filled a glass and carried it back to Trista's bedside.

"Trista," she said firmly.

The child's eyes rolled open, but Trista didn't seem to recognize Elisabeth. She made a strangled, moaning sound.

The prescription bottle recommended two tablets every four hours, but that was an adult dose. Frowning, Elisabeth took one pill and set it on Trista's tongue. Then, holding her own breath, she gave the little girl water.

For a few moments, while Trista sputtered and coughed, it seemed she wouldn't be able to hold the pill down, but finally she settled back against the curved end of the couch and closed her eyes. Elisabeth sensed that the child's sleep was deeper and more comfortable this time, but she was so frightened and tense, she didn't dare leave the kitchen.

She was sitting beside Trista's bed, holding the little girl's hand, when the back door opened and Jonathan dragged in. "Light cases," he said, referring, Elisabeth hoped, to the children in Ellen's sizable family. "They'll probably be all right." He was at his daughter's side by then, setting his bag on the table, taking out his stethoscope and putting the earpiece in place. He frowned as he listened to Trista's lungs and heart.

Elisabeth wanted to tell him about the penicillin, but she was afraid. Jonathan was not exactly in a philosophical state of mind, and he wouldn't be receptive to updates on twentieth-century medicine. "You need some rest and something to eat," she said.

He smiled grimly as he straightened, pulling off the stethoscope and tossing it back into his bag. "This is a novelty, having somebody worry about me," he said. "I think I like it."

"Sit," Elisabeth ordered wearily, rising and pressing him into the chair where she'd been keeping her vigil over Trista. She poured stout coffee for him, adding sugar and cream because he liked it that way, and then went to the icebox for eggs she'd gathered herself the day before and the leftovers from a baked ham.

Jonathan's gaze rested on his daughter's flushed face. "She hasn't been out of my thoughts for five minutes all day," he said with a sigh. "I didn't want to leave her, but you were here, and the others—"

Elisabeth stopped to lay a hand on his shoulder. "I know, Jon," she said softly. She found an onion and spices in the pantry and, minutes later, an omelette was bubbling in a pan on the stove.

"Her breathing seems a little easier," Jonathan commented when Elisabeth dished up the egg concoction and brought it to the table for him.

She didn't say anything, but her fingers closed around the little bottle of penicillin in the pocket of her skirt. Soon, when Jonathan wasn't looking, she would give Trista another pill.

He seemed almost too tired to lift his fork, and Elisabeth's heart ached as she watched him eat. When he finished his meal, she knew he wouldn't collapse into bed and sleep, as he needed to do. No, Jonathan would head for the barn, where he would feed and water animals for an hour. Then, provided another frantic father didn't come to fetch him, he'd sit up the rest of the night, watching over Trista.

Elisabeth woke the child while he was in the barn and made her swallow another penicillin tablet. By that time, her own body was aching with fatigue and she wanted to sink into a chair and sob.

She didn't have time for such luxuries, though, for the fire was waning and the water in the kettles was boiling away. Elisabeth found the wood box empty and, after checking Trista, she wrapped herself in a woolen shawl and went outside to the shed. There, she picked up the ax and awkwardly began splitting chunks of dry apple wood.

Jonathan was crossing the yard when she came out, her arms loaded, and he took the wood from her without a word.

Inside, he fed the fire while she pumped more water to make more steam. Suddenly, she ran out of fortitude and sank against Jonathan, weeping for all the children who could not be saved, both in this century and in her own.

Jonathan embraced her tightly for a moment, kissed her forehead and then lifted her into his arms and started toward the stairs. "You're going to lie down," he announced in a stern undertone. "I'll bring you something to eat."

"I want to stay with Trista."

"You're no good to her in this condition," Jonathan reasoned, opening the door to her room and carrying her inside. He laid her gently on the bed and pulled off her sneakers, so incongruous with her long skirt and big-sleeved blouse. "I'll bring you a tray."

Elisabeth opened her mouth to protest, but it was too late. Jonathan had already closed the door, and she could hear his footsteps in the hallway.

She had to admit it felt gloriously, decadently good to lie down. She would rest for a few minutes, to shut Jonathan up, and then go back to Trista.

The doctor returned, as promised, bringing a ham sandwich and a glass of milk. Elisabeth ate, even though she had virtually no appetite, knowing she needed the food for strength.

Filling her stomach had a peculiar tranquilizing effect, and she sagged against her pillows and yawned even as she battled her weariness. She would just close her eyes long enough to make them stop burning, Elisabeth decided, then go back downstairs to sit with Trista.

There were shadows in the room and the bedside lamp was burning low when Elisabeth awakened with a start. Her throat was sore when she swallowed, but she didn't take time to think about that because she was too anxious to see Trista.

She was holding her breath as she made her way down the back stairway.

The kitchen lamps were lit, and Jonathan sat at the table, his head resting on his folded arms, sound asleep. Trista was awake, though, and she smiled shakily as Elisabeth approached the bed and bent to kiss her forehead.

"Feeling better?"

Trista nodded, though she was still too weak to talk.

"I'll bet you'd like some nice broth, wouldn't you?" Elisabeth asked, remembering the chicken Ellen had killed and plucked yesterday. And even though Trista shook her head and wrinkled her nose, Elisabeth took the poultry from the icebox and put it on the stove to boil.

Although she tried to be quiet, the inevitable clatter awakened Jonathan and he lifted his head to stare at Elisabeth for a few seconds, seeming not to recognize her. Then his gaze darted to his daughter.

Trista smiled wanly at the startled expression on his face.

A study in disbelief, Jonathan grabbed his bag and hastily donned his stethoscope. His eyes were wide with surprise when he looked at Elisabeth, who was grinning at him and holding up the little medicine bottle.

Jonathan snatched it out of her hands. "You gave her this?"

Elisabeth's delight faded. "Yes," she answered with quiet defiance. "And it saved her life."

He looked from the pills to his daughter's placid, if pale, face. "My God."

"It's safe to say He's involved here somewhere," Elisabeth ventured a little smugly. "You should give her one every four hours, though, until she's out of danger."

Jonathan groped for a chair and sank into it. He opened the bottle, this time with no assistance from Elisabeth, and dumped the remaining tablets out onto the table to stare at them as though he expected a magic beanstalk to sprout before his eyes. "Peni— What did you call them?"

"Penicillin," Elisabeth said gently.

"I didn't dream it," he whispered.

She shook her head and spread her hands over his shoulders. A glance at Trista showed her that the child was sleeping again, this time peacefully. "No, Jon—you were really there." She began to work the rigid muscles with her fingers. "You never told me what you saw, you know."

A tremor went through him. "There was a box with women inside," he said woodenly. "They spoke to me."

At the same time she was stifling a laugh, tears of affection burned in Elisabeth's eyes. "The television set," she said. "They weren't talking to you Jon—they were only pictures, being transmitted through the air."

"What else do they have in your world," Jonathan inquired wearily, "besides automobiles that travel too fast?"

Elisabeth smiled. So he *had* seen something of the real twentieth century. "We're exploring outer space," she said, continuing with the massage and knowing an ancient kind of pleasure as Jonathan's muscles began to relax. "And there have been so many inventions that I couldn't list them all—the most significant being a machine called a computer."

Jonathan listened, rapt, while Elisabeth told him what she knew about computers, which was limited. She went on to explain modern society as best she could. "There are still social problems, I'm afraid," she told him. "For instance, we have a serious shortage of housing for the poor, and there's a lot of drug and alcohol abuse."

He arched an eyebrow. "Which must be why you were so angry when I sedated you," he ventured.

Elisabeth's achy throat was tight as she nodded. He finally believed her, and if she'd had the energy, she would have jumped up and clicked her heels together to celebrate.

Jonathan sighed. "There are people now who use opium, but thank heaven it's not prevalent."

Elisabeth sat down beside him and cupped her chin in her hands. "Don't be too cocky, Dr. Fortner. You've got a lot of laudanum addicts out there, taking a tipple when nobody's looking. And the saloons are brimming with alcoholics. In approximately 1935, two men will start an organization to help drunks get and stay sober.''

He rubbed his beard-stubbled chin, studying Elisabeth as though she were of some unfamiliar species. "Let's talk about that fire you've been harping on ever since you first showed up," he said. Then, remembering Trista, he caught Elisabeth's elbow in one hand and ushered her out of the kitchen and into the parlor, where he proceeded to build a fire against the evening chill. "You said Trista and I died in it."

"I said the authorities—Marshal Farley Haynes, to be specific—believed I killed you by setting the blaze. If—" she swallowed as bile rushed into her throat "—if bodies were found, the fact was hushed up. And the newspaper didn't give a specific date."

Jonathan rubbed the back of his neck and shook his head, watching as the fire caught on the hearth, sending orange and yellow flames licking around the apple-wood logs. "You'll understand," he said, still crouching before the grate, "if I find this whole thing a little hard to accept."

"I think I would in your place," Elisabeth conceded, taking a seat in a leather wing chair and folding her hands in her lap. "Jonathan, we can leave now, can't we? We can move to the hotel in town, at least during that week?"

To her surprise, he shook his head again as he rose to stand facing her, one shoulder braced against the mantelpiece. "We'll be especially careful," he said. "Surely being warned ahead of time will make a difference."

Elisabeth wasn't convinced; she had a sick feeling in the pit of her stomach, a sense of dire urgency. "Jonathan, please—you must have seen that the house was different in my time. If that isn't evidence that there really was a fire…"

Jonathan came to stand before her chair, bending to rest one hand on each of its arms and effectively trapping her. "There won't be a fire," he said, "because you and I are going to prevent it."

She closed her eyes tightly, defeated for the moment.

Jonathan's breath was warm on her face as he changed the subject. "I'm tired of lying in my bed at night, Elisabeth, aching for you. I want to get married."

She felt her cheeks heat as she glared up at him. "Now, that's *romantic!*" she murmured, moving to push him away and rise, but he stood fast, grinning at her. Raw pain burned her throat as she spoke, and the amusement faded from Jonathan's eyes.

He touched her forehead with his hand. "If you come from a time where some of our diseases no longer exist," he breathed, "you haven't built up any kind of immunity." Jonathan stepped back and drew Elisabeth to her feet, and she was instantly dizzy, collapsing against him. Her first thought was that the rigors of the past twenty-four hours had finally caught up with her.

As easily as before, Jonathan lifted her into his arms. The next thing she knew, she was upstairs and he was stripping her, tucking her into bed. He brought water and two of the precious pills, which Elisabeth wanted to save for Trista.

She shook her head.

But Jonathan forced her to swallow the medicine. She watched, her awareness already wavering, as he constructed a sort of tent around the bed, out of blankets. Presently, the air grew close and moist, and Elisabeth dreamed she was lost in a jungle full of exotic birds and flowers.

In the dream, she knew Jonathan was looking for her—she could hear him calling—but he was always just out of sight, just out of reach.

12

Jonathan's fear grew moment by moment as he watched Elisabeth lapse further and further into the depths of the illness. As strong and healthy as she was, her body had no apparent defenses against the virus, and within a matter of hours, she was near death. Even the wonder pills she'd brought with her from the future didn't seem to be helping.

He was searching her dresser before he consciously acknowledged the desperate decision he'd made. Finding the necklace in a top drawer, under a stack of carefully laundered and folded pantaloons, he went back to Elisabeth's bedside and fastened the tarnished chain around her neck.

For a long time, he just stood there, staring down at her, marveling at how deeply he'd come to cherish her in the short time they'd had together. Even when he'd thought she was demented, he'd loved her.

The daylight was fading at the windows when he finally looked up. He turned and went rapidly down the rear stairway to check on Trista.

Earlier, he'd given her a bowl of Elisabeth's chicken broth. He found her sleeping now, and her fever had finally broken.

Jonathan bent and, smoothing back his daughter's dark hair with a gentle hand, kissed her forehead. "I'll be back as soon as I can," he promised in a husky whisper.

Upstairs again, he lifted Elisabeth from the bed and carried her down the back stairs into the kitchen and then up the other set of steps leading to Trista's room. Within moments, they were standing at the threshold.

Although he'd never been a religious man, Jonathan prayed devoutly in those moments. Then he closed his eyes and stepped across.

The immediate lightness in his arms swung a hoarse cry of despair from his throat. He was still in his time—the same pictures hung from the walls and the familiar runner was under his feet.

But Elisabeth was gone.

Miss Cecily Buzbee hovered and fretted while the young men from the county hospital lifted Elisabeth's inert form onto a gurney and started an IV flowing into a vein in her left hand.

"It's a lucky thing I came by to check on her, that's all I can say," Miss Cecily said, following as Elisabeth was carried down the stairs and out through the front door. "There's something strange going on in this house, you mark my words, and Sister and I have a good mind to telephone the sheriff...."

The paramedics lifted the stretcher into the back of the ambulance, and one of them climbed in with it.

"Heaven only knows how long she's been lying there in that hallway," Cecily babbled on, trailing after the second man as he walked around to get behind the wheel.

"Does Ms. McCartney have any allergies that you know about?" he asked, speaking to her through the open window on the driver's side of the ominous-looking vehicle.

Cecily had no idea and it was agony that she couldn't help.

The young man shifted the ambulance into gear. "Well, if she's got any family, you'd better get in touch with them right away."

The words struck Cecily like a blow. She didn't know Elisabeth well, but she cared what happened to her. Merciful heavens, the poor thing was too young and beautiful to die—she hadn't had a proper chance to live.

Cecily watched until the ambulance had turned onto the main road, lights slicing the twilight, siren blaring. Then she hurried back into the house and began searching for Elisabeth's address book.

"Jonathan?" The name hurt Elisabeth's throat as she said it, and she wasn't sure whether she was whispering or shouting. She tried to sit up, but she was too weak. And she was immediately pressed back to her pillows by a nurse anyway.

A nurse.

Every muscle in Elisabeth's limp and aching body tensed as a rush of alarm swept through her. Her eyes darted about the room wildly, looking for the one face that would make everything all right.

But there was no sign of Jonathan, and the reason was painfully obvious. Somehow, she'd found her way back into the twentieth century, though she had no conscious memory of making the transition. And that meant she was separated from the man she loved.

The nurse was a young woman, tall, with short, curly, brown hair and friendly eyes. "Just relax," she said. "You're safe and sound in the county hospital."

Elisabeth could barely control the panic that seized her. "How long have I been here?" she rasped, as the nurse— the tag on her uniform said her name was Vicki Webster—held a glass of cool water up so that Elisabeth could drink through a straw.

"Just a couple of days," Vicki replied. "One of your friends has been here practically the whole time. Would you like to see her?"

For a moment, Elisabeth soared with the hope that Rue had come back from her assignment, but in the next instant, she knew better. Rue was family and she would never have introduced herself to the staff as a friend.

Minutes later, Janet appeared, looking haggard. Her hair was a mess, her raincoat was crumpled and there were dark smudges under her eyes. "Do you know how worried I've been?" she demanded, coming to stand beside the bed. "First I talked to that strange man on the telephone, and then I couldn't get anyone to answer at all...."

Elisabeth gripped Janet's hand. "Janet, what day is this?"

Janet's brow furrowed with concern and she bit her lips. "It's the tenth of June," she said.

"The tenth..." Elisabeth closed her eyes, too drained to go on. Time was racing by, not only here, but in the nineteenth century, as well. Perhaps Jonathan and Trista were trapped in a burning house at that very moment— perhaps they were already dead!

Janet snatched a tissue from the box on the bedside stand and gently wiped away tears Elisabeth hadn't even realized she was shedding. "Beth, I know you're sick, and it's obvious you're depressed, but you can't give up. You've got to keep putting one foot in front of the other until you get past whatever it is that's troubling you so much."

Elisabeth was too tired to say any more, and Janet stayed a while longer, then left again. The next morning, a big bouquet of flowers arrived from Elisabeth's father, along with a note saying that he and Traci hoped she was feeling better.

As it happened, Elisabeth was feeling stronger, if not better, and she was growing more and more desperate to return to Jonathan and Trista. But here she was, too frail even to walk to the bathroom by herself. She fought off rising panic only because she knew it would drain her and delay the time when she'd be able to leave the hospital.

"I'm taking you home with me," Janet announced three evenings later. A true friend, she'd been making the drive to Pine River every day after she finished teaching her classes. "The term is almost over, so I'll have lots of time to play nurse."

Elisabeth smiled wanly and shook her head. "I want to go home," she said in a quiet voice. *To Jonathan, and Trista—please, God.*

Janet cleared her throat and averted her eyes for just a moment. When she looked back at Elisabeth, her gaze was steady. "Who was that man, Bethie—the one who answered the telephone when I called that day?"

Elisabeth imagined Jonathan glaring at the instrument as it rang, and she smiled again. "That was Jonathan," she said. "The man I love."

"So where is he?" Janet demanded, somewhat impatiently. "If you two are so wild about each other, why haven't I had so much as a glimpse of the guy?" She waved one hand to take in the flowers that banked the room—even Ian and his new bride had sent carnations. "Where's the bouquet with his name on the card?"

Elisabeth sighed. She was too tired to explain about Jonathan, and even if she attempted it, Janet would never believe her. In fact, she would probably go straight to the nearest doctor and the next thing Elisabeth knew, she'd be in the psychiatric ward, weaving potholders. "He's out of the…country," she lied, staring up at the ceiling so she wouldn't have to meet Janet's eyes. "And he's called every day."

When Elisabeth dared look at Janet again, she saw patent disbelief in her friend's face. "There's something very weird here," Janet said.

You don't know the half of it, Elisabeth thought. She was relieved when Janet left a few minutes later.

Almost immediately, however, the Buzbee sisters appeared with colorful zinnias from their garden and a stack of books that probably came from their personal library.

"I saw the ghost through the front window one day," Cecily confided to Elisabeth in a whisper, when her sister had gone down the hall to say hello to a friend who was recovering from gall-bladder surgery.

Elisabeth felt herself go pale. "The ghost?"

Cecily nodded. "Dr. Fortner it was—I'd know him anywhere." She took one of the books from the pile she'd brought, thumbed through it and held it out to Elisabeth. "See? He's standing second from the left, beside the little girl."

Elisabeth's throat tightened as she stared at the old picture, taken by the Pine River Bridge on Founder's Day 1892. Jonathan gazed back at her, and so did Trista, but that wasn't really what shook her, since this was a copy of the same book she'd checked out from the library and she'd seen the picture before. No, it was the fact that her own image had been added, standing just to Jonathan's right. Cecily probably hadn't noticed because Elisabeth looked very different in period clothes and an old-fashioned hairstyle, and because she'd been looking at the picture with the careless eyes of familiarity.

"You've seen this man, haven't you?" Cecily challenged, though not unkindly. She poured water for Elisabeth and held the straw to her lips, as though alarmed by Elisabeth's sudden pallor.

Tears squeezed past Elisabeth's closed eyelids and tickled in her lashes. "Yes," she said. "I've seen him."

Cecily patted Elisabeth's forehead. "There, there, dear. I'm sorry if I upset you. You've probably been frightened half out of your mind these past few weeks, and then you let yourself get run-down and you caught—what is it you caught?"

Elisabeth's disease had been diagnosed simply as a "virus," and she knew the medical community was puzzled by it. "I—I guess it's pneumonia," she said. She put her hand to her throat and turned pleading eyes on Cecily. "They took my necklace."

"I'll just get it right back for you," Cecily replied briskly. And she went out into the hallway, calling for a nurse.

Half an hour later, Elisabeth had her necklace back. Just wearing it made her feel closer to Jonathan and Trista.

That evening when the doctor came by on his evening rounds, he took the IV needle from Elisabeth's hand and pronounced her on the mend. His kindly eyes were full of questions as to where she could have contracted a virus modern medicine couldn't identify, but he didn't press her for answers.

"I want to go home," she announced when he'd finished a fairly routine examination. Weak as she was, she was conscious of every tick of the celestial clock, and it was hell not knowing what was happening to Jonathan and Trista.

The physician smiled and shook his head. "Not for a few more days, I'm afraid. You're in a very weakened state, Ms. McCartney."

"But I can recover just as well there as here...."

"Let's see how you feel on Friday," he said, overruling her. And then he moved on to the next room.

Elisabeth waited until it was dark before getting out of bed, staggering over to the door and peering down the lighted hallway to the nurses' station. One woman was there, her head bent over some notes she was making, but other than that, the coast was clear.

With enormous effort, Elisabeth put on the jeans and sweatshirt Janet had brought her from the house, brushed her tangled hair and crept out into the hallway. A city hospital would have been more difficult to escape, but this one was small and understaffed, and Elisabeth made it into the elevator without being challenged.

She leaned back, clutching the metal railing in both hands and summoning up all her strength. She still had to get to her house, which was several miles away. And Pine River wasn't exactly bustling with available taxi cabs.

Elisabeth didn't have her purse—that was locked away for safekeeping in the hospital and, of course, she didn't dare ask for it—but there was a spare house key hidden in the woodshed.

She started walking, and it soon became apparent that she was simply too weak to walk all the way home. Praying she wouldn't find herself hooked up with a serial killer, like women she'd read about, she stuck out her thumb.

Presently a rattly old pickup truck with one missing fender came to a stop beside her and a young man leaned across the seat to push open the door. His smile was downright ingenuous.

"Your car break down?" he asked.

Elisabeth eyed him wearily, waiting for negative vibes to strike her, but there weren't any. The kid kind of reminded her of Wally Cleaver. She nodded, not wanting to explain that she'd just sprung herself from the hospital, and climbed into the truck.

Just that effort exhausted her and she collapsed against the back of the lumpy old seat, terrified that she would pass out.

"Hey," the teenage boy began, shifting the vehicle into gear and stepping on the gas with enthusiasm. "You sick or something? There's a hospital right back there...." He cocked his thumb over one shoulder.

Elisabeth shook her head. "I'm fine," she managed, rallying enough to smile. "I live out on Schoolhouse Road."

The young man looked at her with amused interest. "You don't mean that haunted place across from the Buzbees, do you?"

Elisabeth debated between laughing and crying, and settled on the former, mostly to keep from alarming her rescuer. "Sure do," she said.

He uttered an exclamation, and Elisabeth could see that he was truly impressed. "Ever see any spooks or anything like that?"

They were passing through the main part of town, and Elisabeth felt a bittersweet pang as she looked at the lighted windows and signs. She hoped to be back with Jonathan soon, and when that happened, the modern world would be a memory. If something that didn't exist yet could be called a memory.

"No," she said, pushing back her hair with one hand. "To tell you the truth, I don't believe in ghosts. I think there's a scientific explanation for everything—it's just that there are so many natural laws we don't understand."

"So you've never seen nothing suspicious, huh?"

As a teacher, Elisabeth winced at his grammar. "I've seen things I can't explain," she admitted. She figured she owed him that much, since he was giving her a ride home.

"Like what?"

Elisabeth sighed, unsure how much to say. After all, if he went home and told his parents she'd talked about traveling between one century and the next, the authorities would probably come and cart her off to a padded room. "Just—things. Shadows. The kind of stuff you catch a glimpse of out of the corner of an eye and wonder what you really saw."

Her companion shuddered as he turned into Elisabeth's driveway. She could tell the sight of the dark house looming in the night didn't thrill him.

"Thanks," she said, opening the door and getting out of the truck. Her knees seemed to have all the substance of whipped egg whites, and she clung to the door for a moment to steady herself.

The boy swallowed. "No problem," he answered. He gunned the engine, though it was probably an unconscious motion. "Want me to stick around until you're inside?"

Elisabeth looked back over her shoulder at the beloved house that had always been her refuge. "I'll be perfectly all right," she said. And then she turned and walked away.

Her young knight in shining armor wasted no time in backing out of the driveway and speeding away down the highway. Elisabeth smiled as she made her way around the house to the woodshed to extract the back door key from its hiding place.

The lights in the kitchen glowed brightly when she flipped the switch, and Elisabeth felt the need of a cup of tea to brace herself, but she didn't want to take the time. Her strength was about to give out, and she yearned to be with Jonathan.

Upstairs, however, she found the door to the past sealed

against her, even though she was wearing the necklace. After a half hour of trying, she went into the master bedroom and collapsed on the bed, too weary even to cry out her desolate frustration.

In the morning, she tried once again to cross the threshold, and once again, the effort was fruitless. She didn't let herself consider the possibility that the window in time had closed forever, because the prospect was beyond bearing.

She listened listlessly to the messages on her answering machine—the last one was from her doctor, urging her to return to the hospital—then shut off the machine without returning any of the calls. She thumbed through her mail and, finding nothing from Rue, tossed the lot of it into the trash, unopened.

In the kitchen, she brewed hot tea and made toast with a couple slices of bread from a bag in the freezer. She was feeling a little better this morning, but she knew she hadn't recovered a tenth of her normal strength.

After finishing her toast, she wrote another long letter to Rue, stamped it and carried it out to the mailbox. By the time she returned, carrying a batch of fourth-class mail with her, she was on the verge of collapse.

Numbly, Elisabeth climbed the stairs again, found herself a fresh set of clothes and ran a deep, hot bath. After shampooing her hair, she settled in to soak. The heat revived her, and she had some of her zip back when she got out and dressed in black jeans and a T-shirt with a picture of planet Earth on the front.

Pausing in the hallway, she leaned against the door, both palms resting against the wood, and called, "Jonathan?"

There was no answer, and Elisabeth couldn't help wondering if that was because there was no longer a Jonathan.

There were tears brimming in her eyes when she went back downstairs and stretched out on the sofa.

The jangle of the hallway telephone awakened her and, for a moment, Elisabeth considered not answering. Then she decided she'd caused people enough worry as it was, without ignoring their attempts to reach her.

She was shaky and breathless when she picked up the receiver in the hallway and blurted, "Hello?"

"What are you doing home?" Janet demanded. "Your doctor expressly told me you were supposed to stay until Friday, at least."

Elisabeth wound her finger in the cord, smiling sadly. She was going to miss Janet, and she hoped her friend wouldn't suffer too much over her disappearance. "I was resting until you called," she said, making an effort to sound like her old self.

"I'm wasting my time trying to get you to come to Seattle, aren't I?"

"Yes," Elisabeth answered gently. "But don't think your kindness doesn't mean a lot to me, Janet, because it does. It's just that, well, I'm up against something I have to work out for myself."

"I understand," Janet said uncertainly. "You'll call if you change your mind?"

Elisabeth promised she would, hung up and immediately dialed her father's number at Lake Tahoe. These conversations would be remembered as goodbyes, she supposed, if she managed to make it back to 1892.

The call was picked up by an answering machine, though, and Elisabeth was almost relieved. She identified herself, said she was out of the hospital and feeling fine, and hung up.

Early that afternoon, while Elisabeth was heating a can of soup at the stove, a light rain began to fall and the electricity flickered. She glanced uneasily at the darkening sky and wondered if it was about to storm where Jonathan and Trista were.

Just the thought of them brought a tightness to her throat and the sting of tears to her eyes. She was eating her soup and watching a soap opera on TV when a messenger from the hospital brought her purse. Later, if she felt better and she still couldn't get across the threshold, she would get into her car and drive to town for groceries. Because she'd been away so much, she had practically nothing in the cupboards except for canned goods.

Thunder shook the walls, lightning flashed and the TV went dead. Not caring, Elisabeth went upstairs. Once again, longingly, she paused in front of the door.

There was nothing beyond it, she told herself sternly, besides a long fall to the roof of the sun porch. She was having a nervous breakdown or something, that was all, and Jonathan and Trista were mere figments of her imagination. They were the family she'd longed for but never really had.

She leaned against the door, her shoulders shaking with silent sobs. The hope of returning was all she had to cling to, and even that was fading fast.

Presently, Elisabeth grew weary of crying and straightened. She knotted one fist and pounded. "Jonathan!" she yelled.

Nothing.

She splashed her face with cold water at the bathroom sink, then went resolutely downstairs. Amazed at how simple exertions could exhaust her, she got her purse and forced herself out to her car.

Shopping was an ordeal, and Elisabeth felt so shaky, she feared she'd fall over in a dead faint right there in the supermarket. Hastily, she bought fruit and a stack of frozen entrés and left the store.

At home, she found the electricity had been restored, and she put one of the packaged dinners into the microwave. She hardly tasted the food.

Following her solitary meal, Elisabeth spent a few disconsolate minutes at the piano, running her fingers over the keys. The songs she played reminded her too much of Trista, though, and of Jonathan, and she finally had to stop. And she had to admit she'd been hoping to hear the sound of Trista's piano echoing back across the century that separated them.

Figuring she might as well give up on getting back to 1892—for that day at least—Elisabeth gathered an armload of Aunt Verity's journals from one of the bookshelves in the parlor and took herself upstairs. After building a fire with the last of the wood, she curled up in the middle of the bed and began to read.

At first, the entries were ordinary enough. Verity talked about her marriage, how much she loved her husband, how she longed for children. After her mate's untimely death in a hunting accident, she wrote about sadness and grief. And then came the account of Barbara Fortner's appearance in the upstairs hallway.

Elisabeth sat bolt upright as she read about the woman's baffled disbelief and Verity's efforts to make her feel at home. The words Elisabeth's aunt had written shed new light on the stories Verity had told her teenage nieces during their summer visits, and Elisabeth felt the pang of grief.

By midnight, Elisabeth's eyes were drooping. She closed the journals and stacked them neatly on the bedside table, then changed into a nightshirt, brushed her teeth and crawled into bed. "Jonathan," she whispered. His name reverberated through her heart.

She was never sure whether minutes had passed or hours when the sound of a child's sobs prodded her awake. *Trista.*

Elisabeth sat up and flung the covers back, her fingers gripping the necklace as she hurried into the hallway. Her hand trembled violently as she reached for the knob on the sealed door, praying with all her heart that it would open.

The child's name left her throat in a rush, like a sigh of relief, when the knob turned under her hand and the hinges creaked.

There was a lamp burning on Trista's bedside table, and she stared at Elisabeth as though she couldn't believe she was really seeing her. Then her small face contorted with childish fury. "Where were you? Why did you leave me like that?"

Elisabeth sat down on the edge of the bed and gathered the little girl into her arms, holding her very close. "I was sick, sweetheart," she said as joyous tears pooled in her eyes. "Believe me, the last thing I wanted to do was leave you."

"You'll stay here now?" Trista sniffled, pulling back in Elisabeth's embrace to look up into her face. "You won't leave us again?"

Elisabeth thought of Rue, her father, Janet. She would miss them all, but she knew she belonged here in this time, with these people. She kissed Trista's forehead. "I won't leave you again," she promised. "Were you all alone? Is that why you were crying?"

Trista nodded. "I was scared."

"Where's your papa?"

Jonathan's daughter allowed herself to be settled back

on the pillows and tucked in. "He's just out in the barn, but I heard noises and I imagined Mr. Marley was coming down the hall, rattling his chains and moaning."

Elisabeth smiled at the reference to the Dickens ghost. "I'm the only apparition in this house tonight," she said. Then she kissed Trista again, turned down the wick in the lamp and went downstairs.

Before she went to Jonathan and told him she'd marry him if he still wanted her, before she threw herself into his arms, there was something she had to find out.

13

Elizabeth stood in the kitchen, staring helplessly at Jonathan's calendar. Never before had it been so crucial to know the exact date, but the small numbered squares told her nothing except that it was still June.

The sudden opening of the back door and a rush of cool, night air made her turn. Pure joy caused her spirit to pirouette within her. Jonathan was standing there, looking at her as though he didn't quite dare to trust his eyes.

With a strangled cry, she launched herself across the room and into his embrace, her arms tight around his neck.

"Lizzie," he rasped, holding her. "Thank God you're all right."

She tilted her head back and kissed him soundly before replying, "It was hell not knowing what was happening here. I was terrified I wouldn't be able to get back, and I was even more frightened by what I might find if I did."

Jonathan laughed and gave her a squeeze before setting her on her feet. His hand smoothed her hair with infinite gentleness, and his gaze seemed to caress her. "Are you well again?"

She shrugged, then slipped her arms around his lean waist. "I'm a little shaky, but I'm going to make it."

A haunted expression crossed his face. "I wanted to go

with you, to make sure you got help, but when I stepped over the threshold, you vanished from my arms.''

Elisabeth glanced back at the calendar. "Jonathan..."

He smiled and crooked a finger under her chin. "That's one thing you were wrong about," he said. "It's the twenty-third of June—Thursday, to be exact—and there's been no fire.''

His words lessened Elisabeth's dread a little. After all, she knew next to nothing about this phenomenon, and it was possible that she or Jonathan had inadvertently changed fate somehow.

In the next instant, however, another matter involving dates and cycles leapt into her mind, and the shock made her sway in Jonathan's arms.

He eased her into a chair. "Elisabeth, what is it?"

"I..." Her throat felt dry and she had to stop and swallow. "My...Jonathan, I haven't had my...I could be pregnant.''

His eyes glowed bright as the kerosene lantern in the middle of the table. "You not only came back to me," he smiled. "You brought someone with you."

Tears of happiness gathered on Elisabeth's lashes. Once, during her marriage, she'd gotten pregnant and then miscarried, and Ian had been pleased. He'd said it was for the best and that he hoped Elisabeth wouldn't take too long getting her figure back.

"Y-you're glad?"

Jonathan crouched in front of her chair and took her hands in his. A sheen of moisture glimmered in his eyes. "What do you think? I love you, Lizzie. And a child is the best gift you could give me." He frowned. "You won't leave again, will you?"

Elisabeth reached back to unclasp the necklace and

place it in his palm. "For all I care, you can drop this down the well. I'm here to stay."

He put the pendant into his shirt pocket and stood, drawing Elisabeth with him. "I'd like to take you straight to bed," he said, "but you're still looking a little peaky, and we have to think about Trista." Jonathan paused and kissed her. "Will you marry me in the morning, Lizzie?"

She nodded. "I know it wouldn't be right for us to make love," she said shyly, "but I need for you to hold me. Being apart from you was awful."

He put an arm around her waist and ushered her toward the rear stairs. "I'm not going to let you out of my sight," he answered gruffly.

In the spare room, he settled Elisabeth under the covers and then began stripping off his own clothes. She was grateful it was dark so she couldn't see what she was missing and *he* couldn't see her blushing like a virgin bride.

A few moments later, Jonathan climbed into the bed and enfolded Elisabeth in his arms, fitting her close against the hard warmth of his body. Despite the lingering effects of her illness and their decision not to make love again until they were man and wife, desire stirred deep within Elisabeth.

When his hand curved lightly over her breast, she gave an involuntary moan and arched her back. She felt Jon come to a promising hardness against her thigh and heard the quickening of his breath.

"I suppose we could be quiet," she whispered as he lifted her nightshirt and spread one hand over her quivering belly as though to claim and shelter the child within.

Jonathan chuckled, his mouth warm and moist against the pulsepoint at the base of Elisabeth's throat. "You?"

he teased. "The last time I had you, Lizzie, you carried on something scandalous."

She reached back over her head to grasp the rails in the headboard as he began kissing her breasts. "I g-guess I'll just have to trust you to be a...to be a gentleman."

"You're a damn fool if you do," he said, just before he took a nipple into his mouth and scraped it lightly with his teeth.

Elisabeth flung her head from one side to the other, struggling with all her might to keep back the cries of surrender that were already crowding her throat. Rain pelted the window, and a flash of lightning lit the room with an eerie explosion of white. "Jonathan..." she cried.

He brought his mouth down onto hers at the same moment that he parted her legs and entered her. While their tongues sparred, her moans of impending release filled his throat.

Their bodies arched high off the mattress in violent fusion, twisting together like ribbons in the wind. Then, after long, exquisite moments of fiery union, they sank as one to the bed, both gasping for breath.

"We agreed not to do that," Elisabeth said an eternity later, when she was able to speak again.

Jonathan smoothed damp tendrils of hair back from her forehead, sighed and kissed her lightly. "It's a little late for recriminations, Lizzie. And if you're looking for an apology, you're wasting your time."

She blushed and settled close against his chest, which was still heaving slightly from earlier exertions. Thunder rattled the roof above their heads, immediately followed by pounding and shouting at the front door and a shriek from Trista's room.

"I'll see to her," Elisabeth said, reaching for her nightshirt while Jon scrambled into his clothes. "You get the door."

Trista was sobbing when Elisabeth stumbled into her room, lit the lamp on her bedside stand and drew the child into her arms. "It's all right, baby," she whispered. "You were just having a bad dream, that's all."

"I saw Marley's ghost," Trista wailed, shuddering against Elisabeth as she scrambled toward reality. "He was standing at the foot of my bed, calling me!"

Elisabeth kissed the little girl's forehead. "Darling, you're awake now and I'm here. And Marley's ghost isn't real—he's only a story character. You don't need to be afraid."

Trista clung to Elisabeth's shoulders, but she wasn't trembling so hard now, and her sobs had slowed to irregular hiccups. "I don't want to leave you and Papa," she said. "I don't want to die."

The words were like the stab of a knife, reminding Elisabeth of the fire. "You aren't going to die, sweetheart," she vowed fiercely, stretching out on top of Trista's covers, still holding the child. "Not for many, many years. Someday, you'll marry and have children of your own." Tears of determination scalded Elisabeth's eyes, and she reached to turn down the wick in the lamp, letting the safe darkness enfold them.

Trista sniffled, clutching Elisabeth as though she feared she would float unanchored through the universe if she let go. "Will you promise to stay here with us?" she asked in a small voice. "Are you going to marry Papa?"

Elisabeth kissed her cheek. "Yes and yes. Nothing could make me leave you again, and your father and I are getting married tomorrow."

"Then you'll be my mother."

"I'll be your stepmother," Elisabeth clarified gently.

"But I swear I love you as much as I would if you'd been born to me."

Trista yawned. It was a reassuring, ordinary sound that relieved a lot of Elisabeth's anxieties. "Will there be babies? I'm very good with them, you know."

Elisabeth chuckled and smoothed the child's hair. "Yes, Trista, I think you'll have a little brother or sister before you know it. And I'll be depending on your help."

She yawned again. "Did Papa go out?"

Elisabeth nodded. "I think so. We'll just go to sleep, you and I, and when we wake up, he'll be home again."

"All right," Trista sighed. And then she slipped easily into a quiet, natural sleep.

Jonathan had still not returned when Elisabeth and Trista rose the next morning, but Elisabeth didn't allow the fact to trouble her. He was a doctor, and he would inevitably be away from home a great deal.

While Ellen prepared oatmeal downstairs in the kitchen, Elisabeth brushed and braided Trista's thick, dark hair. After eating breakfast, the two of them went up to the attic to go through the trunks again. The school term was over, and Trista, who was still a little wan and thin from her illness, had a wealth of time on her hands.

Elisabeth found a beautiful midnight blue gown in the depths of one of the trunks and decided that would be her wedding dress.

Trista's brow crumpled. "Don't brides usually wear white?"

Draping the delicate garment carefully over her arm, Elisabeth went to sit beside Trista on the arched lid of one of the trunks. "Yes, sweetheart," she replied after taking a breath and searching her mind for the best words. "But I was married once before, and even though I wasn't very happy then, I don't want to deny that part of my life by pretending it didn't happen. Do you understand?''

"No," Trista said with a blunt honesty that reminded Elisabeth of Jonathan. The child's smile was sudden and blindingly bright. "But I guess I don't need to. You're going to stay and we'll be a family. That's what matters to me."

Elisabeth smiled and kissed Trista's forehead. It was odd to think that this child was her elder in the truest sense of the word. The dress in her arms and the dusty attic and the little girl had become her reality, however, and it was that other world that seemed like an illusion. "We are definitely going to be a family," she agreed. "Now, let's take my wedding gown outside and let it air on the clothesline, so I won't smell like mothballs during the ceremony."

Trista wrinkled her nose and giggled, but when her gaze traveled to the grimy window, she frowned. "It looks like it's about to rain."

There had been so much sunshine in Elisabeth's heart since she'd awakened to the realization that this was her wedding day, she hadn't noticed the weather at all. Now, with a little catch in her throat, she went over and peered out through the dirty panes of glass.

Sure enough, the sky was dark with churning clouds, and now that she thought of it, there was a hot, heavy, brooding feeling to the air. From where she stood, Elisabeth could see the weathered, unevenly shaped shingles on the roof of the front porch. They looked dry as tinder.

She tried to shake off a feeling of foreboding. Jonathan was right, she insisted to herself—if there was truly going to be a fire, it would have happened before this. Still, she was troubled, and she wished she and Jonathan and Trista were faraway from that place.

They took the dress down to Elisabeth's room and hung it near a window she'd opened slightly, then descended to the kitchen. Since Ellen was busy with the ironing, Elisabeth and Trista decided to gather the eggs.

Fetching a basket, she hurried off toward the hen house, expecting to be drenched by rain at any moment. But the sullen sky retained its burden, and the air fairly crackled with the promise of violence. *Jonathan,* Elisabeth thought nervously, *come home. Now.*

But she laughed with Trista as they filled the basket with brown eggs. Surprisingly, considering the threat of a storm, Vera appeared, riding her pony and carrying a virtually hairless doll. After settling the horse in the barn, the two children retreated to Trista's room to play.

Elisabeth joined Ellen in the kitchen and volunteered to take a turn at pressing Jonathan's shirts. The cumbersome flatirons were heated on the stove, and it looked like an exhausting task.

"You just sit down and have a nice cup of tea," Ellen ordered with a shake of her head. "It wasn't that long ago that you were sick and dying, you know."

There was a kind of grudging affection in Ellen's words, and Elisabeth was pleased. She was also enlightened; obviously, her disappearance had been easily explained. Jonathan had probably said she was lying in bed and mustn't be disturbed for any reason. "I'm better now," she allowed.

Ellen stopped ironing the crisp white shirts long enough to get the china teapot down from a shelf and spoon loose tea leaves into it. She added hot water from the kettle and brought the teapot and a cup and saucer to the table. "I guess you and the doctor will be getting married straight away."

Elisabeth nodded. "Yes."

The housekeeper frowned, but her expression showed curiosity rather than antagonism. "I can't quite work out what it is, but there's something different about you," she mused, touching the tip of her index finger to her tongue and then to the iron.

The resultant sizzle made Elisabeth wince. "I'm—from another place," she said, making an effort at cordiality.

Ellen ironed with a vehemence. "I know. Boston. But you don't talk much like she did."

By "she," Elisabeth knew Ellen meant Barbara Fortner, who was supposed to be Elisabeth's sister. Unfortunately, the situation left Elisabeth with no real choice but to lie. Sort of. "Well, I've lived in Seattle most of my adult life."

The housekeeper rearranged a shirt on the wooden ironing board and began pressing the yoke, and a pleasant, mingled scent of steam and starch rose in the air. "She never talked about you," the woman reflected. "Didn't keep your photograph around, neither."

Elisabeth swallowed, contemplating the tangled web that stretched before her. "We weren't close," she answered, and that was true, though not for the reasons Ellen would probably invent on her own. Elisabeth took a sip of tea and then boldly inquired, "Did you like her?"

"No," Ellen answered with a surprising lack of hesitation. "The first Mrs. Fortner was always full of herself. What kind of a woman would go away for months and leave her own child behind?"

Elisabeth wasn't about to touch that one. After all, she'd made a few unscheduled departures herself, and it hadn't been because she didn't care about Trista. "Maybe she was homesick, being so far from her family."

The housekeeper didn't look up from her work, but her reply was vibrant, like a dart quivering in a bull's eye.

"She had you, right close in Seattle. Seems like that should have helped."

There was nothing Elisabeth could say to that. She carried her cup and saucer to the sink and set them carefully inside. Beyond the window, with its pristine, white lace curtains, the gloomy sky waited to remind her that there were forces in the universe that operated by laws she didn't begin to understand. Far off on the horizon, she saw lightning plunge from the clouds in jagged spikes.

If only the rain would start, she fretted silently. Perhaps that would alleviate the dreadful tension that pervaded her every thought and move.

"I'd like to leave early today, if it's all the same to you," Ellen said, startling Elisabeth a little. "Don't want to get caught in the rain."

Elisabeth caught herself before she would have offered to drive Ellen home in her car. If she hadn't felt so anxious, she would have smiled at the near lapse. "Maybe you'd better leave now," she said, hoping Ellen didn't have far to go.

Agreeing quickly, the housekeeper put away the ironing board and the flatirons and took Jonathan's clean shirts upstairs. Soon she was gone, but there was still no rain and no sign of Jonathan.

Elisabeth was more uneasy than ever.

She climbed the small stairway that led up to Trista's room and knocked lightly.

"Come in," a youthful voice chimed.

Smiling, Elisabeth opened the door and stepped inside. Her expression was instantly serious, however, when her gaze went straight to the pendant Vera was wearing around her neck. It took all her personal control not to lunge at the child in horror and snatch away the necklace before it could work its treacherous magic.

Vera preened and smiled broadly, showing a giant vacant space where her front teeth should have been. "Don't you think I look pretty?" she asked, obviously expecting an affirmative answer. It was certainly no mystery that her children had grown up to be adventurous; they would inherit Vera's innate self-confidence.

"I think you look very pretty," Elisabeth said shakily, easing toward the middle of the room, where the two little girls sat playing dolls on the hooked rug. She sank to her knees beside them, her movements awkward because of her long skirts.

Vera beamed into Elisabeth's stricken face. "I guess I shouldn't have tried it on without asking you," she said, reaching back to work the clasp. Clearly, she was giving no real weight to the idea that Elisabeth might have objections to sharing personal belongings. "Here."

Elisabeth's hand trembled slightly as she reached out to let Vera drop the chain and pendant into her palm. Rather than make a major case out of the incident, she decided she would simply put the necklace away somewhere, out of harm's way. "Where did you find this?" she asked moderately, her attention on Trista.

Her future stepdaughter looked distinctly uncomfortable. "It was on top of Papa's dresser," she said.

Elisabeth simply arched an eyebrow, as if inviting Trista to explain what she'd been doing going through someone else's things, and the child averted her eyes.

Dropping the necklace into the pocket of her skirt, Elisabeth announced, "It's about to rain. Vera, I think you'd better hurry on home."

Trista looked disappointed, but she didn't offer a protest. She simply put away her doll and followed Vera out of the room and down the stairs.

Afraid to cross the threshold leading into the main hallway with the necklace anywhere on her person, Elisabeth tossed it over. Only as she was bending to pick the piece of jewelry up off the floor did it occur to her that she might have consigned it to a permanent limbo, never to be seen again.

She carried the necklace back to the spare room and dropped it onto her bureau, then went downstairs and out onto the porch to scan the road for Jonathan's horse and buggy. Instead, she saw the intrepid Vera galloping off toward home, while Trista swung forlornly on the gate.

"There was *supposed* to be a wedding today," she said, her lower lip jutting out just slightly.

Elisabeth smiled and laid a hand on a small seersucker-clad shoulder. "I'm sorry you're disappointed, honey. If it helps any, so am I."

"I wish Papa would come home," Trista said. She was gazing toward town, and the warm wind made tendrils of dark hair float around her face. "I think there's going to be a hurricane or something."

Despite her own uneasiness and her yearning to see Jonathan, Elisabeth laughed. "There won't be a hurricane, Trista. The mountains make a natural barrier."

As if to mock her statement, lightning struck behind the house in that instant, and both Trista and Elisabeth cried out in shock and dashed around to make sure the chicken house or the woodshed hadn't been struck.

Elisabeth's heart hammered painfully against her breastbone when she saw the wounded tree at the edge of the orchard. Its trunk had been split from top to bottom, and its naked core was blackened and still smoldering. In the barn, Jonathan's horses neighed, sensing something, perhaps smelling the damaged wood.

And for all of it, the air was still bone-dry and charged

with some invisible force that seemed to buzz ominously beneath the other sounds.

"We'd better get inside," Elisabeth said.

Trista turned worried eyes to her face. "What about Vera? What if she doesn't get home safely?"

It was on the tip of Elisabeth's tongue to say they'd phone to make sure, but she averted the slip in time. She wished she knew how to hitch up a wagon and drive a team, but she didn't, and she doubted that Trista did, either.

She could ride, though not well. "Let's get out the tamest horse you own," she said. "I'll ride over to Vera's place and make sure she got home okay."

"Okay?" Trista echoed, crinkling her nose at the unfamiliar word.

"It means 'all right,'" Elisabeth told her, picking up her skirts and heading toward the barn. Between the two of them, she and Trista managed to put a bridle on the recalcitrant Estella, Trista's aging, swaybacked mare. Elisabeth asked for brief directions and set off down the road, toward the schoolhouse.

Overhead, black clouds roiled and rolled in on each other, and thunder reverberated off the sides of distant hills. Elisabeth thought of the splintered apple tree and shivered.

As she reached the road, she waved at the man who lived in an earlier incarnation of the house the Buzbee sisters shared. Heedless of the threatened storm, he was busy hammering a new rail onto his fence.

Just around the bend from the schoolhouse, Elisabeth found Vera sitting beside the road, her face streaked with dust, sobbing. The pony was galloping off toward a barn on a grassy knoll nearby.

"Are you hurt?" Elisabeth asked. She didn't want to

get down from the horse if she could help it, because getting back on would be almost impossible, dressed as she was. It was bad enough riding with her skirts hiked up to show her bare legs.

Vera gulped and got to her feet, dragging one suntanned arm across her dirty face. Evidently, the sight of Elisabeth riding astride in a dress had been enough of a shock to distract her a little from the pain and indignity of being thrown. "I scraped my elbow," she said with a voluble sniffle.

Elisabeth rode closer and squinted at the wound. "That looks pretty sore, all right. Would you like a ride home?"

Vera gestured toward the sturdy-looking, weathered farmhouse five hundred yards from the barn. "I live close," she said. It appeared she'd had enough of horses for one day, and Elisabeth didn't blame her.

"I'll just ride alongside you then," she said gently as lightning ripped the fabric of the sky again and made her skittish mount toss its head and whinny.

Vera nodded and dried her face again, this time with the skirt of her calico pinafore. "I don't usually cry like this," she said as she walked along the grassy roadside, Elisabeth and the horse keeping pace with her. "I'm as tough as my brother."

"I'm sure you are," Elisabeth agreed, hiding a smile.

Vera's mother came out of the house and waved, smiling, apparently unruffled to see her daughter approaching on foot instead of on the back of her fat little pony. "It's good to see you're feeling better, Elisabeth," she called over the roar of distant thunder. "You're welcome to come in for pie and coffee if you have the time."

"I'd better get back to Trista," Elisabeth answered, truly sorry that she couldn't stay and get to know this woman better. "And I suppose the storm is going to break any minute now."

The neighbor nodded her head pleasantly, shepherding Vera into the house, and Elisabeth reined the mare toward home and rode at the fastest pace she dared, given her inexperience. As it was, she needn't have hurried, for even after she'd put Trista's horse back in the barn and inspected the unfortunate tree that had been struck by lightning earlier, there was no rain.

She muttered as she climbed the back steps and opened the kitchen door. The forlorn notes of Trista's piano plunked and plodded through the heavy air.

The rest of the afternoon passed, and then the evening, and there was still no word from Jonathan. The sky remained as black and irritable as ever, but not so much as a drop of rain touched the thirsty ground.

After a light supper of leftover chicken, Elisabeth and Trista took turns reading aloud from *Gulliver's Travels*, the book they'd begun when Trista had fallen ill. When they tired of that, they played four games of checkers, all of which Trista won with smug ease.

And Jonathan did not come through the door, tired and hungry, longing for the love and light of his home.

Elisabeth was beginning to fear that something had happened to him. Perhaps there had been an accident, or he'd had a heart attack from overwork, or some drunken cowboy had shot him....

Trista, who had already put on her nightgown, scrubbed her face and washed her teeth, was surprisingly philosophical—and perceptive—for an eight-year-old. "You keep going to the window and looking for Papa," she said. "Sometimes he's gone a long time when there's a baby on its way or somebody's real sick."

Self-consciously, Elisabeth let the curtain above the

sink fall back into place. "What if you'd been here alone?" she asked, frowning.

Trista shrugged. "Ellen would probably have taken me home with her." She beamed. "I like going to her house because there's so much noise."

The old clock on the shelf ticked ponderously, emphasizing the quiet. And it occurred to Elisabeth that Trista had been very lonely, with no brothers and sisters and no mother. "You like noise, do you?" Elisabeth teased. And then she bolted toward Trista, her hands raised, fingers curled, like a bear's claws.

Trista squealed with delight and ran through the dining room to the parlor and up the front stairway, probably because that was the long way and the pursuit could be drawn out until the last possible moment.

In her room, Trista collapsed giggling on the bed, and Elisabeth tickled her for a few moments, then kissed her soundly on the cheek, listened to her prayers and tucked her into bed.

Later, in the parlor, she sat down at the piano and began to play soft and soothing songs, tunes Rue would have described as cocktail-party music. All the while, Elisabeth listened with one ear for the sound of Jonathan's footsteps.

14

The touch of Jonathan's lips on her forehead brought Elisabeth flailing up from the depths of an uneasy sleep. The muscles in her arms and legs ached from her attempt to curl around Trista in a protective crescent.

For a moment, wild fear seized her, closing off her throat, stealing her breath. Then she realized that except for the rumble of distant thunder, the world was quiet. She and Trista were safe, and Jonathan was back from his wanderings.

She started to rise, but he pressed her gently back to the mattress and, in the thin light of the hallway lamp, she saw him touch his lips with an index finger.

"We'll talk in the morning," he promised, his low voice hoarse with weariness. "I trust you're still inclined to become my wife?"

Elisabeth stretched, smiled and nodded.

"Good." He bent and kissed her forehead again. "Tomorrow night you'll sleep where you belong—in my bed."

A pleasant shiver went through Elisabeth at the thought of the pleasures Jonathan had taught her to enjoy. She nodded again and then snuggled in and went contentedly back to sleep, this time without tension, without fear.

Jonathan couldn't remember being more tired than he was at that moment—not even in medical school, when he'd worked and studied until he was almost blind with fatigue. He'd spent most of the past twenty-four hours struggling to save the lives of a mother and her twins, losing the woman and one of the infants. The remaining child was hanging on to life by the thinnest of threads, and there was simply nothing more Jonathan could do at this point.

In his room, he poured tepid water from the pitcher into the basin, removed his shirt and washed, trying to scrub away the smell of sickness and despair. When he could at least stand the scent of himself, he turned toward the bed.

God knew, he was so exhausted, he couldn't have made love to Elisabeth even if the act somehow averted war or plague, but just having her lie beside him would have been the sweetest imaginable comfort. He ached to extend a hand and touch her, to breathe deeply and fill his lungs with her fragrance.

Wearily, Jonathan made his way toward his bed and then stopped, knowing he would lapse into virtual unconsciousness once he stretched out. Before he did that, he had to know Elisabeth wouldn't get it into her head to vanish again.

Picking up a small kerosene lamp, he forced himself out into the hallway and along the runner to the door of the spare room, where she normally slept. The necklace, left carelessly on top of the bureau, seemed to sparkle in the night, drawing Jonathan to it by some inexplicable magic.

Although he knew he would be ashamed of the action in the morning, he scooped the pendant into his hand and went back to his own room, where he blew out the lamp and sank into bed.

Even in sleep, his fingers were locked around the necklace, and the hot, thunderous hours laid upon him like a weight.

Somewhere in the blackest folds of that starless night, Elisabeth awakened with a wrench. She had to go to the bathroom, and that meant a trip to the outhouse if she didn't want to use a chamber pot—which she most assuredly didn't.

Yawning, she rose and pulled on a robe—Ellen and Trista always spoke of the garment as a wrapper—and, after her eyes had adjusted, made her way toward the inner door and down the back steps to the kitchen.

There was no wind, she noticed when she stepped out onto the back step, and certainly no rain. The air was ominously heavy, and it seemed to reverberate with unspoken threats. With a little shiver, Elisabeth forced herself down the darkened path and around behind the woodshed to the privy.

She was returning when the unthinkable happened, paralyzing her in the middle of the path. As she watched, her eyes wide with amazement and horror, a bolt of lightning zigzagged out of the dark sky, like a laser beam from an unseen spacecraft, and literally splintered the roof of the house. For one terrible moment, the entire landscape was aglow, the trees and mountains like dazed sleepers under the glare of a flashlight.

Immediately, flames shot up from the roof, and Elisabeth screamed. The animals in the barn had heard the crash and had probably caught the scent of fire. They were going wild with fear. Elisabeth dared not take the time to calm them. She had to reach Jonathan and Trista.

She hurled herself through the barrier of terrified inertia that had blocked her way and ran into the house, coughing and shrieking Jonathan's and Trista's names.

The short stairway leading to Trista's room was filled with black, roiling smoke. The stuff was so noxious that it felt greasy against Elisabeth's skin. Breathing was impossible.

Beyond the wall of smoke, she could hear Trista screaming, "Papa! Papa!"

Elisabeth dragged herself a few more steps upward, but then she couldn't go farther. Her lungs were empty, and she was becoming disoriented, unsure of which way was up and which way was down. She began to sob, and felt herself slipping, the stairs bruising her as she lost her grip.

The next thing she knew, someone was grasping her by her flannel nightgown. Strong hands hoisted her into steely arms, and for a moment she thought Jonathan had found her and Trista, and that the three of them were safe.

But then Elisabeth heard a voice. She didn't recognize it. She felt a huge drop of rain strike her face, warm as bathwater, and opened her eyes to look into the haunted features of Farley Haynes.

Looking around her, she saw the man from across the road, along with his five sons. The shapes of other men moved through the hellish, flickering light of the flames, and Elisabeth saw that they'd formed a bucket brigade between the well and the house. Frantic horses had been released from the endangered barn into the pasture.

The barn won't burn, Elisabeth thought with despondent certainty, remembering the newspaper accounts she'd read in that other world, so faraway. *Only the house.*

Marshal Haynes set her down, and she stood trembling in the silky grass, her nightgown streaked with soot.

"Jonathan—Trista—" she gasped hoarsely, starting back toward the house.

But the marshal encircled her waist with one arm and

hauled her back. "It's too late," he said, his voice a miserable rasp. "All three stairways are blocked."

At that moment, part of the roof fell in with a fierce crash, and Elisabeth screamed, struggled wildly in the marshal's grasp and then lost consciousness.

When she awakened, gasping, sobbing before she even became fully aware of her surroundings, Elisabeth found herself in a wagon, bumping and jostling along the dark road that led to town. She sat up, twisting to look at the man who sat in the box, driving the team.

She raised herself to her knees, hair flying wildly around her face, filthy nightgown covered with bit of hay and straw, and clasped the low back of the wagon seat. "Jonathan and Trista," she managed to choke out. "Did you get them out? Did anyone get them out?"

Marshal Haynes turned slightly to look back at her, but the night was moonless and she could see only the outline of his tall, brawny figure and Western hat. The rain that had begun to fall after she'd been pulled from the house started to come down in earnest in that moment, so that he had to raise his voice to be heard.

"That's somethin' you and I are going to have to talk about, little lady," he said.

Elisabeth remembered the sight of the roof of Jonathan's house caving in, and she closed her eyes tightly, heedless of the drops that were wetting her hair and her dirty nightgown. Nothing mattered, nothing in the universe, except Jonathan and Trista's safety. She knelt there, unable to speak, holding tightly to the back of the wagon seat, letting the temperate summer rain drench her.

Only when Farley brought the wagon to a stop in front of the jailhouse did Elisabeth's state of shock begin to abate. Bile rushed into her throat as she recalled the events she'd read about—the fire, no bodies found in the ruins, her own arrest and trial for murder.

And despite the horror of what she faced, Elisabeth felt the first stirring of hope. *No bodies.* Perhaps, just perhaps, Jonathan had found the necklace and he and Trista had managed to get over the threshold into the safety of the next century.

The marshal hoisted her down from the wagon and hustled her into his office. While Elisabeth stood shivering and looking around—the place was like something out of a museum—Marshal Haynes hung his sodden hat on a peg beside the door and crouched in front of the wood stove to get a fire going.

"Now, I suppose you're going to arrest me for murder," Elisabeth said, her teeth chattering.

Farley looked back at her over one shoulder, his expression sober. "Actually, ma'am, I just brought you here to wait for the church ladies. They'll be along to collect you any minute now, I reckon."

The guy was like something out of the late show. "You'll try me for murder," Elisabeth said with dismal conviction, stepping a little closer to the stove as the blaze caught and Farley closed the metal door with a clank. "I read it in the newspaper."

"I heard you were a little crazy," the marshal said thoughtfully. His eyes slid over Elisabeth's nightgown, which was probably transparent, and he brought her a long canvas coat that had been draped over his desk chair. "Here, put this on and go sit there next to the fire. All I need is for the Presbyterians to decide I've been mistreating you."

Elisabeth's knees were weak, and she couldn't keep her thoughts straight. She sank into the rocking chair he indicated, closing the coat demurely around her legs. "I didn't kill anybody," she said.

"Nobody is claiming you did," Farley answered, pouring syrupy black coffee into a metal mug and handing it to her. But he was staring at Elisabeth as though she were a puzzle he couldn't quite solve, and she wondered hysterically if she'd already said too much.

The chair creaked as Elisabeth rocked, and the heat from the stove and the terrible coffee began to thaw out her frozen senses. "Jonathan and Trista are not dead," she insisted, speaking over the rim of the cup. She had to cling to that, to believe it, or she would go mad, right then and there.

Farley looked pained as he finally shrugged out of his own coat and came to stand near the stove, giving Elisabeth a sidelong glance and pouring himself a cup of coffee. His beard-stubbled face was gray with grief, and his brown hair was rumpled from repeated rakings of his fingers and wet with the rain. His green-blue eyes reflected weariness and misery. "There's no way anybody could have survived a blaze like that, Miss Lizzie," he said with gruff gentleness. "They're dead, all right." He paused and sighed sadly. "We'll get their bodies out tomorrow and bury them proper."

Elisabeth felt the coffee back up into her throat in an acid rush, and it was only by monumental effort that she kept herself from throwing up on the marshal's dirty, plankboard floor. "No, you won't," she said when she could manage it. "You won't find their bodies because they're not there."

Farley sidled over and touched Elisabeth's forehead with the back of one big hand, frowning. Then he went back to his place by the stove. "What do you mean they're not there? Me and four other men tried to get in, and all the staircases were blocked. We couldn't get to Jonathan and the little girl, and we damn near didn't get to you.''

A headache throbbed under Elisabeth's temples, and she could feel her sinus passages closing up. ''Don't think I'm not grateful, Marshal,'' she said. ''As for what I meant—well, I—'' What could she say? That Jonathan and Trista might have disappeared into another time, another dimension? ''I believe they got out and that they're wandering somewhere, perhaps not recalling who they are.''

''I've known Jonathan Fortner for ten years,'' Farley answered, staring off at some vision Elisabeth couldn't see. ''He wouldn't have left that house unless he was taking everybody inside with him. He wasn't that kind of man.''

Elisabeth felt tears burn her eyes. No one was ever going to believe her theory that Jonathan and Trista had taken the only escape open to them, and she would have to accept the fact. Furthermore, even though the man she loved, the father of the baby growing inside her at that very moment, had not died, he might well be permanently lost to her. Perhaps he wouldn't be able to find his way back, or perhaps the mysterious passageway, whatever it was, had been sealed forever....

Farley fetched a bottle from his desk drawer and poured a dollop of potent-smelling whiskey into Elisabeth's coffee. ''You mentioned murder a few minutes ago,'' he said, ''and you talked of reading about what happened in the papers. What did you mean by that?''

Elisabeth normally didn't drink anything stronger than white wine, but she lifted the whiskey-laced coffee gratefully to her mouth, her hands shaking. ''There hasn't been a murder. It's just that you're going to *think*...'' Her voice failed as she realized how crazy any explanation she could make would sound. She squirmed in the chair. "You won't find any bodies in that house, Marshal, because no one is dead."

A metallic ring echoed through the small, cluttered office when Farley set his cup on the stove top and disappeared into the single cell to drag a blanket off the cot. "Put this around you," he ordered, returning to shove the cover at Elisabeth. "You're out of your head with the shock of what you've been through."

Elisabeth wrapped herself in the blanket. By that time, her mixed-up emotions had undergone another radical shift and she was convinced that Jonathan would come walking through the door at any moment, his clothes blackened and torn, to collect her and prove to the marshal that he was alive. Trista, she decided, was safe at Vera's house.

Farley stooped to peer into her face. "You didn't set that fire, did you?"

She jerked her head back, as though the words had been a physical blow. "Set it? Marshal, the roof was struck by lightning—I saw it happen!"

"Seems to me something like that would be pretty unlikely," he mused, rubbing his chin with a thumb and two fingers as he considered the possibilities.

"Oh, really?" Elisabeth demanded, frightened now because the scenario was beginning to go the way she'd feared it would. "Well, it split one of the apple trees in the orchard right down the middle. Maybe you'd like to go and see for yourself."

"Who are you?" Farley inquired, and Elisabeth was sure he hadn't heard a word she said. "Where did you come from?"

She swallowed. Jonathan had told various people in the

community that she was his late wife's sister, and now Elisabeth had no choice but to maintain the lie. If—*when*—she saw him again, she was going to give him hell for getting her into this mess. "My name is Lizzie McCartney, and I was born in Boston," she said, her chin quivering.

"Yes, I remember that Barbara's family lived in Boston," the marshal answered calmly. "If you'll just give me your father's name and street address, I'll get in touch with your family and tell them you're going to need some help."

Elisabeth felt the color drain from her face. She couldn't relay the information the marshal wanted because she didn't know the answers to his questions. "I'd rather handle this on my own," she said after a hesitation that was a fraction too long.

The marshal took a watch from the pocket of his trousers, flipped the case open with his thumb and frowned at the time. "Now where do you suppose those Presbyterians are?" he muttered.

"I don't imagine they'll be coming by for me at all," Elisabeth ventured to say, and her throat felt thick because Jonathan and Trista were gone and she might have to live out what was left of her life alone in a strange place. "My guess would be the ladies of Pine River don't entirely approve of the fact that I've been staying in Jonathan's house."

"Well, you'd better get some sleep. You can bunk in there, on the cot." He pointed toward the cell and Elisabeth shuddered to think of some of the types who might have used it before her. "In the morning, we'll contact your people."

Elisabeth was shaking, and not in her wildest imaginings would she have expected to sleep, but she went obediently into the cell all the same. When the marshal had blown out all the lamps and disappeared into his own undoubtedly humble quarters out back, she stripped off the wet nightgown, wrapped herself tightly in the blanket and laid down on the rickety bed.

Two sleepless hours passed, during which Elisabeth alternately listened for Jonathan to storm the citadel and cried because she knew the twentieth century would never surrender him. She was tortured by worries about how he was faring and whether he and Trista had been hurt or not. Jonathan was a doctor and an extremely intelligent man, but Elisabeth wasn't sure he'd know how to get help in her world.

What if Jonathan and Trista were in pain? What if they weren't in the twentieth century at all, but some weird place in between? Worst of all, what if they *had* died in the fire and their remains simply hadn't been found yet?

The cell was brimming with sunshine when the marshal appeared, bearing an ugly brown calico dress in one hand. "You can put this on," he said, shoving it through the bars. Actually, he looked rather handsome in an Old West sort of way, with his brown hair brushed shiny, his jaw shaved and his substantial mustache trimmed.

"At least have the courtesy to turn your back," Elisabeth said, rising awkwardly in her scratchy blanket to reach for the garment.

Farley obliged, folding his beefy arms in front of his chest. "Looks like you'll be staying with us for a while," he said with a sort of grim heartiness. "I had a talk with Jon's housekeeper, and she managed to find some family papers in the part of the house that didn't burn. Then I sent a telegram to Barbara's family, back there in Massachusetts. They wired me that they never had a daughter named Lizzie.''

Elisabeth felt panic sweeping her toward the edge like a giant broom, but somehow she contrived to keep her voice even. ''I guess I'm just lucky I didn't end up in the 1600s,'' she said, pulling on the charity dress and fastening the buttons. The thing was a good three sizes too big. ''They probably would have burned me at the stake as a witch.''

''I'd be careful about how I talked,'' Farley advised, turning around to face her. ''The people around here don't hold much with witches and the like.''

''I don't imagine they do,'' Elisabeth remarked sweetly, wondering how the heck she was going to get out of this one. ''Tell me, whose dress is this?''

''Belongs to Big Lil over at the Phifer Hotel. She's the cook.''

''And she's in the habit of lending her clothes to prisoners?''

Farley's powerful shoulders moved in an offhanded shrug. ''Not really. I believe she left that here the last time I had to run her in for disturbing the peace.''

Elisabeth gripped the bars in both hands and peered through with guileless eyes. ''I hardly dare ask what Big Lil was wearing when she left.''

To her satisfaction, the marshal's neck went a dull red, and he averted his eyes for a moment. ''She had her daughter bring her some things,'' he mumbled.

If it hadn't been for the gravity of her situation and all the dreadful possibilities she was holding at bay, Elisabeth might have smiled. As it was, her sense of humor was strained to the breaking point.

''Exactly what am I charged with?'' she asked as Farley went to the stove and touched the big enamel coffeepot with an inquiring finger. "You can't pin a murder on somebody if there aren't any bodies."

Farley stared at her, looking bewildered and just a touch sick. "What makes you so sure we didn't find... remains?"

He'd never buy the truth, of course. "I just know," Elisabeth said with a little shrug. She wriggled her eyebrows. "Maybe I am a witch."

The marshal hooked his thumbs under his suspenders and regarded Elisabeth somberly. "What did you do with them? Drop 'em down the well? Dump 'em into the river?"

Elisabeth spread her hands wide of her body and the horrendous brown dress that was practically swallowing her. "Do I look big enough to overcome a man Jonathan's size?"

Farley arched an eyebrow. "You could have poisoned him or hit him over the head. As for disposing of the bodies, you might even have had an accomplice."

Knowing the townspeople were going to believe some version of that story, Elisabeth cringed inwardly. Still, she had to at least try to save her skin. "What motive would I have for doing that?"

"What motive did you have for lying about who you are?" Farley countered, rapid-fire. "I'll bet you lied to Jonathan, too—told him you were family, so to speak. He took you in, and you repaid him by—"

"Before you whip out a violin," Elisabeth interrupted, "let me say that Jonathan *does* know who I am. And telling people I was Barbara's sister was his idea, not mine."

"Unfortunately, we don't have anybody's word for that but yours. And it wouldn't make a damn bit of difference if we did." He came to the cell door and glared at her through the bars, his hands gripping the black iron so hard that his knuckles went white. "What did you do to Dr. Fortner and his little girl?"

Elisabeth backed away from the bars because, suddenly, Farley looked fierce. "Damn it, I didn't do *anything* to them," she whispered. "To me, Jonathan and Trista are the most important people in the world!"

Glowering, Farley turned away. "Big Lil will be by with your breakfast pretty soon," he said, taking a gun belt down from a hook on the wall and strapping it on with disturbing deftness. "See you don't try to escape or anything. Lil is mean as a wet badger and tall enough to waltz with a bear."

Again, Elisabeth had the feeling that she would have been amused, if her circumstances hadn't been so dire. "I'll be sure I don't try to dance with her," she replied, slumping forlornly on the edge of the cot.

Farley gave her a look over one broad shoulder and walked out, calmly closing the door behind him.

Elisabeth cupped her chin in her hands and tried to remember if the *Pine River Bugle* had said anything about a lynch mob. "Jonathan," she whispered, "where are you?"

When the door slammed open a few minutes later, however, it wasn't Jonathan filling the chasm. In fact, it could only have been Big Lil, so tall and broadly built was this woman who strode in, carrying a basket covered with a checked table napkin. She wore trousers, boots, suspenders and a rough-spun shirt. Her gray hair was tied back into a severe knot at the nape of her neck.

It occurred to Elisabeth that Big Lil might begrudge her the calico dress, and she reached back to pull the garment tight with one hand, hoping that effort would disguise it.

Big Lil fetched a ring of keys from the desk, unlocked

the door and brought the basket into the cell. Her regard was neither friendly nor condemning, but merely steady. "So, you're the little lady what roasted the doctor like a trussed turkey," she said.

Elisabeth's appetite fled, and she swallowed vile-tasting liquid as she stared at the covered food. She jutted out her chin and glared defiantly at Big Lil, refusing to dignify the remark with an answer.

Big Lil gave a raucous, crowing laugh, then went out of the cell and locked the door again. "Folks around here liked the doc," she said. "I don't reckon they'll take kindly to what you did."

Still, Elisabeth was silent, keeping her eyes fixed on the wall opposite her cot until she heard the door close behind the obnoxious woman.

Elisabeth was in the worst fix of her life, but in the next few moments, her appetite returned, wooed back by the luscious smells coming from inside the basket. She pushed aside the napkin to find hot buttered biscuits inside, along with two pieces of fried chicken and a wedge of goopy cherry pie.

She consumed the biscuits, then the chicken and half the piece of pie before Farley returned, followed by a hard-looking woman with dark hair, small, mean eyes and a pockmarked complexion.

"This is Mrs. Bernard," Farley said, cocking his thumb toward the lady. "She's a Presbyterian."

At last, Elisabeth thought, *the lynch mob.*

Mrs. Bernard stood at a judicious distance from the bars and told Elisabeth in on uncertain terms how God dealt harshly with harlots and liars and had no mercy at all for murderers.

Elisabeth's rage drew her up off the cot and made her stand tall, like a puppet with its strings pulled too tight.

"There will certainly be no need to bring in a judge and try me fairly," she said. "This good woman apparently feels competent to pronounce sentence herself."

Mrs. Bernard's face turned an ugly, mottled red. "Jonathan Fortner was a fine man," she said after a long, bitter silence. She pulled a handkerchief from under her sleeve and dabbed at her beady eyes with it.

"I know that, Mrs. Bernard," Elisabeth replied evenly. The marshal made something of a clatter as he went about his business at the desk, opening drawers and shuffling papers and books.

"Which is not to say he didn't make his share of errors in judgment," the woman went on, as if Elisabeth hadn't spoken. She snuffled loudly. "In any case, the Ladies' Aid Society wishes to extend Christian benevolence. For that reason, I'll be bringing by some decent clothes for you to wear, and some of my companions will drop in to explain the wages of sin."

Elisabeth let her forehead rest against the cold bars. "And I thought I didn't have anything but a hanging to look forward to," she sighed.

If Mrs. Bernard heard, she gave no response. She merely said a stiff goodbye to the marshal and went out.

"If you'll just bring a doctor in from Seattle," Elisabeth said, "he'll testify that human bones can't be destroyed in an ordinary house fire and you'll have to let me go."

"I'm not letting you go until you tell me what you did with the doc and that poor little girl of his," Farley replied, and although he didn't look up from his paperwork, Elisabeth saw his fist tighten around his nibbed pen.

"Well, at least send someone out to look for my necklace," Elisabeth persisted, but the situation was hopeless and she knew it. Farley simply wasn't listening.

15

It was the second week in July before the circuit judge showed up to conduct Elisabeth's trial, and by that time, she'd lost all hope that Jonathan and Trista would ever return. The townspeople were spoiling for a hanging, and even Elisabeth's defense attorney, a smarmy little man in an ill-fitting suit, made it clear that he would have preferred working for the prosecution.

If it hadn't been for the child nature was knitting together beneath her heart, Elisabeth wouldn't have minded dying so much. After all, she was in a harsh and unfamiliar century, separated from practically everyone who mattered to her, and even if she managed to be acquitted of killing Jonathan and Trista, she would always be an outcast.

And she would probably be convicted.

The thought of the innocent baby dying with her tightened her throat and made her stomach twist as she sat beside her lawyer in the stuffy courtroom—which was really the schoolhouse with the desks all pushed against the walls.

The judge occupied the teacher's place, and there was nothing about his appearance or manner to reassure Elisabeth. In fact, his eyes were red rimmed, and the skin of his face settled awkwardly over his bones, like a garment that was too large. The thousands of tiny purple-and-red veins in his nose said even more about the state of his character.

"This court will now come to order," he said in a booming voice, after clearing his throat.

Elisabeth shifted uncomfortably in her chair beside Mr. Rodcliff, her attorney, recalling her reflection in the jailhouse mirror that morning. Her blond hair had fallen loose around her shoulders, her face looked pallid and gaunt, and there were purple smudges under her eyes.

She was the very picture of guilt.

Farley stood over by the wainscotted wall, slicked up for the big day, his hat in his hands. He caught Elisabeth's eye and gave a slight nod, as if to offer encouragement.

She looked away, knowing Farley's real feelings. He wanted to see her dangle, because he believed she'd willfully murdered his friend.

The first witness called to the stand was Ellen, Jonathan's erstwhile housekeeper. Tearfully, the plain woman told how Elisabeth had just appeared one day, seemingly out of nowhere, and somehow managed to bewitch the poor doctor.

Mr. Rodcliff asked a few cursory questions when his turn came, then sat down again.

Elisabeth folded her arms and sat back in her chair, biting down hard on her lower lip. Vera was the next to testify, saying Trista had told her some very strange things about Elisabeth—that she was really an angel come from heaven, and that she had a magic necklace and played queer music on the piano and claimed to know exactly what the world would be like in a hundred years.

Mr. Rodcliff gave Elisabeth an accusing sidelong glance, as if to ask how she expected him to defend her against such charges. When the prosecuting attorney sa down behind his table, Elisabeth's lawyer rose with a defeated sigh and told the judge he had nothing to say.

Elisabeth watched a fly buzzing doggedly against one of the heavy windows and empathized. She felt hot and ugly in her brown dress, and even though she'd borrowed a needle and thread from Farley and taken tucks in it, it still fit badly.

Hearing Farley's name called, Elisabeth jerked her attention back to the front of the room. He wouldn't meet her eyes, though his gaze swept over the jury of six men lined up under the world map. He cleared his throat before repeating the oath, then testified that he'd been summoned to the Fortner farm, along with the volunteer fire department, by one of Efriam Lute's sons, who'd awakened because the livestock was fretful and seen the flames.

When he'd arrived, Farley said, he immediately tried to get up the main staircase, knowing the members of the household would be sleeping, it being the middle of the night and all. He allowed as how his way had been blocked by flames and smoke, so he'd tried both the other sets of stairs and met with the same frustration. He had, however, found Miss Lizzie half-conscious in the kitchen and had carried her out.

It was only later, he related, when she began saying odd things, that he started to suspect that something was wrong. When he'd learned she was lying about her identity, he'd filed charges.

While Farley talked, Elisabeth stared at him, and he began to squirm in his chair.

Mr. Rodcliff didn't even bother to offer a question when he was given the opportunity and, at last, Elisabeth was called to the stand. She was terrified, but she stood and walked with regal grace to the front of the crowded schoolroom and laid her left hand on the offered Bible, raising her right.

Benches had been brought in for the spectators, and the place was packed with them. The smell of sweat made Elisabeth want to gag.

"Do you solemnly swear to tell the truth, the whole truth and nothing but the truth?" asked the bailiff, who was really Marvin Hites, the man who ran the general store.

"I do," Elisabeth said clearly, even though she knew she couldn't tell the "whole truth" because these relatively primitive minds would never be able to absorb it. She would be committed, and Elisabeth's limited knowledge of nineteenth-century mental hospitals told her it would be better to hang.

There followed a long inquisition, during which Elisabeth was asked who she was. "Lizzie" was the only answer she would give to that. She was asked where she came from, and she said Seattle, which caused murmurs of skepticism among the lookers-on.

Finally, the prosecutor inquired as to whether Elisabeth had in fact "ignited the blazes that consumed one Dr. Jonathan Fortner and his small daughter, Trista."

The question, even though Elisabeth had expected it, outraged her. "No," she said reasonably, but inside she was screaming her anger and her innocence. "I loved Dr. Fortner. He and I were planning to be married."

The townswomen buzzed behind their fans at this statement, and it occurred to Elisabeth that many of them had probably either hoped to marry Jonathan themselves or had wanted to land him for a son-in-law or a nephew by marriage.

"You *loved* him," the prosecutor said in a voice that made Elisabeth want to slap his smug face. "And yet you did murder, Miss—Lizzie. You killed the man and his child *as they slept,* unwitting, in their beds!''

A shape moved in the open doorway, then a familiar voice rolled over the murmurs of the crowd like a low roll of thunder. ''If I'm dead, Walter,'' Jonathan said, ''I think it's going to come as a big shock to both of us.''

He stood in the center aisle, his clothes ripped and covered in soot, one arm in a makeshift sling made from one of the silk scarves Elisabeth had collected in her other incarnation. His gray eyes linking with hers, he continued, ''I'm alive, obviously, and so is Trista.''

Women were fainting all over the room, and some of the men didn't look too chipper, either. But Elisabeth's shock was pure, undiluted joy. She flung herself at Jonathan and embraced him, being careful not to press against his injured arm.

He kissed her, holding her unashamedly close, his good hand pressed to the small of her back. And even after he lifted his mouth from hers, he seemed impervious to the crowd stuffing the schoolhouse.

It was Farley who shouldered his way to Jonathan and demanded, ''Damn it, Jon, *where the hell have you been?''*

Jonathan's teeth were startlingly white against his soot-smudged face. He slapped the marshal's shoulder affectionately. ''Someday, Farley, when we're both so old it can't make a difference, I may just tell you.''

''Order, order!'' the judge was yelling, hammering at the desk with his trusty gavel.

The mob paid no attention. They were shouting questions at Jonathan, but he ignored them, ushering a stunned Elisabeth down the aisle and out into the bright July sunshine.

''It seems time has played another of its nasty tricks

on us," he said when he and Elisabeth stood beneath the sheltering leaves of a maple tree. He traced her jawline with the tip of one index finger. "Let's make a vow, Lizzie, never to be apart again."

Tears were trickling down Elisabeth's cheeks, tears of joy and relief. "Jonathan, what happened?"

He held her close, and she rested her head against his shoulder, not minding the acrid, smoky smell of him in the least. "I'm not really sure," he replied, his breath moving in her hair. "I woke up, Trista was screaming and there was no sign of you. I had the necklace in my hand. All three stairways were closed off, and the roof was burning, too. I grabbed up my daughter, offered a prayer and went over the threshold."

Elisabeth clung to him, hardly able even then to believe that he'd really come back to her. "How long were you there?" she asked.

He propped his chin on top of her head, and the townspeople kept their distance, though they were streaming out of the schoolhouse, chattering and speculating. "That's the crazy part, Elisabeth," he said. "A few hours passed at the most—I waited until I could be fairly sure the fire would be out, then I came over again, this time carrying Trista on my back. Climbing down through the charred ruins took some time."

"How did you know where to look for me?"

His powerful shoulders moved in a shrug. "There were a lot of horses and wagons going past. I stopped old Cully Reed, and he about spit out his teeth when he saw me. Then he told me what was going on and brought me here in his hay wagon."

Elisabeth stiffened, looking up into Jonathan's face, searching for any sign of a secret. "And Trista wasn't hurt?"

He shook his head. "She's already convinced the whole thing was a nightmare, brought on by swallowing so much smoke. Maybe when she's older, we can tell her what really happened, but I think it would only confuse her now. God knows, it confuses me."

The judge, who had been ready to send Elisabeth to the gallows only minutes before, dared to impinge upon the invisible circle that had kept the townspeople back. He laid a hand to Jonathan's shoulder and smiled. "Looks like you need some medical attention for that arm, son."

"The first thing I need," Jonathan answered quietly, his eyes never leaving Elisabeth's face, "is a wife. Think you could perform the ceremony, Judge? Say in an hour, out by the covered bridge?"

The judge agreed with a nod, and Elisabeth thought how full of small ironies life is, not to mention mysteries.

"Will you marry me, Lizzie?" Jonathan asked, a little belatedly. "Will you throw away the necklace and live with me forever?"

Elisabeth thought only briefly of that other life, in that other, faraway place. She might have dreamed it, for all the reality it had, though she knew she would miss Rue and her friends. "Yes, Jon."

He kissed her again, lifting her onto her toes to do it, and the spectators cheered. Elisabeth forgave them for their fickleness because a lifetime of love and happiness lay before her, because Jonathan was back and she was carrying his baby, and because Trista would grow up to raise a family of her own.

As Elisabeth caught a glimpse of the half-burned house, what in her mind had been the very symbol of shattered hopes now, miraculously, became a place where children would laugh and run and work, a place where music would play.

"Oh, Jonathan, I love you," Elisabeth said, her arm linked with his as Cully Reed's hay wagon came to a stop in the side yard. They'd been sitting in the back, their feet dangling.

Jonathan kissed her smartly, jumped to the ground and lifted her after him with one arm. "I love you, too," he answered huskily, and his eyes brushed over her, making her flesh tingle with the anticipation of his lovemaking. He waved at the driver. "Thanks, Cully. See you at the wedding."

Practical concerns closed around Elisabeth like barking dogs as she and Jonathan went up the front steps and into the house. "What am I going to wear?" she fretted, holding wide the skirts of Big Lil's brown calico dress. "I can't be married in this!"

Jonathan assessed the outfit and laughed. "Why not, Lizzie? This certainly isn't going to be a conventional wedding day anyhow."

Elisabeth sighed. There was no denying that. Nonetheless, she diligently searched the upstairs and was heartbroken to find nothing that wasn't in even worse condition than what she was wearing.

In his bedroom, Jonathan sank into a chair and unwrapped his wounded arm. Elisabeth winced when she saw the angry burn.

"Oh, Jon," she whispered, chagrined. She fell to her knees beside his chair. "Here I am, worrying about a stupid dress, when you're hurt...."

He bent to kiss her forehead. "I'll be all right," he assured her gruffly. "But after the wedding, I'd like to go first to Seattle and then San Francisco. There's a doctor in Seattle who might be able to help me keep full use of the muscles in my hand and wrist."

Elisabeth's eyes filled with tears. "I'll go anywhere, as long as I can be with you. You know that. But who will look after your patients here?" Even as she voiced the question, she thought of the young, red-haired physician who had been summoned from Seattle after Jonathan's disappearance.

"Whoever's been doing it in my absence," Jonathan replied, and there was pain in his eyes, and distance. "I won't be of use to anybody if I can't use my right hand, Lizzie."

Elisabeth watched unflinchingly as he began treating the burns with a smelly ointment. "That's not true. You're so important to me that I can't even imagine what I'd have done without you."

Before Jonathan could respond to that, Trista bolted into the room and hurled herself into Elisabeth's waiting arms.

"Vera said there was a trial and that she testified," the child chattered. Her brow was crimped into a frown when she drew back to search Elisabeth's face. "How could so much have happened while I was sleeping?"

Elisabeth kissed her cheek. "I don't think I can explain, sweetheart," she said truthfully enough, "because I don't understand, either. I'm just glad we're all together again."

"Vera's mother says there's going to be a wedding, and she's bringing over her own dress for you to wear. She says the least Pine River can do for you is see that things are done properly."

Soon Vera's mother did, indeed, arrive with a dress, and Elisabeth was so grateful that she forgot how the woman's child had practically called her a witch that very morning. She bathed in the privacy of the spare room, and brushed her hair until it shone, pinned it into a modified Gibson-girl and put on the lace-trimmed ivory silk dress her neighbor had so generously offered. The fabric made a rustling sound as Elisabeth moved, and smelled pleasantly of lavender. Trista gathered wildflowers and made a garland for Elisabeth's hair, and when the two of them reached the site Jonathan had chosen, next to the covered bridge, the doctor was waiting there with a handful of daisies and tiger lilies.

The townsfolk crowded the hillside and creek bank, and several schoolboys even sat on the roof of the bridge. Elisabeth marveled that she'd come so close to losing her life and then had gained everything she'd ever wanted, all in the space of a single day.

To be married by the very judge who would probably have handed down her death sentence was a supreme irony.

The ceremony passed in a sort of sparkling daze for Elisabeth; it seemed as though she and Jonathan were surrounded by an impenetrable white light, and the ordinary sounds of a summer afternoon blended into a low-key whir.

Only when Jonathan kissed her did Elisabeth realize she was married. When the kiss ended, she was flushed with the poignant richness of life. Instead of tossing her bouquet, she handed it to Trista and hugged the child.

"Now we're a family," Trista said, her gray eyes glowing as she looked up at her stepmother.

"We are, indeed," Elisabeth agreed, her throat choked with happy tears.

After the ceremony, there was corn bread and coffee at the hotel. There hadn't been enough advance warning for a cake, but Elisabeth didn't care. What stories she'd be able to tell her and Jonathan's grandchildren!

Trista would spend the night with Vera, it was agreed, and the Fortner family would leave on their trip the following morning. Once all the corn bread had been consumed and Jonathan and Elisabeth had been wished the best by everyone, from the judge who had married them to the man who swept out the saloon, the newlyweds retired to the room Jonathan had rented.

Beyond the window and the door, ordinary life went on. Buggies and wagons rattled by, and the piano player hammered out bawdy tunes in the saloon across the road. But Jonathan and Elisabeth were alone in a world no one else could enter.

She trembled with love and wanting as he slowly, gently undressed her, and it was an awkward process, since his right arm was still in a sling. "I'm going to have your baby, Jon," she said in a breathless whisper as he unbuttoned her muslin camisole and pushed it back off her shoulders, baring her breasts. "I'm sure of that now."

He bent his head, almost reverently, to kiss each of her firm, opulent breasts. "The first of many, I hope," he relied.

Elisabeth drew in a quick breath as she felt his mouth close over her nipple. "I missed you so much, Jon," she managed after a moment, tilting her head back and closing her eyes in blissful surrender as he enjoyed her. "I was terrified I would never see you again."

He suckled for a long, leisurely time before drawing back long enough to answer, "I was scared, too, wondering if you escaped the fire." He turned to her other breast, and Elisabeth moaned and entwined her fingers in his rich, dark hair, holding him close as he drank from her. If she never had another day to laugh and breathe and love, she thought, this one would be sweet enough to cherish through the rest of eternity.

Presently, he laid her down on the edge of the bed, running his hands along her inner thighs, easing her quivering legs apart for an intimate plundering. She felt her hair come undone from its pins and spread it over the covers with her fingers in a gesture of relinquishment.

Her soul was open to Jonathan now; there was no part of it he was not free to explore.

He knelt, his hands gripping the tender undersides of her knees, and nuzzled the moist delta where her womanhood nestled. "I love pleasing you, Elisabeth," he said. "I love making you give yourself up to me, totally, without reservation of any kind."

Elisabeth's breath was quick and shallow, and she could barely speak. "I need you," she whimpered.

Jonathan burrowed through and took her fiercely, and Elisabeth cried out, her body making a graceful arch on the mattress, her hands clutching and pounding at the blankets.

He consumed her until she was writhing wildly on the bed, until she was uttering low cries, until her skin was wet with perspiration and her muscles were aching with the effort of thrusting her toward him. He drove her straight out of herself and made her soar, and brought her back to earth with patient caresses and muttered reassurances.

She found him beside her on the lumpy hotel bed, after she'd returned to herself and could think and see clearly. Very gently, she touched his bandaged arm.

"Does it hurt much?"

He bent to scatter light kisses over her collarbone. "It hurts like hell, Mrs. Fortner. Just exactly how do you propose to comfort your husband in his time of need?"

She stretched like some contented cat, and he poised himself over her, one of his legs parting hers. "I intend to love him so thoroughly that he won't remember his name," she responded saucily, spreading her fingers in the coarse hair that covered his chest.

Jonathan groaned, touching his hardness to her softness, receiving warmth. Elisabeth guided him gently inside her, arching her back to take him deep within, and his magnificent gray eyes glazed with pleasure.

Slowly, slowly, she moved beneath him, tempting, teasing, taking and giving. With one hand thrust far into the mattress, the other resting against his middle in its sling and bandage, he met her thrusts, retreated, parried.

The release was sudden and ferocious, and it took Elisabeth completely by surprise because she'd thought she was finished, that all the responses from then on would be Jonathan's. But her body buckled in a seizure of satisfaction, and he lowered his mouth to hers, as much to muffle her cries as to kiss her.

When the last whimper of delight had been wrung from her, and only then, Jonathan gave up his formidable control and surrendered. He was like a magnificent savage as he lunged into her, drew back, and lunged again.

Finally, with a loud groan, he spilled himself inside her and then collapsed to lie trembling beside her on the mattress, his chest rising and falling with the effort to breathe. Elisabeth draped one leg across both of his and let her cheek rest against his chest.

For a long time, they were silent, and Elisabeth even slept for a while.

When she awakened, there were long shadows in the room and Jonathan's hand was running lightly up and down her back.

"I think you'll miss your world," he said sadly as she stirred against him and yawned. "Maybe you shouldn't stay, Elisabeth. Maybe you should take the necklace and go back and pretend that none of this ever happened.''

She scrambled into a sitting position and stared down at him. "I'm not going anywhere, Jonathan Fortner. You're stuck with me and with our baby."

"But the medicine—the magic box..."

Elisabeth smiled and smoothed his hair, less anxious now. "In some ways the twentieth century is better," she conceded. "They've wiped out a lot of the diseases that are killing people now. And life is much easier, in terms of ordinary work, because there are so many labor-saving devices. But there are bad things, too, Jon—things I won't miss at all."

His forehead wrinkled as he frowned. "Like what?"

Elisabeth sighed. "Like nuclear bombs. Jonathan, my generation is capable of wiping out this *entire planet* with the push of a single button."

His frown deepened. "Would they actually be stupid enough to do that?"

"I don't know."

He sighed and settled deeper into the pillows. "Do you suppose all the rest of us would die, too, if they did? I mean, the past and the present are obviously connected in ways we don't understand."

Elisabeth was saddened. "Let's hope and pray that never happens."

Jonathan stroked her hair and held her close against his chest. "What else can you tell me about the twentieth century?"

"You're bound to experience some of it yourself, since it's only about eight years away," she answered, entwining an index finger in a curl of hair on his chest. She bit her lip, remembering history that hadn't happened yet. "But I'll see if I can't give you some previews of coming attractions. Around the turn of the century, America will declare war on Spain. And then, about 1914 or so, the Germans will decide to take over the world. France, England, Russia and eventually the United States will take them on and beat them.''

Jonathan stared pensively into her face, waiting for more.

"Then, around 1929, the stock market will crash. If we're still around then, we'll have to make sure we invest the egg money carefully. After that—"

He laughed and held her close. "My little Gypsy fortune teller. After that, what?"

"Another war, unfortunately," Elisabeth confessed with a sigh. "Germany again, and Japan. As awful as it was for everybody, I think most of the scientific and medical advances made in the twentieth century happened because—well, necessity is the mother of invention, and nothing creates necessity like war."

Jonathan shuddered. "Tell me the good things."

Elisabeth talked about airplanes and microwave ovens and Disneyland. She described movies, electric Christmas-tree lights, corn dogs and Major League Baseball games. Jonathan laughed when she swore that a former actor had served two terms as President of the United States, and he absolutely refused to believe that men were having themselves changed into women and vice versa.

When Elisabeth was finished with her tales of the future, she and Jonathan made slow, sweet love.

Later, they ate a wedding supper brought to them by Big Lil's daughter. They consumed the food hungrily, greedily, never remembering after that exactly what they'd been served. Then they made love again.

Early the next morning they rose, and Elisabeth put on the dress she'd been married in, since she had nothing else to wear. Jonathan kissed her, said she was beautiful and promised to buy her as many gowns as she wanted once they reached Seattle.

Elisabeth was nervous and distracted. Finally she brought up the subject they'd both been avoiding. "Jon, the necklace—where is it?"

He paused in the act of rebandaging his arm and studied her for a long moment. "I left it at the house," he said. "Why?"

"There's something I have to do," she replied, her gaze skirting his, her hand already on the doorknob. "Please— tell me where to find the necklace."

The expression in his eyes was a bleak one, but he didn't ask the obvious question. "All right, Elisabeth," he said. "All right."

They drove out to Jonathan's house—their house—in his buggy. "The necklace is in my study," he said. "Under the ledger in the middle desk drawer."

As she hopped down from the rig, Elisabeth surveyed the ladder propped against the partially burned house. Apparently, the repair work had already begun.

She hummed as she went inside, found the necklace exactly where Jonathan had said it would be, and brought it out into the sunshine with her. Her husband stood beside the buggy, watching her pensively.

"I'm about to show you how much I love you, Jonathan Fortner," she said, and then she began climbing up the ladder.

"Lizzie!" Jonathan protested, bolting away from the buggy.

Elisabeth climbed until she reached the doorway that had once led from Trista's room into the main hallway. Holding her breath, she shut her eyes tightly, closed her fingers around the necklace and flung it over the threshold.

She was pleased when she opened her eyes and saw that the pendant had vanished. Holding her skirts aside with one hand, made her way quickly down the ladder.

Elisabeth Fortner had found the century where she belonged, and she meant to stay there.

Take 3 of "The Best of the Best™" Novels FREE
Plus get a FREE surprise gift!

Special Limited-time Offer

Mail to The Best of the Best™

3010 Walden Avenue
P.O. Box 1867
Buffalo, N.Y. 14240-1867

YES! Please send me 3 free novels and my free surprise gift. Then send me 3 of "The Best of the Best™" novels each month. I'll receive the best books by the world's hottest romance authors. Bill me at the low price of $3.99 each plus 25¢ delivery per book and applicable sales tax, if any.* That's the complete price and a savings of over 20% off the cover prices—quite a bargain! I understand that accepting the books and gift places me under no obligation ever to buy any books. I can always return a shipment and cancel at any time. Even if I never buy another book, the 3 free books and the surprise gift are mine to keep forever.

183 BPA A4V9

Name	(PLEASE PRINT)
Address	Apt. No.
City	State	Zip

This offer is limited to one order per household and not valid to current subscribers.
*Terms and prices are subject to change without notice. Sales tax applicable in N.Y.
All orders subject to approval.

UBOB-197

©1996 MIRA BOOKS

New York Times Bestselling Authors

JENNIFER BLAKE
JANET DAILEY
ELIZABETH GAGE

Three *New York Times* bestselling authors bring you three
very sensuous, contemporary love stories—all centered
around one magical night!

It is a warm, spring night and masquerading as legendary
lovers, the elite of New Orleans society have come to
celebrate the twenty-fifth anniversary of the Duchaise
masquerade ball. But amidst the beauty, music and revelry,
some of the world's most legendary lovers are in trouble....

Come midnight at this year's Duchaise ball, passion and
scandal will be...

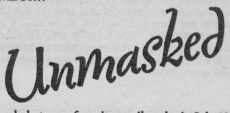

Unmasked

Revealed at your favorite retail outlet in July 1997.